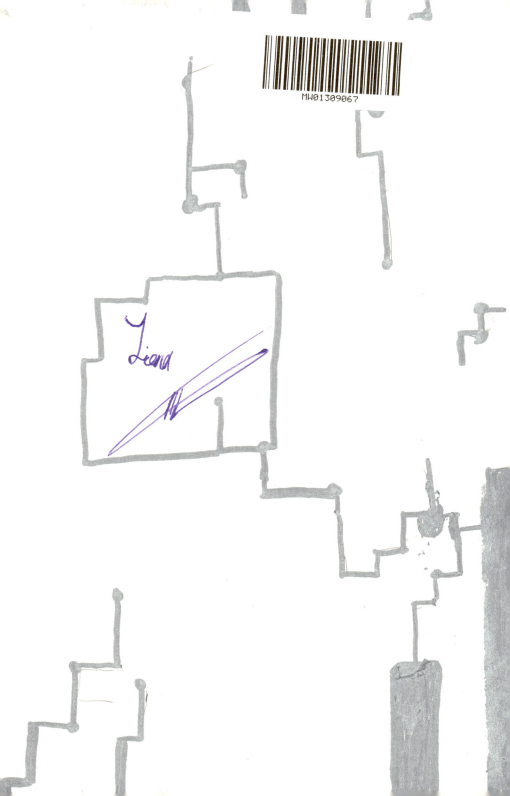

Conquer
Tiana, M

Copyright © [2024] by [Tiana M]

All rights reserved.

No portion of this book may be reproduced in any form without written permission from the publisher or author, except as permitted by U.S. copyright law.

Contents

	Dedication	1
	Content Warnings Please read through these before you begin the story.	3
1.	Chapter 1 Xandria's Past	4
2.	Chapter 2 Aruni	9
3.	Chapter 3 X	26
4.	Chapter 4 Venus's Past	33
5.	Chapter 5 X	45
6.	Chapter 6 Isaiah's Past	50
7.	Chapter 7 X	58

8.	Chapter 8 Aruni's Past	61
9.	Chapter 9 X	70
10.	Chapter 10 Liam's Past	73
11.	Chapter 11 X	88
12.	Chapter 12 X	92
13.	Chapter 13 X	101
14.	Chapter 14 X	112
15.	Chapter 15 Xandria's Past	121
16.	Chapter 16 Xandria's Past	130
17.	Chapter 17 X	147
18.	Chapter 18 Liam	161
19.	Chapter 19 Xandria's Past	165

20.	Chapter 20 Liam	183
21.	Chapter 21 Xandria' Past	194
22.	Chapter 22 X	221
23.	Chapter 23 X	233
24.	Chapter 24 X	244
25.	Chapter 25 Liam	265
26.	Chapter 26 X	268
27.	Chapter 27 X	276
28.	Chapter 28 X	283
29.	Chapter 29 X	294
30.	Chapter 30 X	299
31.	Chapter 31 X	303

32.	Chapter 32 X	321
33.	Acknowedgements	328
34.	Imperfect Black Characters Blog post about Conquer	332
35.	My Social Media	333
36.	My Website	334
37.	Abilities Guide	335
38.	A Rough Sketch Map of Where the Gang has Been.	336

For my Black folk that hide because they feel like they're too much.
You are loved as you are. Messy, broken, and beautiful.
You're not too much. If they can't keep up...
Tell them to get out of your way.

Content Warnings

Please read through these before you begin the story.

- Blood

- Violence/ violent thoughts

- Mentions/ insinuations of sexual assault

- Mentions of abusive scenarios: Including domestic scenarios and child scenarios

Disclaimer
All events in this story are fictional, though they are inspired by real life situations.

Chapter 1
Xandria's Past

Someone or something stole my mom from me. She's here, but I don't see her, and she doesn't see me. Something is stealing us, and it's warping time. Though the days are odd, there was a time outside of this where all that wasn't quite right was just right as it was.

But then someone stole my mom from me, and in turn whatever she was supposed to give me I can't seem to find.

I hope I find it before its absence tears me apart.

Past: January 18th, 2091

City: Unknown

Two moms with the same face can't mean it's the same one. I don't know what happened to her, but it's a dream or a nightmare. I don't know how or why she is a split version of herself, but I miss who she was when I wake up. Her ghost haunts my mind, and I could be better off not having her in my thoughts at all. That way I couldn't compare what I have now to what I had when I was asleep.

This mom is so strange. I never understand why she's so angry or why her emotions glitch around. Sometimes she begins to tell me something and she'll stop mid-sentence, shake her head, and walk away. She'd be calm for a bit and it's nice, but I get too comfortable and end up hurt. Usually, when I ask questions, she gets angry with me. I can't figure her out.

"XANDRIA!"

Here she is again bursting in the room with her wine-stained blue robe, her black bonnet, and I can't forget the look as her dark eyebrows tighten into a grimace. I was sitting down listening to piano and answering questions to tonight's homework. I found this old iPod a while ago when I was in school. It was stuffed under a bunch of junk in a desk, with wired headphones wrapped around it. All that's on it is a playlist filled with all types of piano music. There's a peaceful playlist, jazz playlist and dramatic playlist. Whatever's playing is the medicine for the things I can't put words to; it detangles the emotions I can't quite explain.

I stopped tapping my hand against my leg stuck on how to respond to Monster Mom.

"Sorry." I answer, hoping I snatched the earbuds from my ears fast enough.

"You're sorry?" Maybe if I freeze in place she'll leave me alone.

"YOU DON'T GOT AN ANSWER?"

"Well, I— "

"Xandria, please."

"I . . . you . . . I came in and you said to put your sh— stuff straight down and go to my room, so I did." So, I don't know why you're yelling. But of course, I can't say that.

"You think that means to drop your shit on the floor? Pick it up. Today, please." Getting up from the chair in my room her words fuzz in my ears. Instead, the music flutters in my mind muffling the venom she spits at me. Even without the earbuds, I need to keep the music playing one way or another, even if it's in thought.

After waiting for her to finish picking me apart for the second time today, I get up. Brisk in my movements, collecting my things from the front of the house. They lay next to the gray couch that sits slanted against the wood flooring.

Then I do that weird swaying speed walk thing back to my room and slide past her so I don't accidentally touch her. After I place my things in the corner of the room I sit down in my chair. Without weighing the consequences, words fly out my mouth. "I'm sorry . . . I didn't know . . . I forgot to put my stuff away, I wanted to make sure I followed your directions correctly so you won't—"

I can't not explain myself. I wanna know what the issue is so we can stop this, but I already know how this goes. I don't know why I bothered.

"Won't what?"

"Mom, I'm trying to talk to you, so stuff like this won't happen again but you don't talk to me!" Oops. That wasn't supposed to leave my lips. Here we go.

"Trying? You think trying to pay bills gets them paid? You think trying kept our family from falling apart? Lost to a mistake no one can fix. Xandria, I need you to pay attention! I have but so much time to help you understand—"

She pauses and presses the palms of her hands together in front of her face, leaning her forehead into them. *Pay attention to what?* She's about to have a rage fit, I bet. But for once her stern eyebrows went soft, so maybe not? I don't get it. This happens from time to time, and she almost reminds me of the dream. The dream is too close to memory.

That's not important. What's more important is avoiding sudden movements or gestures. I don't even remember what I was thinking about anyway.

The door creaks shut and clicks after she peels her eyes away from me. Finally. I have homework to finish as usual, so I flop in my chair now that I'm able to concentrate on something other than my mom's every movement. I should go to Homework Help for literary class at least. But I don't need help. I'mma figure it out. The teacher is gonna write all the answers when we go over it, and I'll change all my answers then. In the class, there's a pile of homework on the teacher's desk where every student leaves last night's assignment when they walk into class—every student except me. She picks it up at the very end. By then I have all the answers. Why would I bother wasting brainpower on learning any of this when could simply place my paper on the stack when I pass by.

Tonight, I might dream about my mom and the past I can't remember. That's one of the few times I think I'm happy. sometimes it eases into a nightmare like the one I'm living in.

Maybe when I get older this will change, it could be better. One day I'll look for my actual mom. The one that seems too real to be a dream. The one I see in the cracks of my mom's face because that's not her. It can't be.

Chapter 2
Aruni

April 20th, 2096
Present Day: 1 year and 6 months later
Main City 27

"WAIT! I want some chips."

Every time we walk to the bus stop after school Venus stops at the deli without warning to go get "some chips". Which ones? Nobody knows. It's been this way since she got back to school a few months ago. Like most Fridays, we all stop and wait for her to get whatever she's getting. There was a time where she would say what she just said and everyone would grumble and mumble, but we've grown out of it. We're all going to the same place anyway—might as well go together.

While we wait in front of the deli, the street noise is broken when a large icicle crashes through a transom window. We all tear our gaze from our phones and shift our attention to the street where chaos erupts as cars skid around the mountainous icicle. People either run or whip their heads around to see what's happening after the brief pause at the chaos. I hope that red at its point is not blood. It's probably a neo-human. I don't want to be that guy, but an icicle?

Venus runs out with her bag and chips in hand, wide-eyed, and asks what happened—like we're supposed to know. Before any of us can say anything, we see this girl in an all black sweatsuit with her face half-covered behind locs that peak from her hood. She jumps through the broken window, lands right in front of us then looks out at the street. We know about neo-humans—they've been around for a while. I'm related to one, I never thought I would see one again in person outside of my family, and she's not hiding either.

She turns to us, and her dark-brown eyes study each of our faces, and I'm about ready to make a run for it down the block.

"Guys, why are we standing here?" Venus asks, putting her chips in her tote bag. She's about the same height as Venus, who's a little bit taller than me but shorter than Liam and Isaiah. She looks directly at me and points at a scar on my collarbone.

"What happened to you?" *Nothing I'd wanna talk about right now.* She sounds calm, but who is she? I hadn't seen her in school before. But how would I know, I can't see her face. Before I can think of a reply, we spot BT down the block and the girl in the hoodie disappears into thin air. Isaiah swears out loud asking the same question we're all thinking.

"It's probably best if we aren't here when they are." I look over at Lee as he nods at the trucks and vans that are getting a little too close now. "Good point," Venus replies.

***

"So, we're not gonna talk about the whole girl disappearing through mid-air thing?" Isaiah asks, dropping his bag on the old red couch after we enter his basement.

"You mean the murder we witnessed?"

"No, you mean the murder y'all witnessed, I didn't see a damn thing." Venus corrects both Liam and Isaiah .

"Why would she ask me that?" I ask, remembering how she pointed at me.

"I don't know but I've seen her around before." Venus answers after putting her bag down in an old recliner.

"How?"

"Somehow. Guys, I don't think this is the first person she has went after. Look at this." Venus pulls out her phone, pecks away at the screen, and a minute or two later shows us several stories of people who were murdered and there's one thing they all have in common.

"Ah, so she murders shitty people. Sounds good to me," Isaiah replies, flopping into the couch, but I don't think that's the last time we're gonna see her.

"Ok, but what if we see her again?" We might.

"I don't think we would."

"Liam, she looked into my soul." She's gonna show back up.

"Ok, then we keep an eye out. I'm sure it's not even gonna be a thing by next week," Isaiah replies, sitting up on the couch. That I can work with. I know he thinks he's a neo-human which could be the reason why he's so lax about this, but I'm not buying it.

Later that evening by the time we got home, Auntie has food out on the table for us even though we told her we ate already. She loves to cook so we're never surprised to see full meals being made. It smells so good too, with that tang of lemon pepper chicken. I don't mind eating a little extra. She asks about our day after we put our stuff down. I wash my hands while Liam opens up the fridge even though he's not supposed to because—

"Liam! Wash your hands! Why do you do this every day?" she asks while checking the pot of rice.

"Sorry. Aruni, can you hurry up? You don't need to spend fifteen minutes washing your hands."

"You can wash them in the bathroom." He slams the fridge door shut, and I'm smiling simply because the easiest way to get back at him for complaining about what I'm doing.

"Liam! If my eggs fall off that door, you're cleaning it up!" He doesn't say anything because he probably doesn't hear her from upstairs.

"How's everything with you, Aruni?"

"Eh, school is school."

Liam comes back down and goes to warm up his plate and Auntie asks him the same.

"What about you, Lee?"

"Same. I just wanna graduate already."

"It goes by quick. You should at least try to enjoy it."

"I guess. Can I eat in the backyard?"

Alright, what's wrong with him now? I know my little joke doesn't have him that bothered. After my aunt says he can go, I follow him to the backyard. He's sitting on the swing against the wall of the grassy backyard and I plop right next to him causing him to almost drop his plate of food.

"Oops."

"What is the problem, Aruni?"

"What's your problem, Liam?"

"You. Can I eat in peace?"

"Can I take the bus home by myself? . . . Exactly what I thought. Now what's the issue?"

"What do you think?"

"Well, you heard what Venus said. I don't think it's gonna be a thing."

"Yeah, but when's the last time you've seen a neohuman with multiple abilities? That's not common. It's not something that ever occurs at all for that matter."

"You think she's like you?" I haven't heard him talk about his abilities since we left home. Now's the worst time for him to not be stubborn and let curiosity get the best of him.

"No, but we're both not supposed to exist."

"Lee, just because you haven't seen another mimic doesn't mean they don't exist. You exist. What does this have to do with the girl?" Before he decides to answer my question the girl in the hoodie materializes almost on cue. Without hesitation Liam puts down the plate and jumps up. Her hands emit white smoke, and by that alone I know ice is gonna start flying. The ice slams right into the wall behind the lawn swing and before we turn back to her, she's gone. We both whirl around looking for her and then she appears a couple feet behind my brother and panic swarms my body. What she says next doesn't make it any better.

"So, you're a mimic?" He turns around to face her and she stares back at him with her arms crossed.

"Were you—"

"Listening? Yes, I was, but I've never met a mimic before. Interesting." Then she poofs away before either of us can say anything. It's bad enough for anyone to know someone else is a neo-human, but it's worse that Liam isn't a typical neo-human.

"So, um. Should we tell the others?" Auntie bolts outside after the commotion and part of me is glad that she wasn't here to see everything that happened.

"What's the problem? I went to use the bathroom for five minutes and y'all are back here causing chaos."

Liam and I apologize. As soon as she closes the door, we look at each other. Thankfully, she didn't see the ice on the wall.

***

The next day I sent everyone a text asking them to come by our house. It's evident we need to talk about what happened.

Auntie didn't expect them, but she doesn't fuss about it too much. They're here pretty often and she is already super welcoming. They all call her Auntie 'cause she treats them as her own. Then again, we're over each other's places so often that our parents might as well become short-distance neighbors. After Auntie overstuffed everyone with sandwiches, Liam and I explain what happened, but we tried to keep it vague. There's still a lot to learn so we fill them in on the gist of everything.

"Ok, great so how are we gonna find her?" Isaiah asks.

"Relax. You do realize that she has multiple abilities, right?" Venus shakes her head.

Isaiah looks at me for back up but instead I shrug. Typically, I encourage spontaneous shit, but not if he's gonna get himself caught up in a fight. He can't fight again. Neo-humans belong in New City, but they can't all make it there. When they are here, they're usually caught up with BT labs or hiding. According to what Venus showed us yesterday, it's not easy for them to catch her. While Venus and Isaiah bicker about the last sentiment Liam looks over at me and I already know what he's gonna tell them.

"What if I told you I had them too?"

"No, you don't." Isaiah replies ,I lean back in my chair, and continue listening to the others argue .

Isaiah shakes his head. "I do, actually. You don't."

"Yes, I do, clearly. What are your abilities then?"

"It's complicated," Liam replies and it's true they are complicated.

"Exactly, because you don't have them."

"Isaiah, if you did have any of them, all I need is one good punch to level the playing field." Actually, that is a good point. Isaiah gets out his seat and Venus rolls her eyes.

"We don't have time for this, and Auntie is literally right in the kitchen." Both sit down and before I can think of another way to find her before she finds us—again—Venus holds out a hand.

"What are you do—"

Her arm goes limp, and the plate begins to float. So, she can astral project. Now I definitely don't believe Isaiah because there's no way I'm the only one that didn't get abilities. This shit sucks.

"With that in mind. I'll start looking." Her arm snaps backwards and the plate flies into her physical hand. She sits up in the chair pridefully and I find myself crossing my arms like a spoiled child. *How come I didn't get one!* How did I happen to be in a room full of neo-humans and I don't have a single ability.

"Wait. If we do this, what do we tell Auntie?" Liam asks as we stand to leave.

"We went to the park. What else?" As I said that, I rush out the door with my bag on my back. How do people become neo-humans anyway? And if both my parents had the gene and my brother has the gene then who do I need to see to get this shit checked because something's not right. When I got halfway down the block it's only Isaiah and Liam who catch up to me.

"Where's Venus?"

"Venus went to your room to leave her body." Leave her body? That's such an odd thing to say out loud, but I guess that's what happens with astral projecting abilities.

We go back to the deli, the original spot where we first met the girl. We don't even know what else to do. This is so pointless. How would we know where she is, and what are we actually going to do if we see her? Maybe we should leave this alone or call someone who can help. But who can we call? Parents are out of the question because that'll escalate the situation. BT is an absolute no. Why would I call BT? So, my friends can get caught up? I smooth my puff again because I swear, I'm sweating out the gel.

Granted, they'll give out quite the check for sending in neo-humans, but I wouldn't do that. BT can burn for all I care. I think we need to split up, but Liam is not gonna agree with that idea.

"Lee, maybe we should split up."

"No."

"That's it? No? What do you mean no? You said that like that's supposed to stop me."

"Lee, I'm sorry, but she's right we're gonna be here forever." Isaiah chimes in after looking away from the broken window.

"See, Isaiah agrees." I reply as I swing my arms out at him.

"Then Isaiah can go."

"I didn't ask about Isaiah. I was asking about me." The last thing I will be doing is becoming the sorry-tag-along that has no special powers. They always die in the book, and I will not be that character. I will go look for the girl in the hoodie since everyone else has some big issue going on.

"What about Venus?"

"We don't know when she'll be back. I'll let you know if something is wrong but I'm gonna go."

"Fine, but if you find her don't do anything call me."

"Of course, I will." I'm lying through my teeth. I'm going to talk to her first. Maybe I can figure this out and make sure we're all good, that way we know for sure we'll be left alone. Walking off, my hands swing at my sides as I lift my head. I know what I'm doing.

After gaining a good amount of distance from everyone, I'm stopped in my tracks. Across the street I see what I believe to be a piece of chalk floating down the block? I freeze in my tracks surveying the area. I'm surprised nobody noticed but they're so into their conversations or phones how could they notice? Unless I'm seeing things again, but I've been handling that just fine. How would I know unless I follow it? So, I'm gonna follow it. It could be Venus, it could be the girl in the hoodie that apparently calls herself X based off what Venus showed us. It could be my mind playing tricks on me. I won't know 'til I get there and nothing bad is going to happen. At least I hope not.

I'm led into an old, empty hotel building exit that opens for me and it doesn't sound an alarm. I follow the little chalk through the building, and it writes an X on the door and drops in front of it. Ok, room 238. I take a deep breath and knock on the door. At short notice it creaks open. This is the part where I run out the building because I know damn well I shouldn't be here, but I made it this far. So I walk in anyway ignoring the sweat on my palms.

After I walk inside, the door shuts and locks behind me. That wasn't Venus. I turn back around to see the full face of the girl with the hoodie standing in the middle of the decrepit room with sunlight glowing behind her.

"What's up, Aruni? So, the mimic and your other two neo-human friends are showing up soon, or no?"

"How—How are you finding us?" I ask, smoothing the sides of my puff again.

"I'll explain later. You might want to get comfortable because you're not leaving 'til I get what I need from you and your friends." Nah, let me call them because this is already getting out of hand.

"You can tell them you know. I'm not gonna stop you. In fact, the sooner you do the better."

Ok, should I even call them now? She seems to already know who we are so what exactly is the point of being rebellious? I don't have any abilities, but they do. I hope they know how to use them the way she does, but I know they don't. I'm still gonna text them, I can't stay here alone.

"So, you don't wanna sit? I got a chair over there in the corner"—she says pointing to the rickety chair that looks like it can't hold its own weight—"You want some water? I got water."

"I—No, thanks." She stares with hunter eyes long enough for me to stop resisting and walk over to the chair to sit. Is she gonna stop watching me now? I cut my eyes to her when I sit. I guess that's a no.

"See! Isn't that more comfortable, Aruni?" she asks, lying on her side instead of sitting upright on the couch.

I'm not even gonna look at her, but I'm not gonna act like I didn't see white particles leaving her hand. Now she's making snowflakes. *Why is she making snowflakes?* Squinting at her now I wouldn't have guessed that under the hoodie the girl seems like she could toss that couch at me if she wanted to. She's so calm, probably because she knows more than she should.

"How did you know Liam is a mimic?"

"You'll see." As she says that the door creaks open and in walks Liam and Isaiah. As soon as they fully enter the room, she poofs from the couch.

"Mimic and Patches. But where's the ghost?" she asks as she appears in front of them. Liam goes to touch her shoulder to take her abilities, but she disappears and reforms from dust back into the same spot. Isaiah goes to throw a punch, but she stops it so effortlessly. In shock, I hold my head in my hands, wanting to yell "don't you embarrass me," at both of them. Liam thinks quickly and adapts Isaiah's abilities, but he freezes for a minute before he pushes her to the side. Guess he was right after all.

Her hands start smoking and I watch in awe. Multiple abilities and I couldn't get one? More disappointed than I was earlier about not having any abilities.

Isaiah and Liam both go around her but when they do, she disappears and reappears around the room, and every now-and-then she laughs a bit as if this were a game. Every time they get close, she disappears. Liam stands by to think for a minute, but Isaiah charges at her and she gracefully steps out the way and with a sharp wave of her hand, there's a shot of ice. Isaiah, idiot, ends up iced on the wall behind her.

"You gotta do better than that, Patches."

Isaiah is pissed. He's frozen to a wall with nothing but his head free. Liam hurls one of the chairs at her, she snatches it out the air and launches it back. He almost gets caught like Isaiah after the chair flew above him, but he ducks out the way. He stops a few feet away as the arm she put out in front of her goes limp.

"Nice to see you out of body, Venus," she says aloud. She's talking to Venus? Liam manages to almost get close enough to copy her abilities, but she snaps her working arm toward him and he ends up with an arm iced to the floor.

She laughs comically then sternly says, "That was entertaining, but I'm not here for that. You guys are gonna help me break into a house in New City."

"No, we're not." At Isaiah's rebuttal I shake my head.

"Whenever you figure out how to manage your abilities." She continues, "That was a very quick fight for four neo-humans. But I can work with that you just need more practice. Venus is here if you haven't figured that out yet." Four? She means three...right?

"You're supposed to be helping us?"

"Yeah, of course. Look at where you are right now, you need help. Desperately." she replies looking down at Liam struggling to pull his arm out of the ice.

"What do you mean by four neo-humans? I'm not a neo-human."

"Yet. But if your brother is one, I suspect that you'll come across yours soon." X turns to Isaiah struggling to get out of the cold ice and I can see in his face that he can't stay there much longer. "Patches, maybe I could let you out of the cold ice if you would stop struggling so much."

"Stop calling me Patches."

"Ok, fine sorry. Patches. Here's the deal. You all meet me here at noon tomorrow."

"And if we don't?" Liam asks and X glances down at him.

"And if you don't I hope you can mimic enough abilities to outrun me before I find you."

* * *

When we all meet at the abandoned hotel, everyone's fidgety including myself. I smoothed the sides of my puff for the tenth time. I don't have the hair tie I usually pluck at on my wrist. She could be wrong about me, but she could be right, but if she's right what's taking me so long to find out what I can do?

"Guys, are we sure this is the only option?" Venus asks, leaning off the wall.

"I think it is. Look on the bright side, you guys get to learn how to use your abilities. That's pretty cool right?" And I get to see if I have any.

My efforts at lightening the mood are brushed off, so we all head to room 238. If I can't do anything, the least I can do is make someone smile or make myself smile. When we get there, the door is open, and when we walk in we find a folder on the kitchen counter labeled Xandria. Then she appears out of thin air. I still jump when it happens as if this hasn't happened already. Before she says anything, Venus asks a question.

"So, your full name is Xandria?"

"No. Not anymore. Just X. So, you guys wanna know what this folder is for or not?" she asks with her arms crossed as she stands firm. She pauses as if waiting for us to actually answer but the silence grows tense. She sighs and pulls four sheets of paper from the folder and hands one to me first. I glance at her before I take it.

"Whether you want to believe it or not, your abilities come from what's listed on those sheets. It's pretty self-explanatory."

Isaiah tosses his sheet back on the counter and sits down on the couch in the living room.

"What does this have to do with anything?" Venus asks. I don't even need to know which ability it is if the illusions are associated with the memories that happened back home. Memories I'd rather not rehash.

"Your abilities. Like I said."

"Right, but how is this helping us?"

I don't know how being reminded of this is supposed to help me understand how to access these abilities—maybe she's wrong about me.

"Would you guys rather learn the right way or the easy way?" The right way is what I would've said if I spoke up before Lee.

"What's the easy way?" X smiles ever so slightly at him. This could be a great idea or a horrible one.

Chapter 3
X

He wanted the easy way out and I took the silence from the others as an agreement. What they don't know is there is no easy way to learn. I'm gonna make sure they get the point today. I don't have time to sit around this neighborhood waiting for these lab people to show up again.

In the stolen car, pulling my hair back into a low wide ponytail I wait for them to get in. We need to go somewhere we cannot and will not be seen. If anyone finds out about them, they're gonna have a bigger problem than me to deal with. After about twenty minutes of driving, we're in between the borders of New City and Main City. Out here there's mostly trees and junk metal which is perfect because that means we can stay hidden. When we exit the car, I walk ahead and they follow behind me. We walk for a few minutes until we're not too far but far enough.

"Alright, Patches, you're first. " I nod forward and I hear him shuffling behind a few moments afterward. He's too impatient and I wanna see something. After making our way past a few trees I can still see his friends talking about what's going on in the distance as they point in my direction. It doesn't bother me, but this is gonna bother him. "So, before we get started there's one thing I need to know."

"I thought you knew what you needed to know already since you've been stalking us in ghost form."

"Funny but no. On a scale of one to ten, how good are you at puzzles?"

"What?"

Before anything else is said, I dig my hand into the dirt to make a maze of ice. There's water in the dirt to pull from. I don't need to dehydrate myself to create this. The ground ripples and shakes as ice erupts from the ground in the formation of walls and halls. I don't keep track. When I'm done with the maze, the ice smokes amongst all the settling dirt. Even though it prickles against my skin, I've been around it so much that I've got used to it. It won't make me as uncomfortable as it may to someone who doesn't have these abilities. I can't remember what I made now but I can teleport out of here. He on the other hand has to figure it out.

"Good luck, Patches!"

I appear in front of the crew and their conversation halted. Their gaze glued to the maze. It was close enough for them to make out Patches maneuvering his way throughout the ice labyrinth.

"Aruni, you're next."

"No, Aruni is not next. Where's Isaiah?" I expected some pushback from Liam but I have something for him when I'm done with everyone else. I'm not a mimic but the same way I'm a strange case, so is he, and I wanna know how.

"Relax, Mimic, Isaiah is fine, the ice isn't that cold, and if I really wanted to add you to my kill list, I would've done that a while ago."

"I'll be fine. What's the worst that can happen?" Aruni asks, shrugging her shoulders.

"See, you should think more positive like your sister."

Right as I said that a box of ice rose around her. Liam and Venus immediately swarm around the box talking over each other to Aruni. I nod at them answering their "are you ok?" questions while they crowd around the box.

"Yeah, we're done."

"Take it easy, Liam." I can't do what I gotta do if he's gonna have a problem with everything. I slide past to lean next to the box to help Aruni out. Whatever she can do it'll show up in an intense situation.

"You cold?"

"Obviously! Yes!"

"Ok, good." Then I turn around and lean my head toward Venus.

"Me next?"

"Yes, you ever took up running as a hobby?"

"Why?" The moment she asks her eyes mirror the gray of a storm cloud. I don't know what she's running from, but her brain will fill in the blanks for her except there's no ghosting this time. I've seen her out of body more than she's in it. I get how that could be an addictive habit but it's a deadly one too.

By then I'm on to the next person and he waves a hand in front of Venus who is still processing the mindscape. I'm only explaining this one more time because I need him to focus.

"She's fine, Liam."

"How? She is staring into space, Aruni is in a box, and we don't know where Isaiah is!"

"If you would shut up maybe I can figure this out faster!" I look at Aruni in the box and nod at her in agreement.

"They're fine. Now it's your turn. So, how many of my abilities could you copy before they all figure themselves out?" I disappear and reappear amongst the trees until he soon figures out the pattern I'm flashing in. He copies my teleporting ability by getting a hold of my arm, but he freezes for a minute, why? I watch him study something I can't see, squinting as if it'll reveal itself but it doesn't. I'll ask him later." Yeah, I don't think we should keep—"

I stop him in the middle of his sentence when a log goes flying in his direction. He disappears out the way but reappears in the air and lands on his back. After a good while he figures out how to copy each ability. But every time he does, he freezes and goes into a trance. *What's he seeing?*

By the last ability mimicked, Venus has come out the illusion and Liam takes both Aruni and Isaiah out of the parts of the forest I've put them in. He's not bad and if he had as much experience as I did, I think we may have a fair fight. Why is he pausing in between copying abilities?

After several illusions are used to distract Liam, everyone else watches as he copies the last ability by getting a hold of my shoulder. It was nothing serious this time. Random duplicates of me dashing through the trees and random hunks of metal. While I was hoping he would fall for it, he didn't. At least not longer than he needed to.

Right when he can get used to the new ability, I realize what I did. The last time I saw my mom I was in a BT building. The same happens with him but it's different, it's almost as if he wasn't even here. I make my way to Liam as I watch him sit against a tree with his eyes squeezed shut and his head in his hands. His friends see the chaos and rush over. They push past me to kneel next to him, but they can't help. So, I have to, especially because this was my mistake. "You can't help, let me talk to him."

"How are you gonna help? You caused it!" Venus and the others have every reason to be upset but if they don't move, I can't help. Then again, I don't know how to. When this happened to me I went through it till it stopped. I apologized and explained a second time that I can't help if they won't let me. Hesitant, they let up and I took a knee in front of him, but the chaos ceased.

"I'm so sorry." Why? What did he see?

At that point I froze, in confusion and poofed to the car. I can suspect what he saw based off of what I know, and already I find myself regretting my decision. I let out a heavy sigh and lean my head back on the seat.

I could've done this myself but the house in New City is heavily guarded, and I need to get in. When they finally climb in the car we silently ride back to my broken-down motel. Surprisingly, they don't disperse, and they all follow me back to my room. I can't question why they did if I wanted to.

"I'm sorry about what happened today. I have experience but I'm not the best at teaching. However, you did agree to doing this, but it's clear that rushing this was a bad idea."

"You think?" Isaiah blurts out. Even though it's understandable I did warn them this wasn't the best way. At least I thought I made it clear. I wouldn't wish for anyone to deal with an overload of abilities unless they deserved it.

"X, I don't know who you are, but whatever you need to do needs to not end with someone getting hurt. Otherwise, this is all pointless." All I could do was nod at Venus before they all began to make their way out, but I called Liam back. I have questions about what the hell happened. Well, not really, but I wanna hear him say it. To my surprise he stays back and they all stand at the door staring at me before it closes.

"What did you see out there today? Every time you copied an ability you paused. Why?" I asked straightening my back and crossing my arms.

"Guess they forgot to mention that on the sheet... I don't just mimic abilities, I see what caused them apparently."

"What did you see?"

"How long have you been running from BT?"

"I asked a question first."

"I think I answered that already." Whatever caused my abilities. That's what he saw.

"We'll do something different next time." If I can figure something else out. That's too much information to give away.

"If there is a next time. You kinda pissed them off."

"I know. Listen we got off on a bad foot, but this could help you all as much as it could help me, so at least think about it and I'll think of a better way to help. I'm not the teacher type."

"X, not that I am telling you what to do but you might want to try and take it easy. If the papers you showed us are true, making them panic isn't gonna help. Just sayin'," he says, raising his hands up and shrugging. I don't like how casual this conversation is and he already knows too much.

"Good point. So, what about you then?"

"You don't need to worry about me."

"Yeah, we'll see. Well, you can get the hell out of my room now." I stand by the door to open it. I'm ready for this to be over with so I can come up with a new plan.

"By the way I expect everyone back here same time tomorrow, unless you want me to show up at one of your houses." And I slam the door for dramatic effect. They'll be back, I know they will.

Chapter 4
Venus's Past

October 3rd, 2095
Past: 6 months ago
Main city 27

I don't know anybody in linguistics class but from what I heard eventually we're gonna have to do some group work. I'd much rather do this myself, but unless I make up a person that doesn't exist, this two-person dialogue isn't gonna write itself. As I listen to instructions, before scanning the room at the desk next to me is the guy in the navy-blue hoodie. He's tapping a screen when I notice his brown hands spotted with white patches.

"Hey, before he answers another question that was asked three times already, do you wanna work together on the next assignment? 'Cause I don't wanna stand up to look for somebody to work with."

"People repeat questions because they don't pay attention and right now—"

"Right now, what?"

"Well, you're not paying attention."

"I am, actually. You can't say, yes or no?"

"No, because he just said to turn to the person next to you to avoid getting up and you would've heard that had you been—"

"Alright, alright, I get the point." I don't mind working with people I don't know but it really is a hit or miss sometimes.

The work got done, well almost got done, so we had to do the rest for homework. The second we exchanged numbers he was already halfway out the classroom. Damn. He could've said something first but I'm as ready to go as he is. For once I can go straight home after school since there's no tutoring today. On a lighter note, I won't have to stay up till the dead of night to do homework.

"Hey, Mom!"

"Hey, V, did you get the paperwork to apply for that college program?" Of course, I forgot something. Why would there be a day where I can simply go home after school.

"No, but I will tomorrow." Or maybe I'll mysteriously forget again. Everything I did sign up for is a lot already. Honors classes are already dense, tutoring takes up an extra hour of my time, and I like the debate club because I enjoy arguing. We need to talk about it if we're gonna fix it, the next thing is doing something about it. But I'mma be honest, nobody is standing up to BT, but I'm not gonna shut up about it either.

My mom hands me the phone and I know who it is based on the chaotic background.

"Hey, Dad, you still stopping by this weekend?" My mom cuts her eyes at me as a way to say I'm rude for leading with that question. With all the chaos in the background it's a constant reminder about why that can't happen every weekend. So, yes, I asked.

"My bad, how was your day?"

"Busy, you?"

"Busy." It's always busy. Part of me wishes I had an excuse to slowdown and do nothing. I shouldn't wish to catch a cold or fall sick but that would definitely give me a week to lay in bed and do nothing. I'm doing all this stuff and when I talk to my family, or almost anyone for that matter, they assume I know exactly what I'm doing. I don't. I'm as lost as the next person, but last time I told my mom that we had a whole conversation about why we can't afford to be lost. She says my older sister, Victoria, being lost is the reason why she actually ended up lost.

Before he can answer my question, he tells me to hold on and sets the phone down. I can hear him in the background dealing with his kids who are doing all that yelling. This wouldn't be as irritating if I had met them. And honestly, I don't want to, especially not at this point. Let me go do my homework. I won't know if he's stopping by this weekend 'til I get the phone call on Saturday morning either apologizing or telling me that he's outside.

Every time I walk past Victoria's room, I pretend it's not there because my last memory of her resurfaces and reminds me why she left. She was going through it when she was here. Her room was always a mess, her laundry was hardly ever done. The window curtains remained closed most days unless Mom barged into her room to yank them open. They would argue back and forth about any and everything. My mom's final straw was when she found pill bottles behind Victoria's bed. After they argued about that, I found myself wishing for the petty arguments we had about who borrowed who's sweater.

As much as we nagged each other and stole clothes from each other's closets, if someone were to ask me about Victoria right now, the first thing I would bring up is the real reason why I'm so outspoken in debates and history class. Last time she was here I wasn't exactly good at debating. I wasn't speaking up much for that matter, but she sat with me and talked about what I studied. I'll never forget how her face lit up when she said, "Venus, people are inspired by how you are when you speak... Whatever voice you put on when you get out there, drop it, and watch everybody move out the way because of your gift."

I was timid before, but over time those words grew on me. If people are gonna monitor my tone, my face, or my emotions when I say what needs to be said, I might as well say it the way it is meant to be said. Now I lead it, and I know I'm good at it. I would never open my mouth to tell anyone about the unread text I sent my older sister hoping to hear her say, I told you so, one more time.

I'll never forget doing each other's hair. Shit. Learning each other's hair. I'll never forget the brief silence after we got in trouble and laughing because we made a joke about something that wasn't supposed to be funny. I remember the arguments we had before she lost herself. Though the memories of her worst are what's closest to me in time, her best is highlighted in memories easily forgotten. It was forgotten on days when she was right down the hall from me. I go into the bathroom without an argument now and who knew a lack of arguing would leave me crying in the shower.

November 3rd, 2095
Past: 5 months ago

As we leave the diner I throw on my rose gold bomber jacket and we head to the bus stop. I asked Aruni what she uses on her hair to make it grow so full. My curls aren't damaged or unhealthy, I was curious because her puff is so cute.

"My mom actually has a friend who used to buy some coil custards and send it to us, but now that we're here I don't know where to get it." Aruni answers smoothing the sides of her puff.

"Wait, I think I know what you're talking about. There's a beauty shop by my building and whatever you think you can't find, I'm sure she has it. We should go after school on Monday."

"Yeah, but I'mma have to ask my aunt for more money to carry."

"Girl, don't even worry about it, my mom and I have been going for years, the owner will cut you some slack."

"You think they sell whatever lip gloss you're wearing too? Mine doesn't look that."

"I'mma tell you what my sister told me. Brown liner." She smiles and nods at me understanding exactly what I'm talking about before she starts typing on her phone. Then at the mention of my sister her loss looms over me, and tears prickle at my eyes.

"I thought you had tutoring today. Why are you out here?" Isaiah asks.

"Oh, I quit and I'm not taking those college courses either."

"Damn. You gonna quit the debate thing too?"

"No, because that's the one time I can say what needs to be said without tiptoeing over people's opinions." Right after I said that the quiet drags out instead of the conversation continuing. "Was that too heavy? Cause that pause was—" Before I can over explain my sentiment, I get scattered no's and bouts of reassurance. I drop my shoulders after hoping this wasn't another case of Venus you're doing too much.

"Oh, ok cool, cool. I like you guys. You're not too bad."

***

When I walk into the house, the first thing my mom does is lecture me about quitting half of my extracurricular activities. I let her because I'm tired of explaining I'm tired. I don't wanna waste energy on something I'm not enjoying when it's something I don't even have to do. When I volunteer my time, I have to care about what I'm doing or it's gonna show up in my work. Which it was. My grades were dropping, and I've been missing out on hanging with my friends. I don't wanna be the last person out of school all the time. If it was for something I enjoyed sure. But I'm not enjoying it and it's becoming more of a burden than the supposed stepping stool it was supposed to be.

"Do you understand what I'm saying, Venus?"

"Yeah." No. I wasn't even listening.

"I only say this because I want you to be the best you can be, ok? We need to do more for a chance to even start. We'll work towards those college programs next year."

"K." I love my mom, but I wish she understood we aren't the same person, and I am not Victoria. I'm not gonna crash like she did but I'm not gonna be what my mother is either. Supervising in her office or whatever, while debating with these higher ups about how much money the cities get from The Outlands. It's not allocated evenly between Main Cities and New Cities. I know that she knows that—everyone knows that—but all this talking leaves us chasing our tails. I don't mind talking about it, in fact I enjoy it, but at what point do we pair that up with something productive? I'm not a neo-human, but if I was one, I would be pretty fed up with this by now.

***

Later that night my friend called me around 9:00 p.m. about a house party. I would've asked my mom had I known about this earlier but asking her now isn't gonna get me out this apartment. Not only does she want me to be and do everything, but she's paranoid anytime I leave the house—calling and texting questions about any and everything. Then asking her to go to these parties is always a quest in itself. If I asked now, she would lose it but I'mma go anyway. She doesn't need to know and I'm positive that she's asleep.

I snatch my bonnet off my head and spray my curls, then got real cute. Before I step out the door, I fix the strap on my violet Dress. To stop any noise from being heard, I covertly ease the door shut and the soft click lets me know it's secure. OK! Let me ring for a driver and be on my way!

***

When I get to the party, I call my friend to open the door. From the sound of the base no one's gonna hear a knock or doorbell. The door swings open and we scream each other's name and fall into a hug.

From that point it was a wrap and whatever was keeping me awake or would've kept me awake fades away into the music as I dance with my friends with a drink in my hand. I need to use the bathroom, though. I lean over to Jessica who let me in earlier to ask her to come with me, but she shakes her head. I would've asked somebody else but that pissed me off so at this point I'll go by myself; I'll be quick.

It's hot, crowded, and loud while people pack together, and the bass shakes the floor. A few minutes ago, this didn't bother me, but now it is. My face is itching from sweat and people keep bumping into me. Soon enough, I make my way to the staircase and head down.

However, when I get downstairs I see a man by the bedroom door, I should've taken that as a sign to go right back upstairs. Maybe even go right back home.

December 5th, 2095
Past: 4 months ago

"Three times! I shouldn't have to go to that damn building three times to build a case around this!" My mom has been yelling in the car like she did the last two times since I told her what happened a month ago. She knew I snuck out, and when she saw the bruises on my neck I didn't have the mental compacity to lie. I wish I could forget exactly what happened that night. I haven't been able to properly eat or sleep since. I've been wearing the same grey sweatsuit combination all week. And I'm still at a loss for words. I haven't been back to school either—my mom set up something where I can do the work remotely. I haven't spoken to anyone else other than those people I last sat with at the diner. I recently told Aruni what's up and she checks on me almost every day, sometimes her brother says hi in the background if she's in the same room as him. I only heard from Isaiah about the homework because I think we both know I'm not willing to say much of anything right now.

I was tired. Which is why I quit all the things I quit, but now I'm tired and angry. And anger doesn't begin to describe why it's best for me to be still. No one really knows the whole truth about BT, the New Cities, or the Main Cities, but from what I've gathered the lack of resources out here are exactly what's stopping us from even making a case. We don't even know where he is, but if I knew where to find him to avenge myself I would.

"I'm going back to town hall after work tomorrow. They will have to shoot me dead before I stop nagging them about this. You hungry, V?" "No, thank you." No would've been an appropriate answer, but "no, thank you" has been the preprogrammed response for a while now. I eat 'cause I have to eat, but my stomach is tight. I don't want food right now.

My mom sighs as we both get out the car and I walk into the apartment building, then into the elevator, back out, and down the hallways to get home and go to my room. I sit on the edge of my bed and bury my face in my hands, finally letting my emotions swell. When I said I wanted a break to do nothing, this is not what I meant. When I said I wanted to slow down and not worry about anything else, this is not what I meant. I wanted to draw near to whatever was calling to me, but this snatched it right out of my hands. And he just disappears?

I don't get to disappear. I don't get to run. I have to carry and live with this shit in my body wherever I go. Flinching anytime abrasive memories occur. The ghost of unfamiliar hands on my body jolt me awake where I am greeted with the sound of my own screaming. I don't get to disappear; I don't get to leave this and move on. I have to sit with it, and I can't even get to him or find a way to take the justice I should've gotten already.

I stand and pace the floor, biting my stubbed nails as I let my mind roam and allow my rage to run hot under my skin. I don't get to disappear. I never did. At that I begin to frantically sweep an arm across my nightstand but halfway through the objects falling on the floor I fall back . . . I'm still standing . . . I look down at my hands and I can still see the mess of perfumes and makeup through them but when I turn back, I look back at—at myself. I have heard stories of neo-humans before but didn't expect to be one.

I look down at my feet floating above the ground surrounded by a purple light haze. And what are these glowing things? I touch one and it travels up my arm. I sway back and forth. I'm so light. Light in more ways than one.

Then I realize, if this is me as a ghost and nobody can see me, I can go wherever I want. I can do whatever I want and no one's gonna stop me this time. Nothing is gonna interrupt me this time.

My mom always talks about good habits and how it'll bring about a successful life. I got a new habit, but it isn't gonna be a good one.

Chapter 5
X

Present day: April 22nd, 2096
Main City 27

I've been sitting in my chair eating a subpar wrap I made from some stolen groceries and in walks my class. I was gonna give up and either handle this myself or find someone else to help me. I could, maybe I should, but here I'm thinking about helping them instead. The other two options are too risky. Besides, I have a lesson plan now and I'm not gonna waste all the effort I put into planning this. Whether they like it or not they better get comfortable because this is gonna take some time.

"New plan everyone!" I announce hoping up from my couch. "You are all going to stay over here while I teach one of you how to not be lousy at using your abilities. I'll come back to get you when I am ready."

"Alright, X, that's cute, but after yesterday I don't think that'll be happening."

"Funny you say that, Venus, because you're first." Lately I've been practicing teleporting, but I never tried it on a person like Liam did yesterday. The car isn't optimal right now so it's worth a shot. Nevertheless, without warning I grab Venus's arm and we disappear. When we get back to the trees, I can imagine the shocked look on their faces. Venus gets all steamy when she realized what I did.

"What the hell was that? What if someone got hurt!" She snatches her arm away as she replies.

"I promise you, I am the very least of your problems. Now if we are gonna do this, I need you to answer this question."

"What question, X?"

"How much time do you spend outside of your body in a day?"

". . . Why do you care?"

"Because from what I know, you almost completely disconnected from your body several times. If you stay out of it too long, you die."

"Yeah. It's . . . it's just really addicting."

"I'm aware. Been there, done that." What I'm about to ask her to do isn't easy, but it's gonna be the first step to helping her.

She can't use her abilities if she accidentally kills herself. She needs a reason to come back, she needs something to come back to. I have my reason—my other gifts. But Venus, even though she holds it together, is so lost. She's no use to me if she's dead.

"What do you do other than ghost in your free time?"

"Um . . . Nothing now. I used to do debates, but I quit everything else right before I got my abilities."

"Great, now what did you like about the debate thing?"

"I don't get how this is teaching me anything, X."

"When was the last time you looked at yourself in the mirror? Like really looked at yourself."

"Yeah, this isn't helping. At all." She shakes her head and pulls her ponytail of curls tighter. Ok, she got me on that because I don't know where I was going with that either.

"Venus. You need to come back in five minutes. K?" I say giving a thumbs up.

"Great, so I can leave my body now— "

"Listen, if you go over time, whatever you saw in that illusion yesterday will continue to haunt you."

"I think that's a bit much."

"Yet, it's coming from your brain. There are two types of illusions and this one was free enough for you to fill in the blanks without my help. I don't know what you're running from, but you need to come back. Got it?" I need to work her out of this addiction. Whether we agree or not, it ends where it began, if we can't get that we won't get anywhere. I count the time in my mind by the amount of songs that play. Leaning against a tree to relax.

Seven minutes.

Seven minutes have passed by the time she's back in body. She shakes her head at whatever the illusions are making her see.

"Ok, I'm done now, right?"

"No, we're not. We're goin' again and this time for four."

"WHAT? I don't know what this is for!"

"You know what it's for, Venus? You gave up on yourself! You don't see a reason to come back to your body, so you hurt yourself by staying disconnected from it. You need to find a reason to come back and then the illusion will repair itself accordingly." Someone pulled the plug on Venus's tear ducts. Before I can alter my brashness, Venus's face is soaked. Ok, I didn't mean to make her cry, but I don't regret what I said. Everything I'm saying to her are the things I wish someone said to me. I had to learn a lot of this on my own and I'm still learning like she is.

"You don't know me, X," she says muffling the break in her voice.

"I don't need to know you to know you're hurting. You try your best to hide it but, Venus, if nobody else understands, I do. I'm only asking you to try. It's not easy but it's not supposed to be. That's exactly why it shouldn't have happened." I should take my own advice, but this isn't about me.

"I can't. I wasn't sure what to do with my life before, but now I can't find the need to bother with it."

"Then let's find a reason to be bothered with it! You can't do that if you run away from yourself and your emotions. Sit with it and you'll find new and better ways to keep going. One that won't waste your life." The same way mine was wasted. Broken up into parts I can't remember correctly. *Get it together.* I turn to wipe my face where she can't see. I'm here to build them not show them I'm broken.

"Ok, look, we'll start with six minutes instead of five."

"Seven?"

"VENUS JU—" I sigh and drop my head before rubbing my eyes to continue saying this in a teachable way.

"Six minutes."

She leaves again but this time I hold her body up when she falls back so she doesn't collapse. We do this a few more times but she sits up against the tree, so she doesn't fall on the ground when her body goes limp. We only made it to four before she showed signs of slacking. She closed her eyes and leaned her head against her knee. This is gonna take time. The difference between me and them is that they actually have it.

Chapter 6
Isaiah's Past

October 3rd, 2095
Past: 6 months ago
Main City 27

If my shit keeps going missing and I end up in BT's graveyard, I'm taking every person involved with me. I can't leave anything on my desk and look away for more than five seconds without spending the rest of class looking around to see where it keeps disappearing to. Unless there's a neo-human in here, I don't know about. Actually, there's this same kid that keeps taking my headphone case off my desk but if I get up to look for it there it is again.

I looked inside the opening of the desk to make sure I didn't drop it in there and forget, but it's not there. But I know it's not, I looked three times already. I look to the front of me and I don't see my headphones near him, but I know he probably has them because this has happened enough times for me to know. I could give less of a shit about BT or suspensions right now because the one-time people seem to get the point is when childlike actions turn into a fight.

I get up from my desk to go get it back and as I push back my chair it screeches and someone calls me from the other side of the room. I don't know him, so I don't know why he's calling me, but when I turn to him he tosses me the case I was looking for. Right after I caught it, the guy I was walking toward turns to confront the thief about whatever form of entertainment he interrupted.

"You ruined it, Liam." Either he's ignoring them or didn't hear them because he continues looking at the tablet on his desk. I would sit back down at my seat but I think I'm just about over the same thing happening everyday. The only other seat is by Liam though, but I don't want him to think this is a sign to have a conversation either. But that's gotta be better than this. I sit in the desk spaced out next to his and of course...

"You know if you would put the case in your bag that wouldn't happen."

"Or maybe they shouldn't have had it in the first place. You're still on the first page of the assignment since this class started and you're not even supposed to be in here."

"What's that have to do with what I said?"

"Exactly. Do you see why we should mind our own shit now? I had it handled."

"No, you did not. You were about to walk into a fight you can't fight, and then get one step closer to BT."

"I can fight."

"No, you can't. Everyone saw what happened the last few times, so really a 'thank you' would've been fine." Ok, maybe, but I'm not gonna say that.

"It shouldn't take twenty minutes to answer that first question." He snatches his earbud out his ear as I take the tablet out my bag to do the questions I would've answered already had I not been preoccupied. He has to be a transfer student because we did that last week.

"So, do you know the answer then?" I purse my lips together then hand him my tablet, after he copies the answer he hands it back. It took about fifteen minutes before he asked me about another question.

"What? I can't take the class for you!" I reply after I glanced at him.

"Alright, but I'm already behind though, and I don't understand any of this."

"Gimmie the damn tablet." This is gonna be the first and last time I hand off any answers to him 'cause he's gonna learn how to do this himself.

October 27th, 2095
Past: 6 months ago

At this point I can't even blame the fact Liam's behind on the assignments on the transfer student situation because he missed this class several times already. I understand getting to your first class late but getting here a whole class later is crazy. I wasn't gonna show up either. I woke up this morning and felt sore enough to lay back down, but my parents weren't hearing it so now I'm here. I was gonna call him knowing he's either asleep or got up late, but my phone's not in my pocket.

"Ay, Isaiah! Catch." He better not throw my phone across this damn classroom. Of course, the inevitable happens and that's exactly what he does. The sleek phone glides through my hands, crashes on the floor, and I know the screen is cracked. I heard it. I've had that phone for years. It doesn't help that it's an old model from where my dad works either. I'll get up and get the phone but Liam's not here to stop me from making my way across this classroom.

The thief is laughing hysterically as if this was so damn funny. As I walk up to him in the middle of a belt of laughter, I land one punch on the side of his face, but I didn't expect him to stumble, nor did I expect to see a tooth flying. I didn't even get a chance to process what happened before I saw a fist fly at my face. When I swayed out the way, we look at each other and I look back at the floor. That actually worked? Everyone's standing up and watching me and the toothless thief throws his hands up when I hear the teacher walk in.

"ISAIAH!"

***

By the end of the day, I was in the office listening to my mom yell at me over the phone. Something, about how she doesn't wanna hear the TV on tonight because of what I did and about BT and suspensions and everything everyone says over and over again. I'm not sure what else she's saying because I'm still thinking about what happened earlier. I couldn't fight before but that's because I couldn't, but I sure as hell can now.

"You hear me, Isaiah?"

"Yeah."

"Good. Your dad said he picked up something for you at work today by the way and really you shouldn't get it, but I suppose it's a decent hobby to have, so it's not too bad."

"Is it a new phone?"

"No, I got the new phone. I don't know what he's bringing home today. Which by the way, please, keep the phone in your pocket, please."

"Alright and thank you."

"Mmhmm. Ok, I gotta pay attention on this road with this self-driving business. Love you, bye." Then the phone clicks.

* * *

When I got home my dad was already at the door fumbling with the keys and balancing what is supposed to be a computer, but it's entirely too massive to be one. There's cords all over the place and there's about three pieces to it. I rush up the steps to take it from him in case it drops on the steps and we have a mess of gears and coils to clean up. I hope this isn't the thing mom was talking about.

"Thanks. That thing is heavy, but it could work perfectly fine once you sit with it for a bit."

"Dad, I can't fix this."

"Why not? You fixed the whatever that thing is called, holographic-cubic-cubit."

"The holo-cube?"

"Yeah, the cubit-cubic." That's definitely not even close to what I said. He's still fumbling with the keys tangled up in one of the cords. This looks heavy but it doesn't weigh heavy. It's a possibility that I could be a neo-human, but if that's the case should I tell them? The door finally opens and I was gonna put the computer down on the coffee table but. . .

"Uh, uh, don't put that monster on my good coffee table, that table's older than you. Put that in your room." Ok, then. I freeze in place and swivel toward the kitchen to get to the hallway leading to my bedroom.

"Woah, what is that?"

"Not yours." I back into my room nearly dropping the oversized keyboard before I hear the cousin, I can't remember the name of, calling my mom. I don't know when or what part of my family dropped their orphan child here but they gotta come back and get them. Why do we always get caught up babysitting somebody?

Now what am I supposed to do with this? I reboot the holo-cube one time and now they think I'm a technician. On the other hand, I have nothing else better to do except for the homework I don't want to do, so I guess I'll sit with this. Just by opening the keyboard I know I'm gonna be here for a while. This dust is gonna kill me before BT can find me. What the hell? I'm waving a hand in front of my face when my phone rings. It's Venus asking about the work I haven't looked at.

"Um . . . I didn't get to it yet, I just got home," I reply after putting the phone on speaker and setting it on the floor. There's so many cords to detangle.

"Why?"

"Principal's office."

"Oh, who kicked your ass today?"

"Nobody this time."

"Wait that kid that lost a tooth—"

"Hell yeah." Then there's dead silence. I lift the keyboard up to get a better look. What is this, man?

"EH! I'll believe it when I see it. I got the answers to the test tomorrow though, but I'm not sending anything if you can't send me the homework." "Yeah, yeah, I got it." Then she ends the call. I put down the keyboard when I see a text from Liam with a picture someone posted of the mess I made in the 8:00 a.m. block.

That shit's sick. Where was this earlier?
I don't know. This is new to me too.

I know this is all the more reason to not get into fights but it's very tempting knowing that that's the damage I could do. I bet that'll be the first and last time my shit goes missing or ends up broken.

Chapter 7
X

Present Day: April 22nd, 2096
Main City 27

When I return to Room 238 with Venus, I find the other three eating from a box of pizza. I don't care that they're eating in my room, but I'm taking a slice. They all watch, frozen in place as I grab a piece of pizza. That's not half-bad actually.

"Nice work, Venus." She nods and I take another bite of pizza before scanning the room.

"PATCHES! You're next."

"Call me Patches one more time and this will be the last time we'll be stuck here with you."

"Patchy?" I shrug, sarcastic with the question. I get a kick out of aggravating him, but it's with a purpose. His first reaction is always to immediately hit back comparable to how he just tried to throw pizza crust at me. He was too slow though.

"Ooooo, bad through, Patches."

"Alexandria or whatever your name is, I don't know if you've stalked us enough to know this, but I will—"

"What? Throw more crust at me? I know you like to fight, Isaiah, but you never had to deal with someone such as myself. " With that being said, I slap a hand on his shoulder and we are back at the trees.

"So, Patches, you should be able to push this over." The wall of ice shoots up from the dirt and knocks hunks of metal out the way as it flakes.

"I can move that. That's light work."

"Prove it."

He smirks. He thinks it's gonna be easy, but I'mma ice a chair for myself so I can get comfortable and watch him struggle as I enjoy the last of my pizza.

"You think there's an easier way to do that other than pushing it over?"

"I think if you let me focus, I could find out."

"Yeah, but here you are doing the same thing, and it hasn't budged." By the time I finish my pizza he still hasn't knocked over the wall. He's taking forever and we don't have all day. I wave him off and step in front of him to take a knee. I dig my fingers under the wall and the ice leaving it stuck to the floor crackles as I pull it apart. The wall begins to fall over after it's separated from the ground. Before it falls over, I reach out a hand to take the ice back through my palm. That way it doesn't crash, make a bunch of noise, and we end up caught.

"Half your problems would be solved if you thought about what you were doing before you did it. Just because you can hit back doesn't mean that's your only option." I explain, after the last of the ice dissipates into my palm.

"It is. It's the quickest way to solve a problem."

"And it's the quickest way to run into something worse. I'm just saying there are better ways to get back at people who do you wrong."

"X, if you suggest any form of homicide, I'm reporting you to BT."

"No, no. I don't think any of you are capable of doing such things, but I'm talking about getting back productively. My mom used to say I had sticky fingers." I rambled on wiggling my fingers. *Why'd I do that?*

"Your point?"

"Steal their shit back. There's a few shops out here where you can turn stuff in and make a little extra cash. If you're gonna risk trouble make it worth something at least."

"So, why are you murdering folks then?"

"I'm a trained professional, Patches. I can do stuff like that. You on the other hand need to watch yourself before you make a decision you can't undo."

Yes, I'm being ever so slightly hypocritical, but I've dealt with BT long enough to know that that's not a group you tease. BT's involvement isn't a risk to take unless they come after you first. It makes no sense to attract their attention so carelessly and for such a small reason too. It's not worth it.

Chapter 8
Aruni's Past

October 27th, 2095
Past: 6 months ago
Main city 27

Why would I need any neo-human abilities when I can keep these hair ties on my wrists. Every morning there's this girl that asks me the same question. "Why don't you talk, Aruni'?"

The simple answer is silence, which I thought would be the equivalent of "maybe I don't want to talk to you because you're obnoxious and annoying." Most days the silence is enough to watch her greasy ponytail swing behind her head as she prances back to her seat like a tiny dog. For whatever reason today, she decided to put her orange fingers on my tablet screen and now I've just about had it. Yes, I keep hair ties around my wrist because I typically keep my afro in a puff, but it's also so I can shoot that iced coffee off her desk.

While I listen to the directions the teacher's giving, her voice slowly fades as I pluck the hair tie wrapped around my thumb and index finger. I need the teacher to turn around for a few seconds. As soon she does, I set my elbow on the desk and bend my thumb forward, eying her drink.

Thwink!

The drink flies off the desk and slams on the floor. Immediately, I slap my hand over my mouth to muffle my laugh. The look on her face is priceless. I think it splashed on her too. I wasn't sure if I would hit it this time but the fact, that I did is what makes this funnier than it already is.

"See! This is why I don't like having drinks on the desk in my class!"

"But I didn't spill it!"

"So, who did? It's on your desk." The ponytail girl reaches for the black hair tie in the small pool of coffee stretching across the floor and she snaps her head back to me. Damn.

***

After the hair tie incident, I ended up making my way down the hallway to the principal's office. This has happened before, though. Well not while I've been here, I've only been at this school for a month. I was gonna lie to defend myself, but I don't know if they have the patience to listen to me explain. That's why I don't say much to people unless I know them. Most people don't have the patience to let me speak, and if they do, they stopped listening two pauses or ums ago.

As I walk in the office, another kid walks by with a dark-green hoodie pulled over his head— though he's looking at his phone—I steal a glance, catching a partial image of his face. He has a white patch of skin under his eye though he's about the same umber skin tone as me. This is the second time I've seen him here since I've been at this school. Is he in trouble again?

"Aruni." That's not Auntie. I catch her face in the doorway, her twists are tied back in a bun behind her head. Anytime she crosses her arms and makes that face with her narrowed eyes, she reminds me of Mom. My puff reminds me of Mom as well since we have the same hair texture. Part of me misses her and wonders about what happened the day we left. Then again, I shouldn't have to wonder much based on the way my aunt heavily turned to us with a sorrowful look the moment we walked through the door. Everything happened so close together during those days. It made me resent BT more than I did before because now it's personal.

I swiveled on my heels to turn back out the door and she clears her throat. Ok, I'm gonna turn back around. Sitting in the chair in front of the principal's desk as she sits next to me, my hands find my hair tie as it wraps around my fingers, and I pluck at it as if it were a guitar string.

"Aruni, what's this with you and the hair ties? I didn't want to call your aunt, but I'm looking at your records and this seems to be a regular thing?" I open my mouth to say something, but I don't even wanna bother. I'm gonna sit here and attempt to make a point and it's not even gonna matter afterward.

"Look, you're a good kid. I haven't heard anything bad about you except for this. Your grades are decent. You're almost too quiet in class"—the principal pauses and exhales a heavy sigh of disappointment—"just don't let it happen again, alright?"

In the middle of the principal's speech, my eyes drift to the corner of the room. Her voice faded into nothing while I eyeballed the blue paint turn into watery swirls reminding me of an ocean. It smells like there's a tinge of sea salt in the air too. Auntie nudges my shoulder and I stop tilting my head at the wall to address the principal, but what did I see?

"Ok." I look back at the corner of the room and it's gone. It's probably nothing, maybe I'm sleepy.

My aunt and I leave the office, and everyone floods the hallway since the day is done. Liam probably left already if he knew our aunt was picking me up. I could take myself back to the house but that's one of those things where there's not much to debate about. Same as the day I told him I was going with him to the borders. Everybody is always nagging me about being responsible and explaining why Lee sticks around, but I'm good. I wanna do my own thing because I can if they would let me. I'm not reckless and irresponsible. Ok, I am, but I can handle myself. I enjoy a good laugh and being spontaneous every now and then.

November 3rd, 2095
Past: 5 months ago

Where is he at? I could've left and been home already. This is ridiculous. I sit against the lockers reading the book I downloaded onto my phone because what better way to pass time than reading a good fantasy book? From the corner of my eye I catch a glimpse of Liam walking down the hallway, but who is this with him? What's the green-hoodie guy doing here? Except now it's a gray hoodie but still.

Liam opens the locker—I told him he would share with me—and I stand up and clear my throat. He looks over at me and I dart my eyes toward the new kid because I do not know him and its gonna be awkward to eat at the diner if I don't know who this is. He could've at least warned me first.

"What? That's Isaiah. Isaiah, that's Aruni. See ,now you know each other." He hands me my black jacket and closes the locker.

I walk ahead to catch up with him while new guy walks on the other side. Then as we leave the hallway through the double doors here comes another new person.

"Hey, Isaiah, I had meant to ask you for the last few answers for the homework before we left class. I want to hand it in now and you're already here so . . ." She may be a new person to me but who doesn't know Venus?

"I already handed it in. I told you we should've done that before the group work."

"Ok, but that was before I realized I missed those questions. I thought I had it, but I have 'til tonight to submit it before it's late. Besides, I did you a favor by telling you what was on that test before the last class of today." She stopped and looked between each of us.

"Where are you guys going? Can I tag along and get the answers?" No. This is too much, I don't know these people! Isaiah swings his bag in front of him and unlocks the tablet and hands it to Venus who takes a picture of it before she hands it back.

"Thank you. Oh, are you guys going to that diner place? I heard the food was better now and I didn't each lunch." She looks over at Liam and I, and all it took was Liam's nod of confirmation for her to stick around. No wonder everyone knows Venus, she makes herself known apparently.

We sat down at the table in silence. From the moment Venus sat next to me, she has been on her phone texting away. Since she seems to be an extrovert, I was hoping she would start a conversation because sitting here and pretending to look at a menu I basically know-by-heart is making me antsy. I wanna get up and go to the bathroom, but I'll have to come back later. I don't even need to go, it's just that I'm typically talking to Liam about whatever by now but we're sitting in silence . Everyone talks at a restaurant, and we look misplaced as shit.

"What're you guys getting?" I asked the question in general, but I happened to look up at the new guy.

"I'm about to get this infinite ice cream bowl. Do you know that if you finish, like the whole thing, they'll only make you pay half the price for all the meals at your table?"

"Ah, I did that before. Tried and failed actually. Don't do it. I did and still had to pay for my whole meal along with the ice cream. I haven't been back here since, I had to recover from that hefty check they put on our table," Venus replies.

"I'll do it," I say, and Venus holds her hands up at me which showed off the hot-pink nails she has on. "Alright, but I can't help you." I love ice cream, it can't be that bad.

"I don't think you should."

"Because you told me not to, Lee, that's exactly why I'mma do it."

After we place our orders, we put the tablet back, and sit and wait. It's too quiet again. I was looking at my phone but the table behind Isaiah is melting. It's drooping as loose clay would and vapors rise from it. Nope, it's all in my head and I'm going to ignore it. I have a genuine question for new guy anyway.

"I saw you once . . . by the principal's office—well twice. It seems like you spend more time there than in class."

"HA!" Venus belts out before she can catch herself. "I'm sorry." Embarrassed, she folds her glossed lips back closed and continues looking down at her phone. Part of me feels bad for even saying all that. I don't say much either; I didn't want to make anybody uncomfortable. Sitting and talking is the only thing stopping me from seeing the oddities. I glance at the table and it's back to normal. It's fine. I'm fine. If I panic Lee's gonna panic and he's already paranoid. I can deal with it.

"Weren't you there the same day? What did you do?"

"Well . . . I shot a hair tie at someone's drink, but I didn't think I would actually make the shot. I was teasing at the thought and I ended up knocking her drink over. It was still funny though. She asks me the same question every day on purpose. What she didn't know is these hair ties are lethal." That got a slight smile out of the new guy as I popped the hair tie in between my fingers. It was all good until Liam decided to give his two cents.

"You could've ignored her."

"That's no fun, Lee, and I can't wear headphones in that class. And why are you wearing headphones if you're not listening to anything?" Isaiah was able to engage in this conversation the whole time with those buds plugged in his ears.

"Same reason why you shot the girl's drink off the table. Except I took your brother's advice."

"You should too, before you get another suspension and get sent off to BT," Liam replies to Isaiah without looking up from his phone. Then, I realize why I saw him in the office that day.

"I'm not getting sent to BT. It's not even that serious." It is, though, but Liam doesn't talk about those friends from the border much or at all since what happened last time.

As he replies, the ice cream platter is placed in front of me. The waiter says, good luck, as I struggle to stare above the mountain of scoops. Let me take my hoops off. This is gonna be a lot.

"You know what, new guy, this was your idea. Either you're gonna help me or you can deal with this."

Chapter 9
X

Present Day: April 22nd, 2096

Main City 27

y the time we got back to 238, Isaiah had left the room. Which is cool with me, I would've left too; to go clear my head. I didn't say much, instead I look to Aruni wondering how I'm gonna help her figure out what her abilities are.

"Ok, Aruni, you ready?"

"Yes. Actually, I was gonna show you yesterday before whatever happened with Lee." I apologized once already, I'm not apologizing again. I place a hand on her shoulder and we both disappear.

"Alright, so what'd you wanna show me?" "Wait. Before I do this, are you an avid reader?"

"No, but if I had time to sit around and read, yeah sure . . . Aruni, I'm gonna be completely honest, my patience is running very thin. Can we get to it please?"

"Alright fine, but you're not gonna understand a thing you see since you're too boring to read a good book."

I'm not boring. Am I? I'm preoccupied. Why do I even care? Before I could kick myself for being offended by something so small, I see a light brown fuzz, faze into view in my peripheral. What is that? I whip my head around to see something that looks completely out of place.

"It's a Pegasus!" Aruni swings her arms out at it with a wide grin on her face, proud of what she made, and I'm still at a loss for words. My eyes dart over the horse with wings—a Pegasus? After tilting my head hoping to understand, I lay a hand on its back and shit, it feels like—like a horse. Pegasus. Whatever.

"I'm guessing you've seen something better before. You haven't said anything."

"Aruni, how long have you been using your abilities?" I ask finding comfort in petting the silky soft coat. I've seen some crazy illusions and even dreamscapes but touching it? It shouldn't be this tangible.

"Since yesterday! You wanna see what else I made? There's this book I read with dragon hybrids that— "

"Aruni, stop. Hold on for a second." I snatch my hand from the fake animal to close my eyes and take a breath. The horse thingy is still there when I open them. "There's no way you did all of this yesterday."

"Why not? What's so unbelievable about me being good at something?" Are they all this sensitive? I swear I'm being nice. I know I am.

"I didn't mean it like that. It's... typically these things take time."

"Well, it didn't for me. When I was in the ice box the other day, I saw something. It was a ball of light and I thought I was hallucinating but—but I wasn't! Those are illusions! I'm an illusionist, X! It makes sense now!"

As she replies we both flinch at the sound of a screech coming from the sky. Thick gray clouds swarm and thunder and lightning fill the middle. It's going to rain, or worse. Either way, I don't wanna find out, so I lay a hand on Aruni's shoulder and we both poof back to the room. From the room window, the sky is clear. Walking toward the window, I squint at the sky. What was that? The borders aren't that far from here, how is the sky clear all of a sudden? How did it get dark all of a sudden? After staring out my window I look back at Aruni who's staring out the window as well.

"Ok, so maybe I should've mentioned that I don't exactly have complete control over what I make." It never crossed my mind that *that* was an illusion. I looked back out the window and the sky is still clear. There's no way this all happened yesterday, all from the little ice box?

"Right. Ok. You, Liam, let's go." I wave him over and rub the pressure in my eyes away. That is not normal. Then again, her brother isn't, and neither am I.

Chapter 10
Liam's Past

September 4th, 2095
Past: 7 months ago
Main City 15

Most people know neo-humans are meant to be in one of the New Cities but that doesn't change the fact a lot of them end up stuck in the Main cities. It's not all that easy to cross over and run into New Cities from here without knowing someone or having a hefty amount of cash on hand. No matter the case, it doesn't stop them or me from hanging around the bordering areas to look out at what could've been. Maybe even wonder what life would be like if we didn't have to watch every corner for BT. They can't go into the New Cities because BT labs aren't supposed to be in any of the New Cities.

"Did you ask your mom about your cousin in New City 15, yet?" I've been asking Aaron the same question for the past week and the answer is usually the same, but I wait for a response as if I don't already know. Eventually it may change. It needs to, because hiding from BT in the middle of an empty field of grass when the road isn't too far ahead makes it very easy to spot us. They're not usually out here but they've been riding by along the edge of New City a lot more often. I told them we should probably stay hidden in the trees, but we end up in the bordering areas looking at the place we can't go to every time.

"You know his mom said he can't go out there." Very typical of Sade to be so pessimistic, but I get it that isn't that simple or sweet.

"Yep, but when I get a job I'mma save up and I'll leave by myself." I wish I could believe him but saving for that would take years, and as a neo-human they don't really have years. The sooner they can leave the better.

"That's expensive, though." Sade replies as she takes a knee into the grass and places her palm in the dirt.

"But at least you don't have to pay for travel. Since you could appear there." I would love to just appear in places if I could. I wouldn't have to worry about getting home late or getting caught up out here if I didn't have to account for travel time. Then again, I don't wanna be isolated anywhere to the point where I develop that ability anyway.

"That's true. Matter fact, did you know I could teleport objects?" He walks over to a stone in the ground and picks it up. It evaporates, and reappears in the air next to me. It falls into my hand after it pieced itself together from dust.

"You think you can use that on a person?"

"He will turn you into dust, Lee." Or maybe we'll be fine. I kept that to myself as I shook my head. The main reason why she's here every day is to drain some of the plants of its life, leaving patches of brown in the green. She takes it back home for the reason she refuses to share. She doesn't have to. I can guess and assume she's doing that for someone who's sick back home. If her dad has the same abilities she has, I'm assuming it's her mom that needs the help since she has no other siblings. If she asks, I'll pretend I don't know. She has a good reason for not sharing, I'm sure. She stands back up from the now brown patch of grass and dusts the dirt off her hands.

"Shit, Lee should be worried about you with the poor plants you kill out here every day." She flicks her hand forward and I take a step back as the grass grows wild in front of me and back over to him.

"Well, now that problem is solved."

"You're gonna stop doing that when I learn how to teleport people," he replies pushing past the tall grass.

"We'll be forty by then so I'm not worried." Is that a BT van? No, those are BT vans. Walk away from the group to get a better look, their banter fades in the background. That's BT's blue and green logo.

"Ay! We gotta go!" I yell, but he's too busy teasing her with the phone she's trying to get from his hand.

"For what?"

Why argue instead of—whatever. "BT, IT'S BT!" They freeze in place as my jog turns into a run. We rush to grab our bookbags and run off into the trees as the blue uniforms hop out the trucks. For the most part, we're all running at the same pace. We hop over branches and boulders, we swerve in and out of trees, but I know BT people are closing in.

"You think you can teleport us?" We can't keep running like this, there's seven of them and three of us.

"WHAT?! No, that's a horrible idea!"

"We need to try! We can't outrun them!" I look back again and I see two blue uniforms have split from the group. They're gonna cut us off.

"Make a left!"

"How—"

"MAKE A LEFT!" I run between them both and grab their wrists to take lead. They weren't listening fast enough. Up ahead I can see a small cave and I let them both go so we can hide inside and figure this out.

"You gotta teleport us." I ask without asking for a second time. It could be the running or BT's presence making the air seem thin right now.

"I can't!"

"Try." Neither of them look at me while I make my suggestion but instead, they look at each other.

"Ok, look. You run back to the Main City and Aaron will teleport us out of here."

"Are you sure?" She's taking way too long to respond.

"Yeah, I'm sure... He can barely teleport himself, there's no way he can take both of us back."

"You're gonna be fine, Lee, those BT people are slow as hell compared to you." He nods and Sade spares me a half-smile, but this isn't right. Either they're telling me a half-truth or they know this isn't gonna work.

"Are you sure?"

"Yes, now hurry up before you get snatched up." Aaron pushes my arm, failing to reassure me. I shake my head before leaving the small hiding spot under the stone. I sure hope this works. In the corner of my eye, I saw a flashlight so I run like they said, but when I looked back...

The flashlight was pointed right at the hiding spot and BT members from all directions flock toward it. I can't go back now. All I can do is hope they return tomorrow.

***

It was dark by the time I got home, and I found myself scanning every block and corner, keeping an eye out for BT. I would be grateful to be home now but it's 9:00 p.m. and I was supposed to be home two hours ago, but walking through all those trees, stepping over stones, and roots take time. It also doesn't help when the buses stop accepting school passes after 5:00 p.m., so I had to walk. I don't do this every day either so it shouldn't be that serious. But If I say it, it's gonna make this worse than it needs to be. As I approach the house, I'm reminded I still need to fix the white chipped paint on the door. From the moment I walked through the door my mom is sitting in the chair waiting.

"You're lucky your dad is asleep." Now should I tell her the truth or should I make up something? What did I say last time? There's a tutoring program after school. Thing is I don't go to that shit. I'm in school for eight hours a day, what I look like staying? I'm going home after those eight hours. What time does that end though? Three or four? I can't make an excuse for four. Did they even meet today?" You're not gonna answer?" No. I should've thought about this in the three hours it took me to get here. I was more worried about those BT trucks.

"Liam, where were you, and don't say tutoring because I called them and they said they've never even met you."

Yes, they have—once. I'm already in trouble but I can't tell them I was by the borders with neo-humans. Last time that turned into a whole event I'd rather not relive.

"I was at the park with some friends"

"Which friends and which park? The one by 85th?" she asks raising an eyebrow.

"Yeah..."

"Liam, that park closes at 7:00 p.m. and it's not that far from the school for you to be getting home this late."

"If I tell you the truth, you're gonna tell Dad?"

"We both already know the truth so what's the difference? I know you know; you're leaving to your aunt's house this weekend. I also know you know that you was supposed to pick up your sister today—which you didn't—so she walked home by herself. By the way did you know about the whole hair tie situation?"

"No." Yes.

"Well, your sister has been shooting hair ties at people. Why must you do all this the day before you leave for the weekend? Did you even make sure everything's packed? Did you check you and your sister's plane tickets?"

"Alright, no, but— "

"Listen." She holds her hand up and shakes her head then smooths the sides of her puff. At this point there's no point in talking.

"I know you were back at the borders with those neo-humans again, and I'm beginning to wonder if you want to go where they go." No one, neo-human or not, wants to go where they go but at this point what does it matter? I don't even know if they got away or not. I would call them but what if the phone ringing gets them caught, I'll see them tomorrow.

"Go ahead, go to your room. You gotta get ready to get out of here tomorrow."

"Can you at least tell me why we're leaving? It's not even close to summer yet so why fly there for just the weekend?"

"Go get your stuff together, Liam."

I don't understand why I can't get a definite answer. The only time we go there is for the summer or if it's a week or two-week-long break. To fly there only to be there for three days makes no sense, and we have no details on why we're leaving.

"Put the pillow down, Aruni." As I flick on the lights to the bedroom I see her grinning face on the top bunk like she wouldn't be the first thing I see when I walk in.

"You got in trouble for hanging out with your neo-human friends again?" she asks, tossing the pillow to the side and laying on her back. "Why are you flicking hair ties at people?"

"It's funny, they're annoying, and that class is boring. At least your dad is sleep."

"He's your dad too."

"Nah . . . I got caught by him today." I sit on my bed and rummage through the duffle bag but I get back up, already knowing what that meant. She leans over the bed to show me her arm and I can see the dark purple mark around her dark-brown forearm.

"Your pops has an iron grip." She jokes about this more than she should, and every so often we laugh about it because there's nothing else we can do. That doesn't work when it's bad like this and I wasn't here so its not as easy to laugh.

"That's not funny, Aruni."

"It has to be funny . . . We live here." She rolls back on her bed and all I could do is shake my head. Maybe it's a good thing we're leaving, we'll be far away from him.

"I don't know about that; I don't think this trip is for a weekend."

"Why not?"

"Mom seems anxious, and why would dad be asleep this early unless he had to get up extra early in the morning. If it's the two of us going then we should be the only ones that need to get up that early."

"Hm . . . What time is that flight for?"

"11:00 a.m."

"We can leave late."

"No, we shouldn't. We need to get through customs and all that." I also need to check the borders before we leave, so if anything, I'm leaving earlier than when we're supposed to. If I miss that 8:00 a.m. bus I'm not gonna make it there. I told Aaron and Sade I would meet them by the borders before I left, and now I really gotta go see if they made it back or not. I hope they're there. They're always there.

I sit back down on the bed and pack the rest of the clothes I left out, ignoring the possibility of whatever spontaneous idea she has.

"Nah, I wanna see what's going on and I know you do too." I'm not even gonna entertain that but of course a pillow hits the top of my head.

"You listening?"

I was before she did all that. "Yes and no. We're not doing that. And next time you hit me with a pillow, I'm throwing them out the window."

"Okay."

"Don't touch my phone alarms, Aruni."

"I didn't say I would."

"I'm serious. I'm tryna go back to the borders tomorrow morning before we leave."

"Really? You could call them though."

"Not this time."

"BT didn't' catch them, right?" I hear her sit up in the bed before she leans over to look at me. I don't even bother to look up.

"I'm going with you."

"No."

"Yes, I am. The airport is closer to that part of the borders anyway, and you won't have to come back to travel with me. I'll tell mom we're both leaving early to get through customs."

"It's too dangerous to be out there and we don't have any abilities."

"I don't care, I'm going with you. No debates this time."

***

When morning came, our parents were up already. Down the hallway I watched my dad pace back and forth as the floorboards creak under the carpet. They whisper-argue about whatever they didn't tell us. I stopped in the hallway before entering the bathroom, I need to hear what they were saying.

Dad sees me and I scurry inside, dropping the idea to listen in at all.

By the time I got out the bathroom, Aruni was standing by our bedroom door with her duffle bag in hand probably to listen in as well. I wonder if she was able to hear anything. When I walk into the room, she shakes her head. She heard as much as I did. Watching them panic quietly doesn't happen often unless something is about to go wrong and we aren't supposed to know about it.

"Maybe we should leave." Aruni says shrugging.

"Nah, we got time."

"Didn't you say we have to catch your bus?"

"Yeah, but why they panicking like that?" As I ask, I hear the front door crash open and both me and Aruni run down the hall to find someone we don't know. He has on a blue suit and two BT workers follow him and begin to flank Mom and Dad at their sides.

"Aruni, you see Mom's hands too, right?"

"No! They're not there, they're practically dust! When was she gonna tell us she's a neo-human?" She whips her head to us as we stand on the other end of the room then looks back to Dad. I'd never seen Mom look so afraid, she walks over and takes a knee in front of us.

"The plan wasn't to tell you anything and there's a lot you don't understand, and you may understand one day but right now I need you to keep the questions to a minimum and leave."

"But can't you teleport away? Your hands—"

How and when did this piece of metal get in her shoulder? When she shows us everything else stops. There's a small red light blinking on it and she doesn't need to say much more for me to know how these people got here, and why it's not easy to leave. They would find her as long as that thing's flashing. If that's the case, then why is my dad still here? Either he decided to stay, or he has one too. But if he has one too then—Is he a neo-human?

"Mom, what's gonna happen after they leave?" She takes a hold of my hand and the same way I felt yesterday at the borders is the same sense that heats underneath my skin. This can't be happening again where I end up running and people tell me half-truths about them being ok. She's not ok. None of them are.

"Look out for your sister for me, ok?" She looks at me with glassy eyes and Aruni hasn't stopped staring at the strangers who haven't stopped watching us. Before she lets go of my hand there's a pang of pain in my head. A scene of someone slamming their fist against the door and yelling flashes before my eyes. I snatch my hand away and she stares at me, her hands frozen. I'm as confused as she is. What did I see? Who was that?

"Lee?" Instead of replying I grab my bag and Aruni's hand and we both rush out of the apartment and the people in the suits watch us leave closing the door right behind us.

"Liam what was—"

"We gotta catch the bus." We couldn't stay there. Those people in suits are from BT, who else would they be?

That was the last time we spoke. After we got off the bus, we remained quiet and the leaves from the ceiling of trees crunched beneath our feet. We lug our bags in our grip, step over stones and overgrown roots as we trudge through and head for the border.

My hands have been burning since I left the house, but it wasn't bad 'til we got here.

"Liam! Your hand!" You've gotta be shitting me. Now I get abilities? Looking at where my hand should be, I drop my bag to see the other one hasn't disintegrated into floating dust, but it will. The cracks in my skin sting as they pull apart. "That's what happened to Mom back home! Where was this earlier? I thought when—when a neo-human has two neo-human parents their abilities manifest around age ten?"

"Does that matter right now? What happens if I disappear!"

"Then don't!" How did this even happen? *I saw something when Mom touched my hands and then as soon as I left . . .*

"Liam! How are we gonna stop you from disappearing? We need to catch the plane!" I can't figure this out right now, the slight burn hasn't gone past my right hand and the other one is fine. I'm gonna hope for the best. I need to see if they're there and then we can leave. So, I continue ahead in hopes that Aruni will give up on calling me.

By the time we got to the borders it was fifteen minutes after the time we said we'd meet and they're not here. They should've been here already, but I knew they wouldn't be. I knew they'd be taken. I know there wasn't much else to do but we could've come up with something or maybe we should've stayed hidden like I said. Then none of this would've happened.

The burning I nearly forgot about creeps up my arms. Even the bag in what was my hand looks like dust floating in the air. It's noticeable enough for me to look at particle pieces of hands and notice that it's not getting better overtime. I shake one out but, that's not gonna stop it.

"Your arms are disappearing! You can't control that? Stop it or something!"

"What do you think I'm tryin to do?"

"Well, it isn't working!" If I'm gonna disappear I can't leave Aruni here. "Hold on to my shoulder."

"NO! I'm not—"

"Aruni!" She takes a hold of my shoulder and lets out half-a-yell before we both disappear.

When we reappear, we end up right in front of the exact hangar we were supposed to be at. The burning has ceased and I look at my reformed hands and Aruni looks at me breathing like we ran a mile. All we could do was stare up at the sign unsure of what to do. Unsure of what this means for our parents and my friends who are now missing. And for me and Aruni. I can't run away from myself. What am I supposed to do with uncertainty? And what am I supposed to do with this new ability I know nothing about.

Chapter 11
X

Present Day: April 22nd, 2096
Main City 27

I can't make sense of how it took Aruni a day to do what I would assume could take months to learn—maybe even years. I can't make illusions like that and I've known about my abilities for a while now. It could've been almost six months, if I count from the day I left the lab. There was hardly a way to track the time in the mindscape or whatever it's called. I would've needed to be outside of it to make sense of that.

I lay a hand on Liam's shoulder, and we make our way back to the slew of trees. I don't know how to approach this but there has to be a better way to do this without unintentionally oversharing.

"Ok, so how exactly do your abilities work? Can you skip all the informational stuff or?"

"I know as much as you do but when you find out, you let me know."

"Yeah, but I'm not a mimic. You've never used your abilities before?"

"... Once maybe but that's it."

"How long ago was that?"

"Almost 7 months ago." Wait, so he's had these abilities this whole time? Well, if he's not around other neo-humans then I guess it's not much help.

"What happened the first time? Don't give me all that shit about, 'why do I need to know' and all that because you already know way too much."

"How much do you know about BT?"

"Too much." He paused, squinting at me with curiosity. "Why do you keep asking me that?" I ask out of my own.

"It's not nearly the same as what happened to you, but I've been around them before. I used to hang out around the borders a lot with other neo-humans I knew."

"They got taken." — My shoulders drop at the realization— "But why would I know anything about that? What did you see?"

"You knew someone from BT."

Ok, I walked into that. I did know someone and that was enough for me to know what he saw. I take a breath, lean on the tree, and stare into the sky. What could I have missed to and how I could've avoid so much information being shared? Circumstances I'd rather not remember at all, let alone have some stranger know about it.

"Why don't you find somebody else, because I can't change the fact that—"

"I can't. Going to New City and asking for help is like asking to go back. Looking for people in the Main Cities and recruiting them is like pulling teeth because they're either deep into some shit or they get caught too easily. You four are the only people I've come across where I might actually have a chance at making this work."

"So . . . I don't know. Should I sit this out? And what do you mean go back? You've been there before?" I push myself off the tree with my leg to meet him eye-to-eye and narrow my eyes as if that'll help me read him better.

"You ask too many questions, Liam."

"You leave too many questions unanswered." I cross my arms and he crosses his.

"First of all, stop doing that. Secondly let me answer two of your plethora of questions. You're not gonna sit this out because you can copy multiple abilities. I hate to admit it, but you might somehow be the most useful being a mimic. To answer your other two questions, I will say what you once said to me. You don't need to worry about me."

"So, I can't copy you, but you can copy me?"

"Exactly. See, I answered another question." He uncrosses his arms and an ever-so-slight smile appears on his face. I pretend to wipe my nose to not do it back. I'm not here to be friendly, I'm here to get my shit handled so I can find my mom before she finds me. She's out here. I don't know where, but the BT worker in New City does.

"So, what're we doing about the flashes then?"

"I don't know anything about how your abilities work so I don't know. What I will say is to keep it to yourself. I don't wanna hear about it and nobody else should, and if I find out you said something then I might have to stay true to my threats."

"Your empty threats."

"They're not gonna be empty if you try some shit, and I promise you I will know, and I will keep my word."

"Yeah, I believe you. You convinced me. I got another question though." Really? Is written in the way I tilt my head to the side. Why am I entertaining this? I got too much to worry about.

"You always hang out by that hotel?"

"Why?"

"So, I know where to go to ask you more questions." My hand slides down my face to hide the smile that keeps creeping in. He's gonna piss me off. I'm not sure why but he is. I place a hand on his shoulder to signal we're done with this. I can't stand him not one bit. I can't wait till this over.

Chapter 12
X

It's early in the day, so if I had to guess, I'll be meeting with the squad in a few hours. I'm about to get ready to leave 238 'cause I need to find something to eat, and now would be a good time to hit up a few places since the streets are busy.

It took almost no effort for me to fit into this lifestyle, it's like I was built for it. Maybe I was. I did wake up in a lab. Who knows what they did to me in there.

As I'm about to walk out the door there's a knock. Why though? They're not supposed to come until later. I crack open the door and see Liam wearing a sweatshirt combination blue and black like most people our age do out here. See. Already he's being a nuisance, because why is he over here?

"Can I help you? You're super early and I have stuff to do." Right after I finish my poor attempt at shooing him away, he lifts up a bag of groceries. Why would he do that? I didn't ask for that.

"Aruni and I thought you could use some stuff."

"I don't need anything. I'm fine."

"X, your fridge is empty." Why were they in my fridge? They could've made all the ice melt out.

I snatch the bag of groceries and open the door; I might as well let him in. *What did he bring me anyway?* He really brought food, like canned foods.

"Do you think this is a joke?"

"No, X, it's just food."

I stare at the bag for a while then look back at him. I didn't ask for that. I put the groceries on the table in what's supposed to be a kitchen.

They playin' games with me. I bet they need something, and guess what? They're not gonna get it. *Who told him to do this? What is he up to?* No, I was right before. This is a team effort but I'm not sure for what yet.

"Liam, what do you want?"

"I have some questions, actually."

"Of course, you do."

"When you teleport, is it supposed to feel like your skin is burning off?"

"For me it's more of a pinch so, yes? Maybe?"

"Is it normal to not be able to coordinate your steps afterward?"

"The first few times, yes. Sometimes." I should put this stuff in the cabinet, I'm standing here talking when I could be doing literally anything else. Which reminds me, I still gotta get some more soap and toothpaste before it runs out. I like having it when I need It.

"The out of body thing. Venus said it could kill you?"

"Well, not necessarily. If you stay out of body too long then, yes, probably." I turn around to face him when he begins the next question and I lean on the counter. I wish he'd hurry up and be done so I can go about my day.

"What about those orb things? What are those?" he asks, rolling his hands in the air creating an air sphere.

"When you said you wanted to know where to go to ask me more questions, I thought you were joking. You're giving me a headache."

"It was a partial joke."

Running from BT is stressful. Being stuck in an artificial world for most of my life is stressful but *this*. This might be the one to take me out. I search my mind for a reason to react in anger but I'm not gonna find it. This was my idea and he's playing along with it. At least I could appropriately react to my other problems, I can't with this.

I sit on the beat-up couch and nod at the empty space next to me so for him to come and sit. It's best if I show him around rather than being asked fifty-million questions about these abilities. I hate that I have to do this, but this is the only way we know how to copy the ability. So, I let the heat of the soul underneath my body rise its way to the surface of my skin. In front of him I offer a hand covered with purple aura and he analyzes it instead of accepting the gesture. This could be because of what happened last time we did this. It didn't end well for either of us, so I get it.

"Well, are you going to copy the ability or are you going to stare at my hand?" I need to find a tad of empathy so I can get past this. But I made up my mind a while ago on why I don't do that. Now all of a sudden, I end up in a space where I'm being eased into searching for something I stored away. It's gonna take me a while to recognize it under all the dust, but I'll know it when I find it. I know I'm gonna have to be patient with all four of them, I hope they can be patient with me too. But I'm not gonna tell him or any of them that.

After, I have to invite him a second time to take my hand, he holds it like it's glass and I immediately leave body because I don't want the moment to last longer than it should. After another few seconds, he pretty much stumbles out of body. This is the one time I'll allow myself a good laugh as it bubbled up from my ghost body.

"Take it easy, alright? It's startling at first. You're gonna be lighter here." After watching me laugh at him he whirls around at the orbs, and I'm reminded of my first time being here.

"If you think this is cool, we should go outside." Without saying anything, I float to the roof of the building and Liam follows after me. One of the orange orbs dances in front of my face. When the tip of my finger touches the edge of the sphere it flows into my arm.

"Go ahead," I say as I gesture for him to do the same. He touches a blue one and looks taken back. Without saying a word, he takes a red one and does the same.

"What do you think?" I ask, wondering what's going on in his head.

"I think, the blue one is sadness and the red one is anger."

"Liam, what?"

"You don't feel that?"

"No. Its ... a ball of hot air." What is he talking about? I tap a green one and I'm staring at it still not understanding. I've been here before and It's only his first day out here, so I know what I'm talking about. I side-eye him and he lets the other ones go without instruction and turns to me with a yellow light dancing in his hand.

"Joy."

"Joy? Liam, you think these things are emotions?"

"Maybe, but it could be other stuff too."

"No." Then he gives me the same *"really?"* look I gave him yesterday and I roll my eyes ignoring the teasing again. He holds out his hand and I guess it's for me to take the yellow lights. In an act of rebellion, I'm not going to. Funny enough he did the same thing to me earlier, the only difference is I'm not budging so my arms remained crossed.

"There's one over there, if you wanna take one that way." He walks away and I turn around to see where he's going. He stops in front of a yellow one and I side-eye him again because I can't undo my stubbornness. How does he know what this is? What if he's wrong? We shouldn't even have been out here for this long. Eventually after looking at the yellow and cutting my eyes back at him, I uncross my arms. I slap a lazy hand through the yellow light after rolling my ghost eyes again.

"You were saying?" There's still no difference.

"Ok, what about this? You know where your heart is or would be? Since we're not—"

"I know 'cause we're out of body. Why'd you ask?"

"Put the yellow light there."

This is such a waste of time. I roll my ghost shoulders back still with a deadpan expression on my face but then warmth crawls over me causing my eyebrows to knit together. Then there it is; alight in my chest and under my face.

"Joy," I breathe. My eyes widen and I stand up straighter and let out half-a-laugh as I look down at the traces of yellow inside of my arms. This is . . . something. Something I couldn't put words to even if I knew every word to use. I look at him and my smile drops when he crosses his arms at me.

"Don't look at me like that. How was I supposed to know? How did you know, actually?"

"I don't know. I wanted to know what it was, so I took my time to find out." Took his time—the irony. That could be a sarcastic joke at my impatience or it's an actual word of advice. I was ready to leave earlier to be onto the next thing but now I seem stuck here, but I want to be. I'm noticing things I didn't notice before like how the clouds in the sky resemble the waves in the ocean or how the pink flowers outside ruffle in the breeze. For once I can take it all in as if time was on my side. This new sentiment feels good, especially when time has been more like an enemy than a friend.

Maybe he's not as annoying as I thought or it's this yellow light making me think opposite of what's going through my conscious mind. He isn't half-bad though and he learns quick. I just learned something from him.

"You sure you've never been out here before?"

"Positive. I only knew what Venus told me."

"So, Venus told you?"

"No . . ." *Yes, she did.* I'm gonna see for myself later.

"But you can find out yourself when you see her later." And there it is. This orb stuff isn't influential enough to stop me from narrowing my eyes at him. How did he meet Isaiah and Venus anyway? I was around them enough to know basic stuff like their names and where they're from, and where they hang out and stuff, but I don't know how they met.

"How'd you guys meet?"

"Well, Venus met Isaiah first, so she kinda showed up and long story short, Isaiah was gonna get himself sent to BT if he kept up with the fighting in class."

"That sounds about right. Why did you care though? I get why you'd care now but why care then?"

"I had careless friends like that before. We were at the open part of the borders, I told them we should stay hidden but they said they couldn't see New City 15 from there. BT rolled by, I told them we should leave but they didn't leave 'til I told them it was BT. We were running from them on foot which isn't easy to do in the trees obviously. I had one friend who could teleport but he didn't think he could make it with both of us, so we hid. Then they told me to run and ensured me they'd be ok. I asked them twice if they were sure but when I went back the day after..."

See I would say what he said to me the other day but I don't believe that an "I'm sorry," fixes anything. Sorry doesn't give me a redo at life, and sorry isn't gonna bring those people back.

"Well, I guess that's a good reason to not wish that on anybody else... unless they deserve it. BT isn't given enough credit for how destructive they actually are. As plucky as Isaiah is you did him a favor by keeping him off their radar."

"The people you went after are all from BT?"

"No, not all of them. Not anymore. It doesn't stop me from killin' them anyway. Anybody that has the heart to do shit like that deserves what I deliver, and I happen to be really damn good at it."

"Yeah, I can see that. You threw a giant icicle through a damn window and left that shit in the street. Had people skidding off the road and running into it. You quite literally stopped traffic, and then you stepped out the window of the building and disappeared. Meanwhile, I was tryna get home."

Alright I'll spare him a laugh for that one. "Typically, I'm a little more discreet but that one gave me a hard time. She was a neo-human, the strong kind, I needed a little extra flair." Alright, it's time to let this yellow go cause I'm sitting here laughing with him like I don't have something else better to do.

"Ok, let's get outta here. I gotta go pick up some stuff from the store." I sink back through the floor, and it takes him a few seconds to follow me.

"You mean steal stuff from the store." I hear him say as he rises from the couch, now that were back in body.

"You gonna call BT on me?"

"Wouldn't even bother putting them through that." I huff out a small laugh, stand at my door, and swing it open so we can cut this short. "You still gotta be here later."

"Wasn't thinking about skipping out on it."

What am I doing? I'm not supposed to be cool with him or any of them for that matter. I'm not gonna get attached to these people. I don't know them and they don't know me. They have full reason and capability to lie me in a ditch before I even get a chance to find my mother. I know what I need them for and we're gonna keep it at that. I close the door behind me pushing away memories of what happened this morning. Of all the things I don't remember and all the things I do, this comes across so much more nuanced. I can't rest in the yellows of today because the yellows from yesterday led me to a place where it does not exist.

Chapter 13
X

Present Day: May 9th, 2096
Main City 27

Spending too much time around them welcomes too many changes, and it's only been two weeks. As I lie on my couch noticing things I didn't notice before, my mistakes are haunting me. I rehash cases where blood is on my hands. All those people I left behind. The victims of these cases don't disappear, they stay and take the blame. If I'm not around who else could've done it? At that, I sit up on the couch and bury my face in my hands recalling the blurry faces of victims I left a mess to. I shouldn't have left them there. But what was I supposed to do? I couldn't take them all with me, but anything is better than being claimed by BT. I should've at least helped them hide. I'm gonna fix this. I'm nothing like the people I killed. It unsettles me to know that I left them to a new type of torture. *What's the point then?*

I peel myself off the couch and cover up before I make my way out to find a BT van or truck to follow back to a lab. I said

I would never go back but I'll go back to give myself some piece of mind. They've been through enough already and they deserve freedom too.

I walk outside and slither in between buildings. Maybe, I can catch on to one that may be heading back. I have to do this right the first time or I'll be stuck with BT *again. Maybe I should plan beforehand.* After a moment I decide against it, I can't plan something like this on my own. I would need someone else on the other side or have someone run with me. *I got this, I always got it, I'll be fine.*

The sour smell from this dumpster is burning my nostrils but the scent dissipates when I spot BT taking someone off the street. It could be one of the people I forgot about. If it is then that just made this easier. The trucks don't have windows to the back, so I teleport myself to the back of the truck and take the ride with them. The captives in the back of the truck sit on benches with black cuffs on their wrist ringed with blue lights. They stare at me wide eyed. I put my fingers over my lips, so they don't make a scene, and for the most part they don't, but they do stare. They could be wondering who would be crazy enough to jump *into* a BT truck.

I don't know if this is gonna work out. I don't know if we're all gonna be ok. The only thing I know is I couldn't stay where I was. I'm not letting BT take more people away from an opportunity to live their lives only to throw them into a place where they pry it from their broken hands. Some may be under in a simulation with little to no control over what they experience and see. Some may be waiting in a cell unsure of what awaits them next while they're asked questions they either can't or shouldn't answer. I understand that and I know what it's like. My story is their stories, and their stories are mine, and they all deserve a chance to continue them. Like I did.

When we got to the lab, the people that were driving the truck waste no time getting to the back. Before they can finish unloading all the people like cargo, I disappear into the building.

I jump into the middle of a bleak, gray hallway. I know nothing about this building so I'm hoping for the best anytime my body fades. I slide into the room closest to me and it's filled with cleaning supplies.

I'm gonna have to walk out of here but I can't go walking around the hallways like this. I could walk around if I had one of those uniforms though. There weren't many people in the hallway, but someone is gonna walk in this room soon. So, I make myself comfortable for a while sitting in the corner of the room until I hear the sound of faint footsteps coming down the hall.

I hop up to slide behind the shelving units and grab a metal bucket from off the shelf. When he walks in I hit him in the head and he collapses to the floor. Quickly, I strip him of his uniform and hold it against my body. This is gonna be a little big on me, but it works.

I leave the closet and push the metal cart he left by the door, and for safe measure I keep my head low under the hat to keep my face as covered as it can be. The captives they brought here are probably somewhere near the entrance right now. There's a lot of storage units though. *So, I'm in a basement.* This could be a basement. I'll find out when I get inside the elevator. The doors are about to close so I pick up my pace. Once I'm inside I wait for the doors to close but it's taking too long and I can see someone running down the hallway. *Where's the close button?* When I see it on the screen I hurriedly tap it until it closes right in her face. A quiet chuckle leaves me before the doors open again.

Is that the kid from the deli? I recognize the face, but I wish I didn't. She looks around swiveling her head around the room with wide, glassy eyes. I'm gonna get them out of here. I follow them for a while but the doors close on another long blank white hallway.

People walk by a lot more often on this floor and some of them squint at me or stare with a question behind their faces. There's a card on this uniform. Maybe I can get in with this. I walk to the door with the cart looking for the scanner. The BT lady that was with them was here but she definitely used her eyes. If I could, I would've snatched her back over here to open this door, but fantasizing about revenge on BT workers isn't gonna get them outta here.

There's a good amount of people walking around right now I can't just poof away unless they're looking at something else. I turn away from the door and tether as many people as I can, most of their eyes cloud with gray. Suddenly the evacuation alarms blare. They all look at each other and begin to scramble as the chaos of red flashing lights and panicky questions build, despite this all being a figment of imagination. That should keep them going for a bit. Now who's eyes are gonna get me into this hallway? I see someone in a blue uniform, and I grab his arm as the gray from his eyes drop.

"No guns. I don't like guns," I say to him before I snatch it and slam it against the wall, crushing it underneath my force. He started to run but I snatch him back by the collar and use my other hand to force his head to the scanner.

I know his eyes aren't closed.

"C'mon now, open your eyes so we can move along." He goes to tap the earpiece. I sigh and roll my eyes before I snatch it out his ear and crush that too. "Look, if this doesn't work with you, I'll have to kill you which would be a waste of both our time. Or I could snatch your eyes out if you prefer that." His eyes are still squeezed shut and I don't like how one of the workers glance at me, nearly breaking from the illusion as the gray in their eyes flicker.

"This is gonna be so gross. You better hope there's a sink behind these doors." He quickly opens his eyes and stares into the eye reader. And the door opens. Now that I think about it, I could've pried the doors open but this is better.

"Oh, thank you! I'm still gonna have to kill you though." Right as I said that I snapped his neck.

Pleased with myself I dust my hands and start down the hallway. Something was lingering in the air, and it smells like gasoline.

I stretched out my hand and nothing happens, so I wave my arm and my skin begins to sizzle. Within seconds the burn gradually burrows deeper into my skin.

"Shit!" I snatch my arm back to assess the new burns. It no longer smells like gas, but I should wait a bit before walking inside. It's gonna reappear before we can get back for sure, but I'll figure that out later.

I fade from one end of the hallway to other. There are two voices approaching from around the corner, so I run down another adjacent hall lined with red stone and a steel door at the end.

I found them. I shake out my hands and the searing burn becomes a simple itch. Digging my hands into the first door I grit my teeth as I tear it down. Behind the door I recognize another face from a case of cryokinesis. I snatch the cuffs off her wrists ready to run down the hall but she hasn't moved.

"I know you're scared but we need to leave. Right now."

"And then what? Where am I supposed to go?" Not back to the house I killed that man in.

"Do you have other family?" She shakes her head 'no,' and tries to wipe tears before they fall. I have to get used to seeing tears again. I can't blame anyone for letting them fall when they remember open sores that have grown too close to the heart.

"I can help you later, but first help me get everyone else out. There are places better than here. Trust me I know." She looks at the burn on my arms and then back at me before she nods and follows me out the room. She rushes past me and to the door on the other side of the hallway. She didn't run, she stayed to help but why? I didn't think she would actually listen to me. She should run but it is better if we stay together. I watch her freeze over the locks on the door which makes it easier to pull the door down. I nod and we pull down another door to free someone else and now there are five of us, but here come the guards.

I wasn't sure if they had abilities until one stopped and let their eyes gray. This might actually work if we keep up this strategy.

There's about ten of us now and we're gonna make it. I look to each side, still unable to believe they were able to stay together for this long, but of course the empathy I stopped believing in doesn't last much longer.

We make it to the hallway but before the word 'wait' could leave my lips one of the neo-humans run in, contorts, and vanishes into ash as each layer of his body is ripped off by the air. From skin to muscle even to the bone. The red from his remains pepper the air and I back away with my eyes frozen wide. *That's a new nightmare.*

Ok, so how do we get down the hall with acid in the air? I should be able to make a sphere and get us through. The guards are gonna get here soon, I can hear pops from their guns in the distance. If I can't figure this out, we'll be on the other end of it. The ice is crackling through my hands but the numbness in my arms and fingers anchor the ice back underneath my skin. There's one person behind me panicking and screams of captives that we're ignorant enough to run away from the group. This isn't working.

Dammit why isn't it working? My breathing weighs heavy on my lungs making me lightheaded. I shake my head while someone's talking to me, I can barely hear them. It's not working. Why isn't it working?

I grit my teeth ready to punch the nearest wall when I hear ice materialize around us and two of the girls with me start running. It forces the rest of the group to do the same since we're all in this ball. The ball of ice crackles as they shoot and the acid gas burns away at it. I hope they can't follow us down this hall but of course they do because they're the only ones able to stop the acid gas.

We get to the end of the hall and they let down the ice, but I put what I can back up out of what they released. The ice reverts from its path back to their hands and packs into a wall blocking us from the workers. They all look at the door and then back to me waiting for instructions.

"Hold this!"

I need them to keep the wall intact in order to get the door open. As I pry the steel doors apart, the group disappears and runs away amid all the chaos because of my illusion. Some I recognize, others I don't. Some of the BT workers break out of the illusions. I yell after the two girls and two other guys to stay with me so we can leave together—it's more likely that we'll get out that way. We're able to fight our way through to the exit but the second that happens we're met with guns.

I would teleport but I can't leave them here. One of the captives disappears—another betrayal. I knew that wouldn't last long. They needed to get far enough to leave.

I construct an illusion of louder alarms and a sharp pain pangs in my head. Not all of the workers fall for it, but we ran the moment we had a chance to. While some BT people scramble and leave, the rest are still after us. It's only four of us left and we need to fight. The only problem is none of them have had practice honing their abilities.

"Get behind me!" I yell. Instead of following my lead another guy runs off. I start to shield us with ice but the surface is thin. The girls press their hands against the shield and reinforce the barrier, now I can teleport us away from here. I put a hand on each of their shoulders and we disappear like dust.

When we break through, we end up next to one of the trucks. I flash into the truck into the driver's seat and open it from the inside. They open the doors and get in the back while I press all the buttons that need to be pressed to get the truck going. Luckily, we were fast enough to skid into some abandoned road mixed up in trees; thankfully, making it harder to see us.

I hope they're ready to walk because I can't leave this truck too close to their homes, they're gonna find it eventually and if it's too close they'll recapture them. Once we we're far enough, we slow down on the empty road and I get out. They hop out the back to follow me and we venture off into the trees.

Now the question is where do they go?

We can walk through these borders for a bit and they can hide between Main City and New City. At least BT isn't there. They didn't say much as we walked, just silently followed me as if they knew I knew where I was going.

While I'm glad I got them out, it really makes me wonder about everyone else. What if I hadn't met Venus, Liam, Isaiah, and Aruni. Would BT have gotten to them first? Or would I have left them behind as well?

***

Finally, we reach a part of the border where there are less trees scattered amongst the abandoned houses.

"There's a market on 34th street, it's small but that's a good thing. It's that way." I point my finger toward the direction they can walk in. "You can use ice to pick the freezer keyhole. Only the back doors, there's no alarms there." I point my other arm in the opposite direction. "That's New city. Don't go to New city. BT lingers on some of the roads in front of it."

I should take them with me but I already have four people under my wing. They'll be ok.

I was ok, and they have each other . . . I hope. I turn to leave and part my lips to say the thing I hate to hear other people say.

An *'I'm sorry'* doesn't change the fact that I'm about to leave them to carry my consequences. So, instead of giving them pity I straighten my back and walk away. My body seems heavier as I'm walking. Teleporting could also exhaust me, but I'd be back to my room sooner if I chose the latter.

When I get to the room, a breath of release burns against my lungs as I flop on my couch. My eyes begin to flutter closed as the sun peaks through my window. My body forces my heavy eyelids to close after remedying what was keeping me awake.

Chapter 14

X

Is that a knock on my door? I roll off the couch and damn near fall before my feet find the ground. I shake my head raking my hands through my hair. I need to at least attempt to look half decent—I fell asleep and never wrapped my locs up last night now they're all over the place. Let me go to the bathroom and get myself together, I'm not ready to talk to whoever knocked on my door. They'll probably leave anyway. It's either Liam, Isaiah, Aruni, or Venus, or all four because I'm pretty sure it's the afternoon based off how high the sun is in the sky. After leaving my makeshift bathroom, I'm ready to be a person again.

I open the front door to look down the hallway and notice someone sitting on the floor.

"Liam? Why are you here? We didn't agree to meet today."

"My aunt made baked mac 'n cheese last night, I thought you might like it . . . everyone likes it," he says, handing me a bag. *Baked mac 'n cheese?* I love baked mac 'n cheese! The delicious smell of salt intertwined with cheese hits my nose. My mom used to make this . . . *My mom used to make this.*

A memory flashes causing me to drift into thought. In the memory, I'm sitting by the table waiting for the plate of steaming mac 'n cheese to be placed on the table by her hands. *"I made it with three cheeses for you."* She's gentle as she slides my braids through her hands.

What was that? That never happened...

"Liam, you don't have to bring actual food. The canned stuff is fine." I hand the bag back to him and drag my feet back into my room. I can't eat that. I don't like where the smell took me.

"If you don't want it, I'll take it back, more for me." He flops on the couch after following me into my room and I can't be bothered enough by it. I really wish he would stop laying on my couch like that, though.

Not too often do these memories come by but when they do it sinks into my chest and stops my whole day.

"What happened to your arm?" He sits up on the couch and I narrow my eyes at him no longer thinking about whatever preoccupied my mind.

"Why does it matter?" He doesn't answer. Instead, he lets out a quiet sigh and leans back onto the arm of the couch and stares out the window. He's not gonna ask me again? Not that I want him to, but he seemed bothered by it enough to ask again. Why is he sitting here?

"No questions today?"

"Yes, actually. You want me to take the mac 'n cheese back?"

"No... its fine. I appreciate it, I just don't think you needed to do all that." I don't wanna be rude because it was nice. I don't know how to say no without it coming off that way. Why did he bring that anyway? He didn't need to and I don't like feeling like I owe people anything.

He looks at me for a second longer, gets off the couch, grabs the bag from the counter, and leaves out the door. So, he's just gonna leave? He could've said something first. Well, it doesn't matter. I want him to leave.

"Hey, Lee!" Yet here I am, leaning my head out the doorway. Why am I doing this to myself? "You think we should get some class time in since you're already here?"

"Maybe, if you have time in your busy schedule for that today." I rub my nose to cover up the silly smile on my face. I can't wait for this to be over. After a bout of persuasion, I convinced him to come back to my room.

I hold out a hand that smokes from cold. He takes a hold of it like he always does and when his hand mimics mine I snatch mine away to cross my arms again.

"Ok, let's start with something easy." In my hand an ice cube materializes. He doesn't say anything but when he tries to copy me it doesn't go well. Instead of an ice cube, it's a bunch of little spikey icicles. I watch him panic and shake the ice off his hands. This is hilarious and it's no use in hiding my laugh.

"Nice cube you got there, Liam." He looks at me glaring. I rub my nose again. I wasn't that good either, but I wasn't that bad.

"How do you deal with that? I felt like my hand was gonna fall off."

"I don't know, you get used to it. It also helps if you keep the ice in control instead of doing whatever that was."

"I would love to see you use this ability for the first time and get that right."

"Lighten up! Even if you almost did it right the first time, I could still do better than that. It's not that complicated. You gotta stop thinking so hard about what you're doing."

"But if I don't think, how am I gonna do it?"

"Simple. You don't have to over analyze the process, picture what you wanna do and do it," I say while materializing a snowflake in the air. The snowflake crumbles back into my hand and he pauses studying the snow as it sinks back into my skin.

"Maybe I could start with that?"

"Not until you get the basics down, Icicle Boy." Damn, he didn't seem bothered by that nickname—that was the whole point. He holds out a hand to make the cube and all I can do is shake my head at the frothy icicles forming in his hand.

"... Liam."

"What?"

"*Relax.* The ice isn't going to go out of control."

"Yeah, but it shouldn't be this difficult." He sits on the couch analyzing his hands and I sit next to him making sure to keep a healthy distance.

"Look, you don't need to get it by today. You just need some time."

"I thought you said you didn't have time."

"I don't but be patient with yourself." Same way I hoped the four of them would be patient with me. Funny enough he's been pretty patient with me even when I'm difficult on purpose.

"Yeah, but what if I need to use this now or if I'm caught up in something. I need to know how to do this. It'll keep me from worrying about it later."

"You're already worrying too much and it's probably the reason why you can't get this right." Despite my efforts he sits back on the couch rubbing his hands down his face. I don't need to ask any questions to know he's worried about BT, and what could happen to his friends and his sister if that situation repeats itself. I didn't have it together either but when I did it was worth it.

It's not easy to talk about my abilities and their origins, but he knows about it already and I have yet to see signs of it being brought up. Besides, this is less about what happened and more about how I got away.

"You know those flashes you get when you mimic the ice?" He looks over at me a nods. I take a breath before recounting the memory. "I don't know if you saw how I got away, but it took me a—a long time to gain enough control over the ice to kill him so I could get out of there. I spent most of my time sitting on that bed pushing myself to keep learning because it was that or stay in the hellscape I once called home. Soon enough when I got it, I lost control of most of it and what I could control was just enough to get me away. The next time BT was after me, I accidentally froze the whole road while I was driving and skidded off into the water."

"So, what you're saying is you were as bad as I was." Turning to look at the ceiling I let a breath of laughter leave. *I hope I hid it well.*

"No, not at all. My point is sometimes it's gonna take you a while. Other times, you do what you gotta do under pressure. In those moments you have to make your way through the chaos as you fight through it."

"But what if you can't?"

"What if you can? It's better than not taking the risk at all. Listen, if you're gonna fall flat on your face, either way you might as well take the leap and figure it out along the way."

"Seems like a big risk. You told me that BT is worse than what it seems the other day."

"It is but if I had the same mindset you did, I would still be stuck under their foot instead of being here now. You'll get it eventually, alright? You're not doing that bad. Worse than me but not that bad."

"Was that a compliment?" *Here he goes.* I roll my eyes distracting myself from mirroring his smile again before I stand up.

"Don't get used to it. Maybe we should leave body for a bit so you won't be so tense." I sit back down so I don't fall on the floor. I only stood up because the tension in my muscles that remind me to keep a distance relax without me knowing. That shouldn't be. I hold out a hand for him to take. "Don't go stumbling all over the place this time." Is the last thing I said to him before I let go of his hand to leave body.

Then, I shoot straight to the roof and my shoulders drop as I gape at the sky.

The sun on the city skyline sits perfectly between the row of small buildings and down the quiet road. The orange rays pierce the orbs, saturating the colors of the lights that flow in place as they dangle in the air. Each stream of light stretches from the sun dipping over the buildings and elongating their shadows. This time I didn't need a yellow to receive this moment as a gift, seeing it was enough to slow time down on its own.

"This—this is beautiful." How many times did I miss a view like this while being caught up in madness?

As I stood, Liam went to sit on the edge of the building for a better view. I watch him take everything in and I shake my ghost arms out to loosen the tension. I want to experience this in its fullness. Not too often do my eyes steal sights like this.

The last few times we've been out here we took brief breaks. He always sits to look at stuff like this. This time I sit with him. As the sky falls into a purple hue, Liam swings his feet like a kid. So I swing mine too, searching for the act of "taking my time," as he once said. This isn't exactly like the yellow but it's similar and I find that relaxing in this new comfort of peace may be worth this small moment.

I want to say something. Words need to be put to this, but I think I understand why he was content with being silent while lying on the couch earlier. Silence is good, it gives me space to sit and experience the entirety of where I am. Like the parallel the other day, that's how he knew what the orbs of lights were.

We've been here for a while, and it still seemed too short. It shouldn't be this short. I look at him like I did before when we first came to the roof together. I have to peel my eyes away from studying the details of his face, the way his umber skin tone sits in the sun slight. The smoothness of his jawline in the profile of his face and the way he sits with his legs swinging over the ledge.

Liam is really a breath of fresh air. As I take in the sun, I think of the way he smiles. How it lights up the room, and for some reason I smile back every time failing to hide it. He always has so many questions, and so much to say but then sometimes he says nothing at all. He just listens. The way he's so careful every time I offer a hand—he has tough hands but not in a bad way.

I shake my head. I shouldn't remember those details. I've always been very intentional about letting go. It can't stay like this. It is nice but I can't stay like this. It's not only because of BT or because of worrisome questions about how this will work out. It's because the last time I felt like this I ended up broken. So as far as I'm concerned, this is not real. It's more intangible than my life before I woke up and it needs to remain that way. I know what I told him about risk, but he wasn't completely wrong. This is one risk I can't afford to take.

I can't entertain the idea of friendships and I most definitely can't entertain the idea of a romantic one. Even if everything was ok, I'm too deep into BT and this chase with my mother. I don't wanna get too comfortable and lead my mess right to them. I'm not built for it. And I made my peace with it. I work better by myself—this is temporary. Though sitting here with him does in fact feel quite alright. It always does.

Chapter 15
Xandria's Past

January 10th, 2095
Unknown City
Past: 1 year and 5 months ago

Today is the day. I did it. on my shoulders lies a purple gown, and underneath I'm wearing a lilac dress I picked out, and on my head the square cap I decorated to match. I looked in the mirror this morning and spared myself a smile—I looked pretty good, actually. My mom never taught me to walk with pride. However, every now and then I'm able to hold my head up when I catch a reflection of myself—I did this for myself. My body, my face, my skin, my hair. My hair, the crown I grew from my head.

As I hear my name, I receive my diploma and walk the stage with my head held high. The auditorium's ACs are on too high, but the lights on the stage and the thought of a new beginning gives me all the warmth I need.

My mom isn't here, but she doesn't need to be. I shouldn't be crying for someone who hated me so much. Ironically, there's this odd desire to keep chasing after someone who didn't even care to chase after me. I look into the audience and see a blur of faces but the one I'm looking for never passes my view. He said he was gonna be here but instead I see the empty seat. Disappointed, I huff out a sigh as I walk off the stage. Instead of going back to my seat I left the auditorium and swiveled into the bathroom to call him. I don't know when I got this phone but I'm glad I have it because I need to know where the hell he's at. I don't know what's up with him, he's been acting funny for a while now. I can't remember the last time we had a conversation without arguing.

"Hey, I walked the stage where are you?" I'm being nice I swear but underneath my even tone a yell bubbles in my chest. He doesn't listen to me and then expects me to care about his opinion when I wanna leave the apartment to do what I wanna do. The piano room was the only place I could go to learn how to play it. After I leave here, I won't have it. I've been looking for places to go so I can continue learning but, it's been real difficult to find. They stopped making instruments decades ago, finding a piano is a million and one chance rendering it pointless unless I can leave the apartment to look through museums and abandoned theatres. He could argue if he wants to argue I'm not staying in that apartment all day waiting for him to come back. I left so I could live my life. I'm not losing that opportunity again.

Maybe I could explain again but I don't know how I'mma do that after this.

"I got busy at work."

"I thought you took off today? Damien why is your job such a secret that you can't just tell me?"

"You don't tell me anything when you leave the apartment either."

"And whose fault is that? I'm not arguing with you about what I wanna do with my time, and maybe I would tell you if I knew where you were at?" I keep forgetting to lower my voice.

"Listen, I'mma come pick you up later, sit tight."

I hear two nodes and squint at my phone screen. There's no way he hung up on me. Taking a deep breath, I remind myself to keep a cool head to avoid another situation. I need a moment of peace for once. These constant conflicts I have little to no control over eat away at me. I'm not asking for much, I wanna do what I do without worrying about obstacles that shouldn't even be present in the first place.

***

When he did pick me up, the street was empty and I was sitting on a bench in front the school. He didn't look up from his phone when I got in the car so instead of giving him any attention I stared out the window hoping this car ride doesn't last long.

"How was it?"

It would've been great if I wasn't by myself most of the day, but instead of answering the question, I continue to stare through the window. What was he doing that he had to miss a day like this? This is nothing like how we were before and because of how unorganized time is here I can't even conceptualize how we got here.

"Where do you work?" The moment the question leaves my lips the car seems to blur and shake. I told myself I wouldn't pay any attention to anomalies anymore but sometimes it shows back up—along with a headache and those bright white walls.

"You know I can't tell you that."

"Why not? I don't know how you expect me to give two shits about your opinions on what I do when you can't answer a simple question." After my statement, the streets outside the car window blur into a blank white sheet but I wasn't the only one that noticed the blur.

"You saw that too?"

"I don't know what you're talking about."

Okay. A small smile and laugh escapes from my diaphragm. I can't keep it together much longer. Now I'm beginning to understand why he wouldn't tell me where he works. Whoever these people are know about this ghost of a virus that's been haunting me and my mom. It was happening closer together when I was still living with my mom and after I left it was easier to forget like I wanted, but every time I leave the apartment...

every time I leave the apartment...

"Damien. Why did you ask me to stay at your apartment?" My eyes briefly widened at the lack of flashes and headaches in that apartment. My concern for time and street names crossed my mind less and less since I moved in with him.

"You needed to get away from your mom so—"

"No, no, that's not it. You're—you're lying to me," I reply, still keeping my voice even; *keep it together*, I know I'm onto something. I stare out the window in front of me and shake my finger at him. My eyes dissolve into the road ahead as thoughts rush my brain. They're of my mom; thoughts of revelation peppered my mind 'til it almost shatters. Yeah, I remember now. I was gonna go somewhere—somewhere that seems far away from here but if I could play close enough attention it's not that far. My mom brought up a lab before I left and said that I was over there with Xavier. The lab has a name and the people that disappear in BT vans are being accused of being neo-humans.

"Do you work with BT?" I shoot my eyes at him, looking at the 'too grown to be in my class' brownskin guy that was a good friend back then. He's unusually quiet and still focused on the road while the dome fades in and out of view.

"BT is the reason why everything is off here isn't it? I know you saw the dome flashing. And not a single traffic light here works. I know you see that and I know you know something's wrong." He doesn't reply, but instead the car speeds up. No, I gotta get out of here, I know something's up for sure now but if I go back to that apartment I'm gonna forget. *I'm gonna forget everything.*

"Let me out the car." The car speeds up again and I can see small townhouses lined up in the distance. Without care for how fast the car is moving I pull at the handle planning to jump out but it's stuck; it won't even move. Shit. The dome flashes in and out of view outside the car. I grab the wheel hoping it would crash and I don't die in the middle of it. At this point I'm willing to take the risk. The car swerves and he grabs my wrist. Eventually we come to a halt where we still end up in front of the apartment. He leaves the car, but before I can crawl to the driver's side he already has a hold of my forearm. I pull away pointlessly and the headache that's forming is making it more difficult. My vision is blurry because of the flashing scenery but I can't go back to that apartment.

I tussle and pull away, whirling around at the way the walls seem to be crumbling to reveal whatever's behind it. My feet are practically dragging across the floor, but I can't shake this grip he has on my arm. I'm yelling and pulling and hitting and his hand is so tight around me I know it's gonna leave a mark. There's a bright flash and a boom that pangs through my skull again and I'm back in his apartment staring wide eyed at the room that looks as if no one lives here. There's a couch in the living room and the kitchen across from it looks as if it was never used. It didn't look like that before.

I turn to the door pulling at the handle knowing my newly found discoveries are gonna fade but the door won't budge. It's as if it's cemented shut. He stands off to the side next to me and I glance at him before I dash off to my room to get to the window. My body heated up with adrenaline takes me to the window fast enough but as the window flies open arms wrap around me. I let out a yell that leaves pressure in my chest, burning against my lungs, but my skin is hot with anger. How could I have been so stupid to have walked myself into an identical situation where I still burn underneath someone else's roof.

I knew moving here wasn't a good idea, but I ignored it believing we could work through the small arguments. I should've trusted my gut. Every time I trust people instead, I end up stuck in another hellscape. He let me go at the other end of the room, and before I get to it he walks back to the window slamming shut. That isn't gonna stop me. No sooner than a second after a hand slams across my face, a chill rushes up my right arm, and I stumble backward. I freeze in place unsure of what to do after being hit like that.

The same nasty feeling I had when I was living with my mom rises in my chest. At the same time, icy smoke begins to rise from my hands. As quick as it dissipates, I clench my fist still processing what happened and the only thing that stops my thoughts is hearing him.

"If you would've stayed put none of this would've happened." I glare at him, tight eyebrows, and my breath quickening. Is he saying this is my fault?

"Don't test me, Xandria," he says as he leaves the room and slamming the door behind him.

* * *

For the rest of that day, I sat on my bed and stared at my hands. What if what I saw is part of whatever this place is doing to my mind? What's this place doing to me, to my body?

Ice crawls under my skin. There's frost under the skin of my hand settling and building causing it to smoke. I'm not crazy. I know what I saw and felt but if I'm one of them what if BT comes looking for me? I burry my face in my cold hands and hot tears press against them.

I'm already with them apparently if I'm here with Damien. I shouldn't have even bothered with him at all. I keep hoping for people to listen to me and be on my side but then I turn around and it ends up being a façade of something I chose not to see. I should've run in the other direction from the time things got out of hand over a hobby I have—had. Speaking of my hobby—*Where's my iPod?*
I jolt up from the bed and tap my pockets in the lavender dress. The phone is there but in the other the iPod is gone. *No. No, I need that.*

"DAMIEN!" I rush to the door to grab the handle but the door wouldn't budge. That's quite literally the only thing that keeps me sane. *I need it.* Pulling at the door turns into running into it. I rush over to the window to open it, but it won't budge either. My arms are sore, but I can't stay. *I can't stay, I need my music.*

Hot tears ache through my eyes again and a knot forms in my throat . . .

Time never makes sense, but I pull at the door, yelling until I've strained my voice in my chest and throat. I didn't know I would fall asleep against it, wishing I could've snuck away to the safe haven in my pocket one more time.

Chapter 16
Xandria's Past

February 16th, 2095
City-Unknown
Past: 1 year and 4 months ago

I don't know how long it's been but despite my memories fading—of whatever happened to leave me stuck here—I can't forget where these scars came from. It's like all that I've been through merged into a blob of torture. Some new trauma happens every couple days but it couldn't have been days. Did all of this happen within days? Maybe weeks or months—it's gotta be months. *But that makes no sense if I graduated and* . . . It doesn't matter. None of this is helping.

I should've listened to myself when I questioned staying before. I should've took note of the arguments we had and the clinginess and possessiveness. But I was naïve enough to see it and ignore it because it was supposed to get better. I hoped it would.

I haven't listened to a single one of my favorite songs since I've been here because I don't know where the iPod is. I can't leave to find it, but I find myself humming as tears stream down my face. When the tears run out, I sit and think, fishing for memories and holding on to the ones that keep my heart beating. The memories that remind me that I need to get out of here.

I don't want to sit and recall what it's been like being stuck here. There are some memories too unsettling to remember but they haunt my nightmares. Some memories haunt me as they take permanent residence on my skin. All from the same person who I will get to one day as soon as I can get this new ice ability together.

The cold in my arms didn't go away after the first time. After Damien left my room the other night, I sat on the bed watching the cold smoke rise through my hands. I still have the phone with no one to call but I was able to learn a lot by doing research on what's happening to me. The ice under my skin will be the undoing of this room, and this apartment, and whatever else BT is hiding from me. But I can't leave while he's here and he won't be because I'mma figure this out. I don't close my eyes to sleep often. Usually, after I shower and get myself together, I sit on the bed and let the ice sit under the skin of my hands.

Studying my them, I slouch over the bed as the cold prickles above my skin. I haven't made anything from this ice yet, but my eyes stay glued to my hands. I don't know how long it's been, but it's been long enough. I've been patient and one of these days something is gonna come from these hands that's gonna get me my life back. I can't stay here and continue spending my life under someone else's foot. That nasty feeling that's been festering inside me is gonna leave him how he left me.

While I become familiar with my newfound gift my ears pick up on movement in the apartment. The clang of keys dropping on the table echo through the apartment and then sound of footsteps heading toward my door—twenty-two to be exact—and then my door flies open.

I miss listening to music, but I wouldn't hear this if I was. "If you were to figure this out. By the time you did they would've had this fixed the glitches you saw already. . ." I stopped talking to him a while ago. I don't know what BT has going on outside of this but while I'm here things are changing out there. Either way, the least I'll do is get outta this damn apartment.

"Ok, look, What I will say is this would be a lot easier if you didn't keep picking at everything." He walks into the room and sits next to me and I immediately jump up from the bed.

"And what you could do is leave me the hell alone." My hands begin to burn from the cold, but I ignore it hoping that a miracle happens if he gets too close to me again.

"Whatever you think that ice is gonna do isn't gonna work out too well. You're not gonna get it before they fix this." He rises to his feet and before I can slide to the other side of the room he grabs hold of my arm.

"I'm about to leave. Don't try some shit while I'm gone—'cause I'll know." I clench my fist and the ice reaches past the palm of my hands. I let out a quiet breath of relief when he lets me go, but his next words put urgency in mind.

"This is gonna go a lot simpler when I get back."

Meaning I have between now and that door creak to get this ice to work in my favor. I sit on the bed letting the ice dissipate, unsure of what I'm doing wrong. It's right there slushing under my skin but it only sits. I flex my hands to gradually bring it to the surface, but nothing happens.

I've been wanting to keep this hidden or subtle to not draw too much attention. I take in a breath to remain calm like normal but what if I stopped?

"Let go Xandria." I swear I heard a familiar woman's voice echoing from everywhere and nowhere. It could all be in my head, yet it compelled me to follow.

I take in a breath and my arms grow cold as I pick through my memories. I pick through all the fights and arguments I had. All the quiet tears and confusion. Memories of happiness spared in the music room overwhelm me with sadness. I want to settle in that again. I sit in what I was afraid to sit in. The craving to hit back, to retaliate without worrying about the consequences. I inhale a shaky breath and the air tastes fridged. There are pinpricks of ice under my skin and suddenly the air that's whirling in circles hazes into white smoke.

I'm gonna get out. I'm gonna get out and I'm gonna get exactly what I want this time. I open my eyes to see the perforations of ice on the floor. Looking down at the smoke on my hands, I place my palm to the ground and the small icicles increase in height and grow into large icicles. Well, shit! I slam my other hand on the ground and the ice widens as they cover parts of the floor and up toward the ceiling. A smile spreads across my face at the monstrosity I made in my room. If I can do that then what else could I do?

I will get out. They just don't know it yet.

With that thought, I lean forward resting my elbows on my knees and form a sharp point at the end of the icicle and grip it tight. Now I wait.

The moon was shining through my window when I heard the door creak. The keys cling and drop.

I hurry to the wall on the side of the door, my face unwavering, and the icicle tight in my hand. Twenty-two steps.

One ... five ... ten ....twenty-two ...

The door opens and my arm swings into the body in the doorway. I let go of the icicle and stand in front of the door and see him stumbling backward.

"I got it," I say, lifting my head, allowing myself to take in the pride. My brain is lights at the rush of rage, it was meant for this to end this way.

"You know, there was a time where I thought my best bet was to lay low, hoping it would grant me the ability to live my life as everyone else does, but seeing you like this, after knowing you're a part of the reason why my body aches, why my head aches, why I have to constantly question my sanity. I regret not speaking my mind and holding myself back hoping that caring about other folks—caring about *you*—would somehow fix this." I watch him fall to the ground.

As I stand over the mess I've made, he reaches for something in his pocket, and I kneel down in the pool of red to take it.

"No phone calls. So, I'll be taking that. And whatever cash you have in your other pocket. What's this?" In his pocket was a silver vile. I open the rubber lid to smell it and the scent reminds me of my mom's room—*it had that same metallic smell.*

"What is this?" He doesn't respond to me and the ice mixes with the heat of frustration in my muscles. "How did you get this?" I lean my hand onto the icicle as I grit my teeth, ignoring the crunch of his bones. *"What is this?"*

I'm not gonna get an answer, he's basically half-dead and part of me wishes I could've asked him this while I still had him as someone I cared for. Cared for so much to ignore everything that was wrong about him

Instead of asking again, I let out a sigh and shake my head. Why do I even bother when I get the same outcome over and over again.

"This would've been so much easier on both of us if you had returned the care I gave you. The grace I gave you." I need to leave soon. I definitely can't stay here. I drag my feet tracking red on the floor and when I get to the sink, I wash my hands clean as I look In the mirror. The scar is still there—the one my mom left me.

I'm spotted with blood I was unaware of, and I huff out a breath of air at the sight. Maybe this is the way it ought to be. Maybe this is what it took to start a journey to finding happiness in my life. I don't need anybody. I did what I did and became what I am by myself. If this is what it has be, so be it.

I wash myself clean and walk past the body without sparing him another glance. I put on a new set of black sweats and grab the bag from my closet before leaving my room. When I pass by Damien's body, memories gather of when we first met, but it doesn't take long for the memory of what happened while I was here to surface. My face tightens. How many times did I attempt to leave and end up in a state where I should've been hospitalized? The reasons why I refused to sit on the bed next to him. He deserved what I did, and I deserved to deliver it.

Anyone that causes this pain deserves to die.

March 2nd, 2092
City-unknown
Past: 1 year and 3 months ago

Ever since I left Damien's place the glitches of the white dome have been back and most of my memory has stayed the same. Like memories of what happened with my mom on the day I left. Unfortunately, memories of what it was like being confined to his apartment have also stayed the same. I also remember BT is the reason why the world flickers the way it does. Whenever it flickers it reveals whatever's beyond it. I've been running from them—the people in the same blue uniform Damien had. The thing with them is this is the first time I'm noticing their uniforms. The pro in this is now that I know who they are, I know when to run. The con, now they know that I know too much. More than I ever have and more than I should.

I've popped the plates off the car since I left, but they still find me. Not having a plate might be making it easier to do so. Wearing an all-black sweatsuit helps especially at night, but they still end up finding me despite it.

As I lay in the hotel bed in nothing but a T-shirt and my sweatpants with my sweater neatly folded beside me, I sort through thoughts about this new runaway dilemma. I watch the snowflakes piece together as particles of snow seep through my skin. I'm running out of money and patience. There has to be a way to catch these BT people off guard and get more answers, but they always show up in large groups. At least when they have tried to catch me. I'm gonna catch one of them when they're not paying attention then I'll go from there. For now, I make it a hobby to figure out what can be done to get me as far away from them as possible.

As that thought passes, I hear a bang on the door. My nerves flare up but a song fills my mind leaving me in a quiet hum. I don't need headphones or the iPod, I still remember every single song. It's with me and its rhythm syncs with my steps anytime I need to run or fight. I know I should pick my battles and not waste time fighting with people I never met but they're pesky—like flies. Sometimes I swat them away with an icicle or two. I know they're not gonna bother waiting for an answer and they're definitely not gonna wait to shoot. So, I roll out the bed and hop onto my feet and I grab what I can. After throwing on my hoodie, I swing open the window to create an ice pathway down and out the building. With hands extended in front of me, I slide down the path. The air around me is crisp as it slides on my face. I crack slight smile before I hit the ground. A part of me loves the adventurous adrenaline rush that comes from these chases.

When I land, without hesitation, I run to the car. I should be panicking right now, but I love this gift so much. It was a little rough at first but overtime its becoming a new part of me. Whatever void my past left in me, this new ability fills it. It pieces me back together.

I almost anticipate the chase sometimes; the pressure is good for creativity. They have to know I'm a neo-human now which is probably why they have the whole damn squad after me every other day. They don't have something better to do? They're so relentless like this is what their whole life is about. I shoot a quick glance behind me. *I swear I've seen similar faces before.* There's no possible way for them to find me this often this quickly. I don't have his phone nor do I have anything in the car for them to track me with. I can almost guarantee this has something to do with the hole I just noticed in the sky. This sick game is falling apart but I can't do anything about that right now.

Finally, I reach the back of building, click the key in my pocket, hop in the white car, and pull off into the neighborhood of identical houses. As I leave the parking lot here come the white vans and trucks with BT plastered on their sides. I should let the thing drive itself, but that's not gonna work if I want to get away. I don't need it to stop and slow down at everything.

Besides, I can out-drive them with a little extra help. Two cars zoom behind me as I fly past an intersection and then another two behind the three that were already there. Three vans, two trucks, and one me. My locs are in my face—they've grown a little past my shoulders—I forgot to tie them back, but I can see just fine. I dangle my hand out the window and flex it as the ice leaves my palm, but maybe I should've considered the road under me would...

"SHIT! SHIT!" My hands grip the wheel tighter and my foot slams on useless brakes. The drivers behind me spin out on the ice, but now I'll spin out into the water if I can't turn the damn car!

Pulling at the steering wheel and tearing my foot through the brakes does nothing to stop me from flying right into the body of water next to the highway. My ears sploosh with the water and I thank myself for leaving the windows down. The pressure of the water adds weight to my limbs as I grasp for the sides of the open window to push myself out of the car. I leave my seat and push myself enough to allow my legs some room to kick to further and push myself to the surface.

My eyes are closed while my legs struggle against the resistance of the water. Pointless kicking turns into a rhythm that gets my head above the chaos. It's like following eighth notes on a music sheet. In 4/4 time.

"Okay, I won't do that again." I look up at the stony hill and all I see is the sky flickering from navy blue, spotted with scarce stars to a blank-white space. Now what? As I continue to kick my legs—because my life depends on it—I reach a bank of land. With all my strength, I use my arms to push onto the hill. I need to sit and catch my breath. I didn't know how difficult it was to move under water. Now, my soaked clothes and hair are weighing me down.

Looking down at my hands, I let the cold smoke rise. How can this get me up this hill? I release snow from the palm of my hand as it packs together into a snowflake. Taking in its details and the points catch my eye. The ice seeps back into my hand and an icicle forms instead. I turn it in my hand and then look to the dirt beside me. I could stab through that.

After I turn over to swing the point into the dirt, a quiet laugh escapes. *See this is why I love this*, what can't I do when at my will ice forms through my hands? Another icicle forms in my other hand and I slam that one into the dirt too. I make another attempt to pull myself up and while my arms slowly numb, a song comes to mind—one I used to play after a bad day or when I was glued to bed. I was learning this one specifically on that old piano—it's the one I ran to the most often.

Tiredness makes my limbs heavy but not heavy enough to find out what else is being hidden from me. These abilities were hidden from me and if *this* is what I found out there must be more to find if I keep going.

There's a bus station not too far from here going to another nameless neighborhood. If what I saw on the hotel lobby map is correct then it's going up north. It's gonna be cold and all I have is my sweatshirt. I'll find a coat somewhere but for now I'll be fine. At least that'll make it easier to wrap my hands in some ice if I need to; especially if it's snowing. That's probably a great place to catch one of these BT people lacking.

After paying for a ticket, I end up sitting on the bus for entirely too long. I was hoping they didn't catch wind of my runaway streak while I was sitting here.

We rode for a while before stopping at a station next to the woods—I've never seen this many trees in one place. It looks so easy to get lost in there.

I shouldn't bother getting off the bus, but I could run into those trees in the worst-case scenario. I really gotta pee and I'm not gonna sit here in pain for however long I have to sit here. *I should go.* Finally, I decide to use the station's bathroom. Before leaving the bus, I cover my face with a black scarf and throw on my hood.

As I step inside the brown tiled room, one of the security guards give me a look, I can see the suspicion in his eyes. *That's not BT. It's a regular security guy.* At least that's what I tell myself, he doesn't even have the right uniform on. I just left, and I'm supposed to be dead, right? I fell. Skidded off into a body of water and now I'm dead—that should be the story. So, I'm good. I hope I'm good.

My next steps are urgent. I use the bathroom, wash my hands, and as soon as I come out there are the blue uniforms. This makes no sense! Where are they coming from? They're like roaches! At this point I'm not gonna be able to get back on that bus. I take long quick strides in the opposite direction before they turn away from their huddle. As I'm leaving, one sees me and shouts "Hey!"

'Oh ok, let me stop so you can drag me off into your lab.' 'Hey' isn't gonna stop me. Why would they bother? Running out the building I head straight into the woods. They run into the woods after me, and I hear more tires not too far away; their swarm growing in size by the second. How did they catch up so soon? Now I don't know what to do. I could do what I did before. Suppose I slip up like I did with the ice under the car— literally. Maybe I should let them catch me then maybe I'd get to see where I end up. Based on my memories, if Damien's job was to keep me ignorant then allowing them to take me isn't a good idea.

My feet are heavy and they're catching up, they're gonna corner me any minute now, and then I'd be done before I even get a chance to figure all this out. To figure myself out. Even now the white dome flickers into view and I shake my head unwilling to go back to where I started. I can hear the crunching footsteps on the leaves, I can hear them through the rustling branches. It hurts to breathe and in between the flickers of the dome my vision spots. My heartbeat echoes in my ears. More eighth notes. I know that song. Everything grows silent and before the folks in blue catch me everything comes to an abrupt stop.

As everything stops, so do they. I turn around and see them standing there, frozen. Do they see what I see, 'cause it was enough to freeze me in place too. Beautiful colorful orbs of florescent light swirling everywhere. Am I dead? I look at my hands and I can see. Right. Through. Them. So, I'm dead . . .

With a reluctant look down I see my body laid out on the floor of brown and orange leaves and the roaches in blue stare 'til one breaks the silence.

"She just dropped."

What do they mean I just dropped? After a few seconds of silence, one of the others tell the others not to worry about it and leave me here. Well shit, I would've faked my death three chases ago if that's what it took for them to leave me be.

As they leave, I whirl around at the lights that have a slight hum to them and each orb is a different color. Should I touch any of them? No, but that's exactly why I'm going to do it. I tap one finger on an orange one and it flows into my translucent forearm

"Nice... Very nice."

I touch another with my other hand, this time it's green and that one does the same. Then there's red, blue, purple, and yellow. I didn't realize how far away I was from my body 'til I tap the blue one expecting it to collect in my arms with the others, but it didn't. Well, that sucks. This is very different from the ice. My eyes dart over my arms. *Where'd this ability take me?*

Through all this beauty, I see my body still lying on the woods' damp floor with no owner. I should leave it and stay here, but if I don't go back, I give up a gift that I love as much as I love this new one. So, I float back into it and the beauty of the other world disappears when I open my eyes.

When I stand up, my mind refocuses on my list of issues regarding what I'm supposed to do since I can't go back to the bus. I don't think I can find it now that I'm out here. But why are my arms... tingling? It's in the same place the orbs went when I was outside my body. Maybe I should let it go, but I already went back, so how would I do that? I can't just leave again, right? How do I find that part of myself to leave again?

Where's my BT roaches when I need them? They should come back so we can reenact what happened the first time. I'm pretty sure that'll help to figure this out. I'm gonna have to deal with it until then, but for now I need to rethink what I'm gonna do. Or I'll take a walk instead.

It's peaceful here now, as peaceful as a broken world can be. Still, it's always infected with the missing pieces in its images. I've tried to reach the open slit glitches in this place, that reveal the dome behind it. I run to them before they close but when I get to them to see what's behind them they disappear. I'mma get my answers. I need to relax for a bit, all that running and new ability stuff is making my head hurt.

The air is nice and it's easy to get lost in here; it's a good place to settle my mind. Some semblance of time passes while I wander around the woods, but out of all the bad luck I've had all my life a sliver of good luck is spared. There's a logwood cabin hidden through the trees. Someone could be there, no one could be there. I don't care, I need to sit down.

The door is open, and it appears empty. The floor creaks as I walk through the cabin to make sure no one is here, and no one is. It's so cozy though and it smells like wood which isn't half-bad compared to that metallic smell from my mom's apartment. Everything is made of the same brown that resembles the trees outside, except the rocking chair made of red cloud-like material, and the bed. This could belong to someone. But it's mine now. I flop into the fluffy chair and practically sink into it. *Oh, I'm never leaving, this is the best thing I've ever sat in.*

I am hungry though. After I rock myself out of the chair, I look through the kitchen cabinets where I find a hot chocolate package. *Nice.* I grab a pot from a bottom cabinet then I put a block of ice in it. In another cabinet lies a box of matches to light the burner. My ice block will melt into water that will soon boil. I set the packet on the counter and sit down on a velvet red chair and kick my feet up on the table. My mom would've killed me if I did this at home, but I can't really call that home can I?

What happened to her? What could've put her in such a state? The random mood swings she had and half-finished sentences. Before I left, she was going to tell me something. She swung forward on the counter before rambling to me about how I should never, *never* do something that's not crossing my mind right now. I need to find her, she knows something. But that's if she can even stay sane enough to get her point across.

Chapter 17
X

Present Day: August 30th, 2096
Main City 27

Four months. That's how long it's been since this started. As I work with them every now and then I catch myself becoming too invested in their progress. I tell myself that I'm only happy to be a step closer to my goals, but warmth settles under my skin anytime I see them get something right. I know none of this is easy. I know the burdens they would carry alone so to witness them win feels like a win for me too—but it's not, I'm here to handle business.

Aruni is being Aruni. I've learned more about fantasy and mythological creatures in the past two months than I ever did in school. She keeps explaining this story she's been reading to me but most times I end up nodding my head and smiling because I can't keep up. She had lent me one of her books the other day and left it on the counter saying that it's a good place to start. I was thinking about reading it at first but that would be me getting too attached to them again.

She loves a good story, she talks about it quite often, but I'm here for her abilities, not to share her favorite hobbies with her. So, it's been sitting in one of the empty drawers in the kitchen.

Venus has gotten better with timing and leaving body. Since I'm also able to leave body, I've been keeping track of her time out when she does go. We agreed someone has to hold her accountable, so for a good week or so I've been guiding her ghost back to her body in a shorter time span; she only leaves if she knows I'll be there. She doesn't speak much about what happened and neither do I, but we've had enough conversations to develop a unique type of empathy that nearly brought me to tears. She's not gonna catch me crying though. I caught her a few times.

I didn't know what to do at first. The most I was willing to do was rest a hand on her shoulder so she felt a little less lonely. I know what she carries. I'm here and I want her to know that I understand. It's one of those things I wish I had but didn't get.

I'm never quite sure if Isaiah is listening to me but the fact he's still here and not at BT says enough. He's also figured out some of the tricks I had up my sleeve as time passed. I don't throw things at him because it's fun, which it is. It's to keep him on his toes and keep him focused.

I also think my nickname is gonna stick. He stopped complaining about it, matter fact he responds to the name the same way he would respond to Isaiah. So, as far as I'm concerned that's Patches.

Someone just threw something at me. I look to my side at the snowball sweating on the ground and back at Liam who clearly threw that at me. Everyone pauses cautious of my reaction, and they should be because I'm not gonna miss when I throw.

I threw one and he disappeared out the way. Then, it was a wrap. Before I know it, more snowballs come flying my way. When did Aruni, Isaiah, and Venus get any? Snow piles up in my hand before I throw it at Isaiah. I let out a laugh from the bottom of my stomach while I point at him getting up from the snow pile.

After I launch a few more snowballs, I stop, and my smile falls and laughs fade in my ears. Yeah, that's enough of that 'cause here I go getting too comfortable again.

"Alright guys, I'm done, seriously." There's a slight pause while I gather myself and I move out the way when another one almost hits me in my face.

"You didn't hear me the first time!" I watch them watch me and I rub my eyes. I didn't mean to yell at them but still! I shouldn't be this comfortable this often and now it's happening too often. I can't do this to myself. I said I wasn't gonna get too attached and we're here laughing together like friends would.

"Wow, X," Venus says tossing the snow to the side.

"You're ridiculous. You can't have fun for five minutes?" Isaiah blurts out. I can't. I can't have fun for five minutes. What is that without consequences? Ones I can't handle.

"I think we should leave." They huddle up to leave but Lee can't take all three of them back, they gotta go one by one. And even then, it's a little too early to leave, right? It's not that early but it seems early. I should let them go ahead.

"Hang on guys. I'm sorry. What about—what about getting something to eat? Don't you guys usually get, like, a pizza or something?" I don't have money for that why would I ask that?

"X, with all due respect, you should sit that out," Isaiah argues as they're about to leave. *I* can't even argue that. I haven't exactly been the easiest person to get along with, but I'm not supposed to be! I've been here too long, and we need to go to New City sooner than later but they're not ready yet.

"Maybe we could do lunch, but it depends on where we're going." I glance at Liam after making a snowflake in my hand. *Is he serious?* Isaiah hits his shoulder, and they all whisper-bicker while I stand off to the side gently sliding my hand against the locs in my grip.

"You know it's cool if—"

"It's fine, hurry up and come over here so we can go back to the room." Isaiah shakes his head after he replies to me. It's one of the few times I let him get away with cutting me off like that.

I take Venus back to the room and Liam brings Isaiah and Aruni. I would've paid that more attention had I not been preoccupied with this "outing". I don't ever bother with asking them to go out anywhere. Maybe I should stay here.

"Are you gonna leave too or no?" Isaiah asks and instead of staying I tag along, and I immediately regret it.

The whole walk there was silent. At the diner they sit at a table with only four seats. I could sit on the booth side. I don't think I like the booth though. I would be sitting behind a partial table space. There's no more chairs though.

"X, you can sit. There's an extra chair at the table behind you," Venus mentions, noticing me fidgeting with my hair. I should stop doing that at some point. After grabbing a chair and bringing it to the end of the table, I fold my hands but it feels odd, so I cross my arms, but that feels weird too, so I end up folding my hands in my lap.

"Alexandria, you like ice cream?" Another reason why the name Patches is gonna stick.

"Isaiah, stop." Aruni looks up from the screen on the table to whisper across the table.

"Why do you ask?" This is why I didn't bother asking, I'm so misplaced.

"SO! There's this ice cream bowl where if you can finish the whole thing, you pay half for every meal at the table."

"No, we can get two combo meals and it's the same thing. Ignore him, X." Venus waves a hand at him. After Aruni puts the tablet back at the center of the table, I pick it up to see what he's talking about.

"So, what you're saying is I make this thing disappear and we pay half-the-price for the food?"

"Yes, and I want a *full* meal so I say you should go for it." Oh, I'mma go for it alright they don't need to know if I ate it, they just need to think I did.

"X, whatever you're thinking—"

"What am I thinking, Liam?" I ask leaning my elbow on the table and resting my head in my hand.

"I know exactly what you're thinking and it's a fantastic idea! I'm gonna double up my meal!" Aruni interjects gesturing for me to hand her the tablet.

"No you're not! Don't do that. Neither of you do that!" Aruni and I glance at each other and she sips her water before ordering the ice cream. We're gonna do it anyway, between me and her no one will know.

"I don't care what you do as long as it works. I'm ordering that burger." Isaiah reaches for the tablet in the center of the table and when it makes its way back around to me, I scroll through the meals. There are too many options to choose from so I end up getting some fries. It smells like they're cooking a lot more than fries here, but I can't make up my mind with all those options.

"So, how are you guys feeling about training?"

"Actually, when are we doing this thing you planned and what exactly are we doing?" Isaiah asks and the rest of them stop looking at their phones to look at me.

"*Actually*, it's gonna be a while. I need more time with you guys. It's gonna be more difficult than you think and all four of you still need work."

"What happened to being pressed for time?" I look at Liam who leans back in his chair crossing his arms. Mirroring him, I cross my arms just as he did. "I am pressed for time, but this is important and it needs to be done right the first time."

"X, I'm gonna need you to explain in detail what this is for and what we are doing because if anyone gets hurt—"

I raise a hand cutting Venus's reply short. "I promise you no one's gonna get hurt. Look I know you guys aren't super fond of me and you have valid reasons, but if you should know anything about me, I keep my word."

Promises said and unsaid have been broken with me before. I won't break my promise with them. I'll make sure they're ok, no matter what. But what happens in a situation where I have to choose between them and finding my mother? This wasn't supposed to be a difficult decision to make but my own words prove it's becoming one.

The waiter comes from the back carrying a mound of ice cream so tall I can barely see their face. Gently, the ice cream is set in front of me and I sit up in my seat.

"Eat up!" the waiter exclaims before leaving. This is such an inhumane amount of food to have in one sitting. It's no wonder they advertise it the way they do—no one's actually gonna finish eating this whole thing! Not even between the five of us. It's a literal mountain.

"Well, Aruni, you got the people at the door closest to you and I got the door across from me on my right. Let me know if you need extra help." Her eyes coat in gray and she looks at the table from across the room. They're looking our way, probably wondering if I'll actually eat this tub of sugar. Aruni grabs a spoon and takes a bite of ice cream and leans back into the booth. Ok, never mind then.

"Wait, but what are we gonna do with this? It can't stay here." I listen to a concerned Isaiah and keep my eyes on anyone looking in this direction, hoping the illusion holds. I actually didn't think that far ahead.

"So, what are you thinking now, X?"

"I didn't think that far ahead, Liam."

"Throw it out." Venus waves her hand, scrunching up her face in a way that makes her seem to hate the sight of the ice cream mountain. She's done this before then.

"We can't throw all of that out."

"What do you think they do with it when we don't eat the whole thing, Lee?"

"Ok, but we haven't touched it. Give me the bowl."

"You're actually gonna eat that?" Isaiah takes his eyes off the door to look at him. Liam shakes his head—he's gonna disappear with that bowl without warning and get caught. Which is why I'm here and they're not ready for the mission because they make silly mistakes like that. I covered up the sight for anyone that could've saw. I hope that the standstill illusion isn't faulty. To everyone in the diner it hopefully appears as though he never left.

When he gets back, the illusion is still holding. I can still see the gray eyes spotting some of the people in the room. It needs to stay that way 'til the food gets here.

"Where did you put it?"

"In some bowls at my aunt's house."

"Matter fact, why don't we go to your backyard today? We can split it when we get there." I look over at Isaiah and I shake my head no. I'm so ready for this day to be over.

Well, not quite. I'm not sure what I want right now.

"I gotta get back to my room."

"Why? It's not even that late yet." Aruni stretches her neck to look past Venus and all I can do is rub my eyes.

"I have stuff to do. Like retwisting my locs."

"OH! I can retwist them, but did you wash your hair?" Venus jumps up in her seat, looks up from her phone and I fold my hands in my lap. I can do it myself, I've been doing this myself since I've had them. "Yes but—"

"Can I retwist your locs, please? My mom used to have locs but she cut them off a while ago. She used to let me help, so I know what I'm doing." It is a lot to do on my own and I don't always want to do them myself, but I do, and I love my hair so it's fine. Luckily, my arms don't get tired like they used to. I'm not even gonna look at her. Instead, I rub my eyes again, so I don't have to watch her smile fade when I say no.

"You can retwist a few BUT THAT'S IT!" Maybe I'll be a little lazy today. It's only a few.

***

We did end up getting the half-price meals but from what I'm hearing it was basically regular priced with the amount of food they got. Aruni ordered extra fries and we don't know where this extra meal came from. No one questioned it, so we took it. When we get to Aruni and Liam's backyard, Aruni almost immediately runs up the steps to go inside and get the ice cream.

"X, come sit." Venus stands by a rusty lawn chair and when I turn around Aruni and her aunt walk out walk out the door.

"Hey, what're y'all doin' back here? I thought you would've been by Isaiah's folks today." She looks like she could be their mom but maybe they all just look very alike. With her braids in a bun I see the resemblance to Aruni's heart shaped face.

"Lee got ice cream," Venus replies, carrying a jar of product I study to make sure it's something I would use. The second she puts my hair up I whip around and tell her to take it easy. Isaiah and Liam are talking to Aruni and their aunt about whatever. Aruni grabs the bowl of ice cream taking a scoop for herself.

"You want some?" Aruni asks me. It's difficult to answer because I'm inhaling deeply to not cuss Venus out for tugging at my hair so roughly. She's not pulling that much but it's irritating me to have my head leaned down like this.

"Um . . . no. No, thank you. Venus, please, with the pulling!"

"Girl, then hold still, your head is on a swivel!" Is it? I didn't notice if it was. I need to see what's happening around me. I can't hold still and see everything!

"What's your name, miss girl? I haven't seen you around." That's their aunt and I wanna look up at her but I can't right now.

"Xandria"—Venus yanks my loc a little too hard—"VENUS!" I call myself X, but I think that would give too much away if I told her that. So, I'll get over it for now and go with the name my mom gave me.

"Stop moving!"

"Oh, a beautiful name for beautiful girl! Alright, y'all better clean up your mess before you leave!" All I heard was scattered okays before the screen door closed shut.

"X, I could get this done so much sooner if you would relax."

"That's true, you should take your own advice." I cut my eyes at Liam since I can't turn my head and I roll them afterwards.

"I can't."

"Then try at least. I get it. You know I do, but if it helps, take it from me if not anyone else. This right here is one of my safe places and my promise to you is that you can relax a bit," Venus replies and suddenly the space is too quiet. When I lift my head a little, I watch them watching me.

I have abilities in common with all four of them and we have similar life experiences. I don't know their whole story but they created this space for themselves when they couldn't have it somewhere else. I've never had other people in my safe space. My safe space was the iPod in my pocket or that room with the piano and then I lost both. I want this to be something I can have but that's not compatible with me. She won't be finished with my head no time soon so for Venus's sake I will sit still even though I refuse to make sense of what she said to me.

Yet anytime I say that I'm not gonna care too much about them I forget about that thought halfway through the day. Then the time gets shorter, and it sits still and my attention goes from pain in my neck to laughing at something one of them said. Hands covering my smile become useless against teary laughs, yelling at Venus about my hair becomes teachable moments. I shake my head lacking tension to handle a loc myself to show her the way palm roll them because it's easier that way.

Listening to Aruni's stories and debates with Isaiah about how functional the world-building is turned me away from anxieties of tomorrow into conversations of today. The yellows of right now don't drown me in the false ones that led me astray in my yesterdays. *Yellows of right now became yellows of right now.*

It took the sky darkening to remind me that todays do end, and by then both Venus and Aruni have their hands in my hair putting it up into a high ponytail. Venus swivels a mirror in front of me and all I could do give was a wide stare and blink.

"Do you like it?" I hear Aruni ask. Instead of responding I still stare unsure of why my eyes are hot right now. It's gotta be another memory. My mom never did my hair but the one from my dreams did. I part my lips and it's too quiet again, but I can't simply say thank you, thank you doesn't describe the intangible gift they gave me. I was supposed to be helping them and all I asked was for them to help me get to the man in New City. I didn't ask for any part of today. *I didn't have to.*

After a day like today of living instead of surviving for the first time, it's too much and not enough to just say, *thank you.*

" . . . Um . . . It's very nice. Very nice. Thank you." I can't stay here. Something's up. And I think I know why. Liam told them about me and they either feel bad or wanna pretend to feel bad to use me for something. I sit up straight and stand up out of my chair revoking all that happened today and how much it lightened the load off my shoulders. He's gonna hear from me because if this was his idea, I'll know better than to fall into the same ditch twice.

Chapter 18
Liam

I know I'm a bit too paranoid about BT. How can I not be after everything that happened at Main City 15 and losing the people close to me because of them. Over these last few months, I've been hoping to learn enough about my abilities sooner than later. That way I won't have to replay hypotheticals in my mind at what to do and how to do it if we were to get caught up with BT. I'm not completely confident that I have it all together but it's nothing like how I started.

Even if I was to be comfortable with my abilities and manage to be good enough to keep Aruni, Isaiah, and Venus safe, I don't worry about them the way I worry about X. It's different when they're being careless or not paying attention. They'll let me be there if I need to be, but X isn't like that. She'll handle her own quietly and say that she's good by herself when I can see differences in her every time she knows she's not alone. She fights it and tries to hide it, but I can't miss it.

I always catch the smile right before her hands fly to her face. I know her laugh without even looking in her direction. The way she crosses her arms at me when I tease her back. Watching how intentional she is about using any of her abilities and how patient she is while explaining everything. The way she sits back and narrows her eyes when listening to someone else explain something on their end like she's taking note of every detail. X has many reasons to not allow herself to be someone else's safe place, but it's never been that easy for me to talk about what happened with me back home.

I'm not sure how long she's had her abilities but watching her is the reason why I always have questions. She's really damn good at it. I'm gonna get it soon 'cause I don't know what's gonna happen if a situation arises where we have to fight or run and I can't keep up. She's not gonna wait for me either which is part of the reason why I need to get it together. I can be by her side when she does attempt to handle things by herself. I know she would, but she shouldn't have to.

Isaiah left earlier when his mom called and X volunteered to teleport Venus home. I was gonna go inside the house after Aruni, but I saw X outside. Good. Because this food is for her. I hand the bag to her and she remains still with her arms crossed, but she's pissed like actually pissed.

"Did I do something?" I drop my extended arm with the food to my side and she stands there watching me like she did the first time we met.

"Did you tell them about the flashes?" And as easy as it is to talk to X, this also makes it difficult. But I understand because of what I saw. I don't mind being patient with her the way she is with me.

"I wouldn't tell them about that. I told you that."

"Just because you said it doesn't mean I should believe you."

"Then ask them. Where is this coming from?"

"... You—"

She rubs her eyes as she takes a breath, but I may know where this is coming from and she's not gonna say it.

"X, if any of this is really bothering you no one's gonna take offense to it. I'm just opening the floor up and saying that if you ever want to ask to hang out or stick around it's fine. But if you don't, you don't. It's up to you." Some things aren't easy to say, and at those times silence may be best. So, I let it be whatever it is and she stares at me studying my face like she usually does. And I do it right back but not for the same reason.

"Why are you like this?"

"Like what?"

"Every time I lose my temper with you. You don't get upset with me like the rest of them do."

"You didn't lose your temper, you asked me a question. I ask you questions all the time . . . Back at the borders though—"

"Yeah, yeah, that was different." And there goes my favorite smile. That would be the reason why I study her face.

"I'll see you tomorrow, Liam."

"You don't have any more questions?"

"No, I'm not like you." After the smile crosses our faces again, I hand her the bag of food and this time she doesn't hesitate to take it.

"You can poof over here if you need to so you can warm it up."

"Yeah. Thank you."

"Anytime, X." She does that thing where she wipes her nose and then disappears. I'm around X because she lets me be and she goes with it. I don't miss anything she says, and she's the same way with me, but even after all that something is still not quite right about her story. Every time I get those flashes something's off about them. I'll ask her about it, maybe not that but where she's from at least. We should all meet at Auntie's house but I'm not telling her business unless she wants to share it herself.

Chapter 19
Xandria's Past

October 29th, 2094
Past: 1 year and 11 months ago
City unknown

Later that night I found time to washup and go to bed. I always use my mom's stuff because it's better than the crap she gets me. Just because I can't buy what I need on my own doesn't mean I have to smell bad until then.

The sun rises, beaming through my eyelids waking me up from my half-sleep. Every morning I lay down longer than I should to make sense of my surroundings. Laying on my self-made bed of clothes, I entertain the thought of skipping school. If I did go, what the hell do I say about this gash on my face? I can't even recall the full memory of how my mom ended up swinging with that ring on.

Then Damien and all those damn questions, I get the concern but why we always gotta talk when he wants to talk? I don't wanna talk sometimes, sometimes I need him to be present without the need to talk. I know he knows what's going on. We both know there's not much we can do about it unless we want BT to get involved and start accusing people of being neo-humans for whatever reason. I'm not one but I wish I was. That would make it easier to leave. What if they accused my mom of being a neo-human? Where would I stay? I can't be homeless then I'll definitely go missing.

Lemme get up, laying down isn't fixing anything.

I drag my feet to stand in front of the bathroom door and I freeze, I don't want to look at whatever she did to my eye last night. This isn't anything new but something about this time was different. What caused the gash was something important...

She shouldn't be home right now—assuming she left for work already— so it'll be easy to search her room for what she clocked me with last night. Maybe grab some cash if I find any, I'll deal with the consequences later.

Instead of going to the bathroom I walk down the hallway and turn into her room. Her bed is a mess like the rest of her room, and it reeks of metal; why that of all things? I wish I knew but it's one of those odd things that I stopped questioning a while ago. I look at her brown dresser where tons of papers and makeup are scattered all over.

When I approach the dresser a glimmer of light bounced in my peripheral. I immediately search the reflection and I spot it. The shine is coming from under the bed.

A ring? An engagement ring. I remember seeing this on her ring finger before, but she hardly wears it anymore. Who is it from? My dad? Doesn't matter I gotta get to class. I also need to figure out how to cover up this gash.

There's a Literacy test this morning and Damien is going to be looking for me after school. I'm not arguing with him again about where I'm at. Sometimes I wanna sneak off to the music room for a bit because it's the easiest time to be myself, but somehow me taking time fuels an argument. I don't have time for that, and I definitely don't wanna talk about the gash. I gotta hide it. He's gonna start asking one-too-many questions that I don't have the energy to answer. We know what happened, what's there to talk about? I shake my head ignoring my frustration with the little arguments that have been bubbling up between us lately. I'll figure him out later.

I grab some makeup that's slightly lighter than my skin, a pair of sunglasses from her room, and the ring. In the bathroom, I do the best bullshit-cover-up job I can. It stings to dab all this stuff on my face, I wince every time I touch it, but I keep going anyway. It's never easy to hide bruises.

I took the ring because if I take this thing to a gold shop I can get some money for it. I know that's gonna get me into some shit and I'll get caught, but I haven't eaten anything of substance since yesterday morning. These headaches and stomach pains could be deemed as deadly. I could ask Damien for some food or money, but I'm not doing that. I need to take care of myself so I can do what I want when I want. I find if I ask for something it turns into an exchange, and I don't want to exchange anything. I want to exist and teach myself to play those songs on the piano at school when I want to. I wanna live or at least feel alive. Right now, I'm surviving but one day it won't be that way.

I slide the ring into my pocket, throw on sunglasses, throw on my black hoodie and sweatpants, grab my bag, and head out the door. Hopefully I can make it to my literacy class on time for once. I clench my fist in my pocket knowing I look so suspicious right now but at least there's no BT people outside.

As I walk down the street, I fight to not get too lost in my thoughts, so I study the trees alongside the sidewalk. They're spaced out to perfection on every block. There's a stoplight at the corner but it's never on which defeats the purpose of a stoplight. There's a stop sign at the one farther down but where are the street names? I swear we had street names out here. Maybe if I could remember them that would help but I got nothing. Did the streets even have names? . . . *This neighborhood . . . What is the name of this neighborhood?*

There's the bus and I'm gonna miss it. I'm running so fast I might bore a hole in my low-top sneakers, but as soon as I get there it pulls off.

I have to either 100-yard dash to my school or wait for the bus that takes the next set of kids to school later, but that's too late so 100-yard dash it is. I've had these gray sneakers for as long as I can remember. One of these days they're gonna disintegrate right off my feet.

Of course, after all of that, I am still extra late to Literacy class today despite my efforts. My chest heaves as I drag my feet to the door but it's closed and locked prompting me to knock like a maniac. Banging my fist on the door as if I was playing drums. I'm tired and sweaty and at this point I don't care how crazy I look knocking on the door.

Despite the urgency of my knock, it doesn't work. Ms. St. Bernard sees me glaring at her through the window but doesn't budge. I can't stand her.

I know I'mma be out here for a minute, so I sit on the hallway floor and stare at the ceiling. That way if anyone walks past, I don't have to make eye contact. Who designed the plans for this school? It doesn't even look like a school. The pale-yellow walls flash in and out the more I squint at them. Behind each flash it's almost like I'm sitting in the middle of a dome with bright white walls. *What the hell is going on?* I sit up from leaning on the wall and the pale-yellow walls return to normal as they solidify. Maybe I didn't get enough sleep.

All the colors here are so washed-out like everything else in this neighborhood, whatever the name of it may be. Come to think of it I don't even know the name of this school. What does it matter? I should be leaving soon anyway, right? How long have I been here? *I'm in my third year, right? No, it can't be, it's been about month. But if it's been a month, how did I—* I should stop thinking so hard before I get a headache again.

I leaned back failing to ignore the spoiled cheese smell, but I hear one of the high school squads coming down the hall. I'mma pretend they're not there, if I close my eyes maybe I can actually disappear.

"Xandria, you better get in that classroom before they call BT on you. I heard if you rack up enough detentions they'll send you right to them."

"Why would they do that if I'm not a neo-human?" I'm not even gonna spare them a look.

"Who do you think gives the school money to keep the lights on? Shoot you make it real easy for someone to make a quick buck off you."

"You plan on calling them?"

"I should, shouldn't I?" she replies, raising an eyebrow at me. She's not going to. I've heard this a few times already and it hasn't happened yet. At first it used to send me into a panic and I would run off somewhere but overtime I learned to not react to them. They only threatened me with BT because of my reaction, if they wanted to do it I would've disappeared already but for whatever reason I'm still here.

If I could, I would fight back... I wouldn't stop, but I can't if I wanted to. Every day I'm here something happens, shoving me closer to an unhinged reaction. Last time I did it was because I couldn't find my iPod for the life of me. That was the closest I got to losing my mind but I found it later on the floor in the hallway. My recollection of the incident is blurry but it's not pretty either. I'm too tired to fight anymore, I need to keep it together 'til I get out.

The group disappears down the hallway when Ms. St. Bernard comes out to lecture me. I stand so I can be less small. I don't have much but I'll use what I got. It helps to fake it 'til I make it—that's if I ever even make it.

"You have been late to my class almost every day since the beginning of the semester and I have had countless conversations with you and your mother about it. What is the issue?" She asks as she crosses her arms and narrows her light eyebrows at me.

"Nothing. Sorry."

Yeah, it's nothing all right. It surely has nothing to do with my abusive mom and half the school calling me out my name and threatening to call BT. Why do teachers call my mom anyway? They don't even know what she looks like. I don't know how this helps. Bullshit. It's always bullshit.

"No, Xandria, you need to speak up now or I will not be letting you into my class anymore when you are late." She scolds me as she waves a finger in my face. Let me take a breath before I get suspended for breaking a teacher's finger. She has some nerve, her nails are gross.

"Miss, it's personal and I'd rather not speak about it." I let out a disappointed sigh because I am about to say something that I may not stay true to.

"Look, I'll do better but I know this test is important and I need to graduate."

"Fine but take those glasses off first. You're in school."

"Miss St. Bernar—Bernadine... I can't." She does look like a Saint Bernard though. Her face is all saggy and stretched out.

"Take them off. Or it's an automatic absence and zero for the day and I'm sure—"My hand snatches the glasses off to stare into her soul with my bruised up half-open left eye. She freezes, surprised like she didn't know it was evident that I was hiding something.

"Well ... I— "

Exactly.

Before she can comment I rush into the classroom ignoring the eyes gawking at my fresh scar. People whisper as I grab a test sheet from the back and sit in my seat. The kid next to me raises her hand and I already know what it's about. The St. Bernard points to her, here we go.

"Can I change my seat?" After she squeaks, I hear scattered giggles around the room and I don't even flinch.

The saggy faced teacher nods and she sits across the room somewhere. Whatever. I need to pass this test.

My life is a mess and if there's anything good that's going to happen, I am going to graduate high school. I'm gonna walk that stage and I'm gonna take my graduation pictures. I'm gonna show that monster of a mother I can accomplish great things without her poor attempt at being a so-called provider. I don't need any help. I'll help myself.

After school I met Damien. He was in a work uniform— a dark blue T-shirt and cargo pants. I asked him about his job before and he wouldn't tell me, but it didn't bother me to not know what he does was, so I left it alone. I find myself wanting to keep the peace more than wanting to have a conversation as of lately but it's nothing serious. He's sitting at the front exit on one of the benches. When he sees me approaching, he gets up to walk with me. *Please don't ask about the clunky glasses.*

"Xandria, what's with the glasses?" Of course. Just my luck.

"You like them? I thought they were cool."

"Right but it's cloudy," he says pointing to the sky.

"Who cares? They look good on me." No, they don't, they've been falling off my face all day.

"Ok. I'm going to ask you what happened, but I need you to not curve my questions."

"You know what happened," I reply with stoic in my face..

"I just want to make sure you're ok."

"I know but I'm clearly not and you know why. Don't worry about it. I don't wanna talk about it right now."

"Xandria, can you at least let me see your face?"

"I gotta go to the gold shop." I need to distract him from the current topic. We can't fix this, why talk about it if we can't fix it?

"Why?" I pull out the ring that's cold to the touch. He looks at me and shakes his head, I can tell by the way he studies me then back at the ring, that he wants to confront me about not telling him anything again.

"You stole that from your mom?"

"Yep. Impressive right?"

"Does she know?"

"Not yet." I was about to wink but my eye is swollen shut so that wouldn't make sense. As we walk, he barely pays attention to where we're going because he's too busy studying my face.

"What the hell did she do to your eye?"

I should've stayed at school and hid in the music room. My thoughts drift to the iPod in my bag and the song I was teaching myself to play the other day crosses my memory. I can see the black notes dancing on the staff. His voice fuzzed into the background noise of other people talking but he's calling me.

"Sorry, I didn't hear you." I did hear him, I was ignoring him.

"You need to get out of there."

I laugh a bit because it's funny that he even brought that up. Where am I supposed to go? I don't know my mom's family and my dad is this mystery guy that I never met. So, I don't really have options here. Homelessness or get beat up as a housing payment, either way I end up stuck.

"How? I have nowhere to go. No other family. Nothing."

"Me."

"No, you don't have to do that," I reply, shaking my head. I don't like people doing me favors. They always want something back when they do me favors. I appreciate his offer, but I already see reasons to not do that.

We've always been good together and at first it was nice to have someone to stick around, but sticking around became clingy. I explained several times why I stay at school so late some days and still he's upset that I'm not outside the school after my last class.

That's my time to just be, and I've been getting less of it because of him. I miss it. Though it feels like I'm talking to a wall when I tell him that. Then there's the incessant questioning of my whereabouts. I don't know. I hate living with my mom, but I know how to deal with my mom. I know exactly what to do to still get what I want and need when I want or need it. With Damien, I don't know if I'll be able to catch a break to do what I want. This is good the way it is, I can navigate this. I don't know if I can navigate sharing a space with Damien.

"That's not true. I do. Xandria, how much worse is this gonna get if you don't get outta there? How much longer do you have?" That's actually a good point and its true. Mom's is weird like that. Some days the beatings are perceived as numb, other days the beatings are numbing, and some days I don't know if I'm going to make it through. Maybe I should go. This is the one person that has stuck by me through everything I've been dealing with. Maybe this is it. Maybe this is how I escape, its different but I'll make it work.

"I gotta get my stuff first and I still have to go to the shop to get the money for this."

"You know you don't have to risk your life stealing from her. You should come to me."

"Yeah but, I had it handled and—Never mind."

We go to the pawn shop, I get the cash, I go home, and it's almost as if the time moved a little too fast. Before I know it, I'm standing outside the doorway and as soon as I come in there she is on the couch. However, something is different about the room, the metallic smell was stronger, and she's sitting too stiff. It's odd to watch her inhumane crunchy movements as she stands up with the gun in her hand.

Before I can collect myself, she speaks as if she we're hissing cold air at me but even that's off, it's like she's forcing the words out her gut.

"Where's my ring, Xandria?" A tear falls from her wide eyes and rolls down her already wet face. I hope she doesn't expect me to care that she's crying. I cried so much, I ran out of tears.

"I don't know."

I had to teach myself how to hold it together in tough situations to protect myself. It didn't change anything or else I wouldn't be in this life-or-death situation right now with my guardian holding a gun.

"YOU DON'T KNOW? Xandria, I've had it. You stole my money. Now my ring. I PAY BILLS TO KEEP THIS ROOF OVER YOUR HEAD! I FEED YOUR STUPID ASS!"

She begins pacing and rubbing the coils on top of her head. My eyes follow her, I have to be ready for anything. Then the room flashes like the pale walls in the school but it stops. It's difficult to mind my surroundings when I'm watching my mom walk around like a mad woman. Something's so wrong and there go those odd questions panging through my mind.

"I'm leaving... for good... but there's one question I have before I go."

"Fine. I don't give a shit that you're leaving but go ahead and ask the damn question." She flails the gun in the air as she talks, and every time she does, I suppress the urge to jump or flinch. She won't look at me, but I look at her. I'm not losing my train of thought this time. I need to know why her actions seems so random. Why people I know blur the lines of dreams and memories.

"Who gave you that ring?" I ask, stopping my voice from shaking. She tightens when she hears the question, is she gonna answer it this time?

"You know what, why not?"

To my surprise, her grimace softens and she stops pacing and the room falls silent. She straightens her back and walks behind the island in the kitchen. Who's my father? Where is he? Where's the mom from the memory-dreams? What happened to her?

"One day, I had made you your favorite meal, the mac 'n cheese with the three cheeses. You remember that, right?"

Hold on. This doesn't make any sense. My actual mom is the one who made that with me, the one from the dreams or are they memories? She was the one who braided my hair when I asked about the braids she had. The one who had no problem with the questions I asked. Questions that aren't important enough to recall.

My mom wouldn't hit me the way she does. The room blurs again, my veins get hot, and a headache covers my skull. This is why part of me hoped I'd never find out because I knew the mom I saw in dreams was the one who lived with me. I didn't want to accept it, so I dismissed the thought. Behind the chaos, she is the mom who only made sense when she wasn't the one I was looking at. *They're not two different moms. They're the same one. The one I live with.*

"Afterward, I went to go get ice cream and left you with Xavier."

Who's Xavier? As a matter of fact, why'd she leave me with him? I know that name though, but that's not my dad, right? The room blurs again and there goes those dome shaped white walls.

"I came home to find you both were gone. To where? I don't know. I called and he said he took you to the park but that's not where you were."

No, it wasn't. Where am I right now? The room shakes and blurs again and I catch myself against the wall.

"Where were we then?" I ask after shaking away the vertigo in my head.

"At a lab. I don't know why but . . ." she massages her head before she continues. I could do the same, my brain is pulsing.

"Your dad is Xavier and before we got here something happened that—" she pauses and holds her head again, straining to get the words out. She was so enthusiastic about hurting me with this story earlier. What changed? She jerks forward and slams both her hands on the counter. Suddenly she rushes to me gently laying her hands on my shoulders.

"Xandria, listen to me. I need to tell you something important before we run out of time. *Don't ever let me find you. You run like there's fire under your feet and if you want to look for me don—*" Her mouth freezes mid-sentence as she shakes her head again and her hands drop from my shoulders. She holds her head. Is the room shaking to her too?

Leaning on the wall, my chest heaves and hot panic tears through my veins as I take in the overload of information my mom rambled off to me. There's loud buzzing in my ears and the room flashes in and out of view showing glimpses of the white dome. *Where are we?*

The buzz of the lights crescendo in my ears. I lean up from the wall and whirl around looking at the room fade in and out. *Where am I? I'm not in an apartment.* I rush out the room and there's a bright flash and a boom before I'm standing right back in the same spot I was standing in before.

No. What happened? I WAS RIGHT THERE! WHERE AM I? At the sound of my mom's voice, whatever I was thinking about sizzles into nothing yet again, and I'm left wondering why my thoughts keep redirecting themselves.

"Where's my dad?" I ask after hearing a mention of him through her mumble of words. She laughs; my tears are her comedic gold and through this laugh she answers another question.

"He's dead. It was his own fault. They had found the body the next day in a dumpster. Now I have nothing but a parasite living in my house. I wanted a child so bad and I get left with something that does nothing but take from me. I was gonna take you with me, you know, but now look."

At this point, nothing and everything boils in my chest at the same time and my hands clench tighter.

"You blame all of this on me? Mom, I'm . . . confused! I don't get where any of this is coming from! I don't think you know where this is coming from! Do you? You don't find it odd that you have little to no reason for treating me like this?" She blinks at me and holds my gaze, but nothing's happening and my mind begins to warp the last events as the conversation continues.

"Yes, I blame you. You distgut—"

"NO! Why would you do this to me?" I yell, pointing at my eye. I lean in close enough so she can see her damage.

"Mom. I'm. Your. Daughter. Why would you do this to me?" Tears I can't control fall hot on my face. I don't care that they do. Not right now.

"ANSWER ME!" I need her to explain. I need her to explain why this is happening. Why days don't drag on like days and years blink by like weeks. Why she does what she does spontaneously. Why my memories fade and walls flash when I ask a question or attempt to get her to understand. She has moments where she is telling me something and seems a little saner but then I lose her. I can't keep up. Part of me wants a genuine answer, an apology, something, but I get nothing but a scared jump back and a fearful stare. She reaches for the gun when I do but I get it first. I could pull the trigger right now and return the pain she gave me but she's my mom, my only family. My mind now floods with memories as they bring themselves into clarity causing my eyes gloss over.

I see her braiding my hair. I see her playing reading me a story. I see her teaching me how to cook. In one memory, I see both her and dad hugging me at some celebration. I see us playing a board game together and all I can wonder in this moment is what happened? How can I fix it? Can I fix it? This isn't fair. Where did these memories come from? I could scream but my throat is already dry. I can't stop crying though, not after all those strange memories skipped by.

Mom, what happened to you? I would've asked out loud if I didn't know the result would get me nowhere.

At this point I lower the gun in defeat and go to my room and gather everything, but still keeping the gun close by. My mom stood frozen in the same position. When I walk into her sight she's glaring at me, her dark eyes filled with malice.
I pick up my book bag and grab another big, plastic bag from the bottom drawer in the kitchen to stuff it with clothes. I put the gun on the coffee table and go to the door to leave. It's cold in this apartment but warm in my body. The gray walls will probably hold the pain that lingers in here for an eternity. I hope I won't, but with the tensity in my muscles now I don't think I'm much different from these walls.

Before I go, I take one last look at my mom, and I say the words I've always wanted to say but refused to because it would make it real in a world where it is not meant to exist. "I love you, Mom. Always have, in some sick strange way I always have. It—it would've been nice if you loved me back. It would've been nice to at least see you try."

At least I loved a version of her, even though it wasn't real. This is why it was always so hard to fight back. The one percent chance I could have her back always lingered at the back of my mind. Still does. But I need to leave. I need to leave my home. After I utter those words, I leave, and close the door hoping that being away from her makes it a little easier to go about my life without wondering why all of this seems broken. I'm not entertaining this anymore, I'm gonna live my life the best I can with what I got.

Chapter 20
Liam

Present day: September 1st, 2096
Main City 27

It took all three of them, including Aruni, an hour to get to our house despite the fact we're not that far away from each other. I should've called or texted them an hour ahead, I knew they would get here late. It's one in the afternoon, they have to be up by now.

By the time they arrive, Auntie had handed me a tray of fresh biscuits to put on the table. We're leaving soon anyway. I told her we were fine, but she insisted on giving us something to eat before we leave.

"So, you called us all the way over here to ask us something you could've asked us through a text?" Never mind the fact Isaiah was the first one to pick a biscuit off the tray even with his complaining.

"Yes, now we can guarantee that we'll all be there."

"Remind me why we care about this to begin with?"

"Well, we have been working pretty closely with X and it's a little odd that she has not a single clock or calendar in her vicinity. She doesn't know about shows and music that almost everyone has at least heard of by now," Venus answers, folding her legs in the couch.

"She tells time by watching the sky and—and she has some other odd quirks about her past too." I should've let her continue her rant. I haven't told them about the full scope of how my abilities work. I don't plan on telling them too much about X, and I definitely didn't plan on sharing that much either. But I might have to at some point.

"What about her past?" Isaiah leans forward from the back of the couch and Venus squints at me. My eyes shift to Aruni and all I can do is lean back in my chair. I should tell them.

"When I mimic abilities, I can see what caused them. So, you remember those papers X showed us? That's what I see."

"Shit, Lee, that must suck," Isaiah replies, grabbing a second biscuit. Honestly, I'mma need another one too.

"Wait so . . . so how much do you see? Do you see everything?"

I shake my head at Venus instead of continuing to explain any further. It's almost too convenient to have the ability to mimic abilities but at the cost of knowing their pain and suffering I would rather have remained as I was. Anyone that got their abilities the painful way rather than through genetics may say the same, but this is different. Every flash bares a burden too heavy for the holder to carry. Every thought on it I carry flashes briefly but having that happen over and over again or even knowing of it is its own breed of fatigue. It's not their own personal burdens that are weighted, though, that leaks through the flashes. It's the fact that multiple people can share their despair with me. That's what makes this difficult. Otherwise, I wouldn't mind these abilities at all. What I haven't told them is over time the more I mimic the same person's abilities the less vivid they get. I barely see X's anymore but it doesn't mean I forget them.

"So, what's so odd about her past? You don't have to give details but . . ." Shout out to Aruni for that save because it was too quiet.

"That's the thing, I don't know, but they seem, I don't know, planted?" Also, I've seen at least two BT members in the flashes I did get. Granted, they weren't friendly but the fact her recollection has these glitchy holes in it along with two BT members makes me wonder.

"Well then now's a great time to go ask her!" Venus hops up and the rest of us don't waste time deciding if we should follow or not. That was the plan anyway. When we walk through the door, X is standing in front of the kitchen counter opening the bag of food I bought for her yesterday.

"You weren't gonna eat that cold right?" I know I offered to warm up the food at my house but knowing her she wasn't gonna do that either. It can't be because she doesn't want to—because who the hell wants to eat cold fries—she's just very apprehensive about taking up space, but it only seems to be in situations like these. She surely has no problem with swinging logs and hunks of metal over people's heads.

"Well . . . I was going to find a way to heat it up eventually, but it was early at the time, and I didn't wanna disturb your aunt if she wasn't up so . . . Actually, forget the food, why are y'all here? I thought y'all wanted to take a break today. You know rest is important."

"X, we have a question." *Really Isaiah?*

"What? Don't look at me like that. That's why we're here."

"About?" She straightens her back and crosses her arms, cutting her eyes at me. I still didn't tell them but she might not believe that.

"You actually . . . X, you don't keep a watch, you don't have a—a phone. Lastly and most importantly, we don't know where you're from because you've never mentioned it. It's—It's a little odd and it's nothing against you. It's just that typically when you meet people these aren't questions that people avoid. Questions that may not come up at all in some cases." After Aruni explains everything, X narrows her eyes and leans forward from the counter.

"And what does this have to do with anything?"

"Well, we've been stuck here with you for a hot minute, X, it wouldn't hurt to know basic information like that." She looks at Isaiah and was gonna reply, but she stops and leans back against the counter. She rubs her eyes with her hands and takes a breath. The room falls silent and we all watch her debate with herself on whether she should answer our questions. I only ask X questions that don't have to do with her past and whatever I knew about it aside from the visions she chose to tell me. However, the fact that there's so much wrong here and she doesn't speak on it could change a lot of what has happened in the past few months. We at least need a *why* for what we're doing because we're caught up in it now. Aruni's caught up in it now.

"Ok... I—I have been through some rough stuff, clearly, and since I've been taking up so much of your time. I guess the least I can do is tell you why I'm doing all of this. The man I'm after is someone who works at a lab. Biology and Trauma Labs, does that ring a bell?"

"Yeah, that's BT. You're trying to catch someone from BT, X? What the hell are you involved with where you're trying to catch someone from BT? Don't they work with New City?" Too many questions at once Isaiah.

She lets out a nervous laugh and her crossed arms drift into her pockets. "Yeah, they work with them alright. Look, BT is doing some scary stuff to people like us. My dad is dead because of them and my mom, she's complicated, but she's missing. I wanna find her and the BT worker is gonna help me do that, but I can't do it if I can't get into his house. That's where the information is located in his computer cube and that computer cube doesn't leave that house."

"X, you're sending us to a place where we'll be easy bait for BT? What exactly is this plan because that doesn't sound right." See, I wanna give her the benefit of the doubt but BT gives away a lot of money to anyone who catches neo-humans, especially if it's successful. That's killing two birds with one stone if she gets paid and she finds her mom.

"How so? Liam, do you think I'm gonna hand you over to them?"

"Well, that's what it sounds like. We don't mess around with BT for very obvious reasons! Why bring us that close to them?"

"Because I need to find my mother?! Why do you think? If you don't wanna help then don't. I'll do it myself then!" She walks over to me.

"Why else would your mother's information be in a BT computer unless she works for BT?" X raises her eyebrows; shocked. "Yes, I saw that! So, why were you going to take us there?"

"Woah, what? X, your mom works for BT? Why . . . Wait do you work for BT?" Venus looks at X with wide eyes and X stops glaring at me long enough to turn her attention to Venus. Her shoulders drop as she looks at everyone. These past few months have been us learning from X and talking to her about shit most people don't talk about. None of this is gonna sit right. It's not gonna sit right with me, but it was inevitable for them. I chose to tell her because I felt like I could.

"X, were those memories planted?"

"What?" She whips around and looks at me, her locs swinging back over her shoulder.

"There are holes in your memories, the flashes. They resemble computer glitches so were those memories planted or did they actually happen?"

"They . . . yes, technically they're planted. But to me they were very, *very* real. So, yes, they actually happened. I—Y'all might wanna sit down. I'll explain everything but it's gonna be a lot." She sat on one end of the couch, and I sat on the other. Everyone else sat in chairs X and I found while walking around that junkyard of a forest. I hope this isn't as bad as I think it is. It could mean I might lose someone else to BT, but in a worse way.

"My past. Sometimes it doesn't feel real. It feels like a dream but doesn't at the same time. All that happened was real enough to still be . . . burdensome. For my whole life 'til eight months ago. I never really considered how much time was passing, I was always too busy running. I'm always running. Anyways, I was in my cabin, and I was real sick, I thought I was gonna die, but I didn't. Instead, I woke up on a damn table in a room with hundreds of other people in it about the same age as the rest of us, if I had to guess. I saw some stuff there like the folder I showed you guys. I also found footage of who I think my actual parents are. I don't even know. And my mom, I know she's the reason why I can do the illusions but it's—it's complicated. I'm looking for her because I need to find her before she finds me." —She burries her face in her hands before she continues. —"Guys, I'm sorry, I really am, if you don't wanna continue, I'll leave you alone. I don't want to drag you guys into it, especially if you don't feel safe." Well, now I feel like shit and I should apologize.

"So . . . it was a simulator?" Aruni asks, breaking the silence.

"Yes. I'm seventeen now, and for the past sixteen years all that was simulation. I think. I don't know for sure yet, that's just my assumption. I don't remember growing up. I remember some things, but I don't know how real they are. Still. I remember most of what caused me to have these abilities. It was back-to-back. Just . . . Yeah don't worry about it. Y'all don't have to stay here, I'll figure it out." She stood and wiped her glassy eyes then disappeared, but I know where to. I need to apologize.

"Lee, where are you going?"

"I'll be right back. Give me a minute." Hopefully, Isaiah listens this time. After I found the staircase to the roof, there she was sitting at the edge we always sit on. I walk over to sit next to her. I'm gonna say what I need to say because putting that together beforehand isn't working out.

"First of all, I'm really sorry for accusing you and thinking you would do something like that."

"Don't be. If I were you, I would've done the same. You lost a lot of people to BT before. Unexpectedly at that."

"Yeah, but I still am though. Also, for bringing up your past. I know you told me not to do that and I did, and I shouldn't have. Don't justify it. I said what I said, and I shouldn't have said it, so that's on me."

"Yeah, it is but it was gonna come up eventually. They ask me about my past all the time when it relates to their abilities. I could never tell them like I tell you, but soon enough the timelines wouldn't have added up. The fact I don't own any type of clock is still strange. It would've come up. Even when we get the information about my mother it would've come up."

"When you said your mom is complicated, what did you mean by that?" I shouldn't ask her shit after all that happened.

"Never mind—"

"No, its fine, maybe you know something I don't. My mom is kind of like how you described your dad. She would have these moments where she'll seem like a completely different person from dreams I had. Not memories, *dreams*. It was so odd, and she would tell me things I wouldn't remember later on. She's off, like that world I was in."

"So, you need to find her first to find out why?"

"Yeah, but really, I just don't want to know what's gonna happen to me if she does find me first. I can't go back, Lee. Every waking moment was basically what you saw in those flashes. It's like living a nightmare. Look, if you really don't want to do this, you can go 'cause I don't want any of you to feel obligated."

"I don't want you to go back either, so I'm staying."

"We're staying too!" We both turn around at the sound of Aruni's voice. The three of them walk out the door to the roof.

"Are you sure?"

"Yeah, well, we don't want to be haunted by you for the rest of our lives. Nor do I want to be frozen to a wall, so yes, we're staying and helping." Isaiah plops down next to me and Aruni sits next to him.

"Besides, I've always wanted to visit a New City . . . city." Venus sits on the other side of X and X looks at all of us before taking in a breath of fresh air.

"Alright. I promise I'm not gonna let anything happen to any of you. I wouldn't wish that on any of you. You have whole lives to live out here and maybe even a better one in New City one day." We can't see New City from here but sitting on this roof refreshes memories of hanging out with old friends at the border. We'd talk about a life that would probably never happen—would never happen with them now—which is why I can't lose them to BT. I can't go through that again. I'm not gonna leave them this time.

"We wouldn't wish that on you either Alexandria. Matter of fact, you think we could also find a way into the city while we're there?"

"Maybe, Patches"—X slaps her hands on her thighs—"WELP! That's enough of that. Since you're here let's get some practice in!"

"No, no, you said today was break day. We're either going to the diner and back to Auntie's backyard or we'll call it a day." After she hops up to head toward the door, I run to catch up to her before she sets her mind on extra days of practice.

"To Auntie's backyard for what?"

"A MOVIE MARATHON! There's this new movie out about—about this girl that gets stuck in a dream and all kinds of weird trippy shit happens. It looks fantastic!" Aruni catches up to us before Venus and Isaiah, and rambles about the plot of the movie as the clouds drip from the sky like running paints.

Sometimes X pretends to be an asshole but seeing her intrigued and smiling as Aruni explains shit she clearly doesn't understand proves she isn't. She'll ask her questions and listen to the conversation regardless of what it is. All the more reason why I shouldn't have doubted her for a second.

Chapter 21
Xandria' Past

December 5th, 2095
Past: 9 months ago
City: Unknown

T he last time I left to the place with the lights the timing was very inconvenient. I went to a grocery store and walked around with a bag on my back searching for a way to get what I needed without spending the limited cash I had in my pocket. I shoved one bar of soap in my pocket and the lady at the front yelled at me. The warm energy in my chest from when I last left body pulled me forward as if it was gonna separate from me on its own. She stood there wide eyed until I got it together and stopped tripping over my own feet. When I was finally still, I glanced at her and rushed out the door. It's not a very convenient ability to have if every time I'm caught off guard I nearly pass out.

I have better control over it now than I did at first but it's because of the other ability. For whatever reason, fidgeting with ice particles around my fingers stop me from misplac-

ing my soul out my body. It's like channeling my nerves through my hands and if I need to leave, I let whatever I was feeling be the catalyst to get me back to where I am now. Sitting against the tree looking at the lights. I'll get more comfortable with both over time. I have to. These abilities are what brought me this far in the first place. It's the reason I can stay at this cabin with supplies I permanently borrowed while floating
around the store. Meanwhile, I rest here without disruption. This same ability could help me find my mom too, but I've been putting it off.

It was easy to say I'll get my answers one way or another, but the answers I needed were so far away. Especially, when I knew I would have to fight more than I already have to get them. These glitches I see in the scenery blink in and out of view and they simultaneously happen when I get a headache—a headache is an understatement now. I find the more often it happens, or the bigger the flaws seem, the more my body aches.

I'm convinced it has to do with whatever's happening beyond the scope of what I see, but if this uncertainty haunts me now, what's gonna happen when I do find out what's beyond this? I don't know the depths of this situation, what if this is worse than I thought? All these damn questions keep growing in numbers the closer an answer gets. But I can't stay here forever. I can't live like this. With the headaches and not knowing the time. I can't live with this eerie feeling that all of this isn't as it should be. I can't stay, but if I go, what will it mean? What will the answer lead me to? I shake my head and float off the tree to woosh back over to the cabin where I last laid my head. I need to find my mom, she's the last person I can go to for an answer. It's a gamble but it's the only one I got. I could've got an answer from Damien too, but I wasn't sitting through that again. I can't. Either way I'm in the middle of chaos.

***

It takes two buses for me to get back to the city and a thirty-minute walk to get to Monster Mom's apartment building. I wait until someone else walks in to follow behind them—I wasn't gonna ring the bell. As soon as I'm in, I head straight for the stairwell. I walk up the steps and I take the scarf off my face. Soon after, the memories of the day I left replay in my mind. The one thing I can't pull from that specific memory is the warning she rambled off before I left.

When I finally get to the door, I take a deep breath and knock once, hoping it's enough for her to hear. My hands are balled into fists and sweaty as the tension continues to build in my muscles. Too many minutes pass. *See, I'm not gonna knock again, I know she heard me. What's taking so long? The apartment isn't even that big.* The door opens and as quick as the emotions well up, they die twice as fast. A short lady with red hair and pale skin answers the door. It sounds like a daycare center in the apartment with the children yelling from the room behind her. *Who's this?* I look around her and into the apartment and then back at her. My eyes narrow at the stranger in front of me. She stares at me while chewing on whatever she just took a bite of, and no words seem to formulate in my mind. I look back at the number on the door. *I'm sure I got the right apartment, but who is this?*

"You need something? My kids are ready to eat and I'm sure you hear all the madness," the red head lady finally says still smacking on her lunch.

"Um. . . Yeah, I was actually expecting someone else. Her name is Marie."

"Marie? Oh, she had to give this place up a while ago."

Give it up? What made her give up the only thing she could possibly afford? "Why? did something happen to her?"

The red-hair lady leans in as if she was telling me a dark secret, and it almost causes me to take a step back. *Why is she leaning in like that ?* Whatever happened can't be good.

"Okay, I'm not one to be in people's business, but you know that funky beige building that's shorter than the ones next to it, it's a couple blocks up from here. I heard that's where folks are disappearing to. What's the logo say? BT? Yeah, she's over there for sure. They ran up by this apartment and—"

"Do you happen to know the exact location?" I ask, shaking my head ready to go looking for her. If she's with BT that means she definitely knows the truth. That's the only reason why they would go after her the way they were after me. Does this mean she's a neo-human too? Maybe she knew I could be one.

"Not a clue, my friend, but hey, I'm sure she's alright. They're just doing their job." She smiles and nods at me and it's almost too robotic for me to believe she knows what she's saying. So, I close the door for her after pulling it in and I watch her smiling face disappear. As if I don't have enough nightmares already.

Now I actually need to *find* my mom. The red-hair lady said there's a building a few blocks up from here, but I've never seen a logo on that building. I would've noticed it. I'm not gonna find anything while standing here so I wrap the scarf back around my face and throw on my hood and head in the direction of the building.

The warm pulse deep in my chest reminds me, I could pass out on the street if I can't get this ability under control. I wish I could twirl the ice around my fingers while I walk the block but that can't happen either. So instead, black notes dance in my mind the rest of the way there. I miss being able to listen to music outside of my memory but between the cold and this new projection thing, I find that I don't drift to it as often. In a different world maybe, but right now this is what I got. When I see the empty building, I look toward the roof where BT is plastered at the top. That wasn't there before. *I need to find my mom.*

As I walked up to the desk, I paid little to no attention to the people who are sitting in the lobby wearing uniforms that resemble the same washed-out colors of the building.

"Ahem," I clear my thought to get the receptionist's attention. "I'm looking for Marie. Is—is she here?"

"Ma'am, I'm sorry she can't take visitors right now," she replies, still peering down at scribblings on papers—*like literal scribblings*—there's no way she's able to read that. More eerie glitches.

"What do you mean she can't take visitors she's my m—" I can't let them know she's, my mom. I bite the inside of my lip to stop myself from losing patience. I don't have time for this. Interestingly enough, any pain I had when I walked in seems louder than before, but the dome doesn't flash into view in here—at all.

"I'm sorry, but we really can't. What is your relation to Marie? "The lady asks while I collect myself.

"If you would answer my question, we wouldn't need to have this conversation! Where is she at?!

When I raise my voice, in my peripheral the lobby people's heads shoot toward me, including one of the workers behind the secretary at the desk—they also have the blue uniform on. Let me relax.

"Okay, I just need to see her for one minute, then I'll leave. I need to ask one questi—"

"No, Miss, you need to leave."

They're glaring at me from all over the room. I didn't even do anything—at least not yet. I'm gonna be in a lot of trouble if I keep pushing it, but I need an answer. They either let me through or I'm lighting this shit up.

"Lady, I'm gonna ask you one more time. Where is my mom?"

"Your mother?" she repeats, raising an eyebrow.

Oops.

She moves the hand that was resting on the paper and I hear a click. I don't need to see what she pressed to know my time is cut short.

"WHERE IS SHE?!"

I yell as I slam a fist into the desk. Then I heard a squeak against the desk. When I look down all I see is a dent the size of my fist. Dammit, if they didn't know I was a neo-human before it's obvious now. When I look up, I see the secretary's face, eyes wide and mouth agape.

I couldn't look at it for long before the people sitting in the lobby just so happen to have that same BT uniform on. *Where did they come from? They weren't wearing that before. Are all these people BT? Have they always been?*

Tears well in my eyes and the soreness dances over my muscle. Before I know it, one of them grabs my arm jerking me away from the table. I yank my arm away then another roach in uniform tries to hold me back. I rip his arms off me because I'm stuck on the fact none of this would've happened had she let me through. More guard's rush in the lobby, I lose track of exactly how many fail to hold me back. Determined to know this new ability, I pull loose from each and every one of them.

I want one thing and they're all in the way. I'm already here so I might as well fight. The pulling turns into pushing and the pushing leads me to toss one roach into a wall. I did a double take but I need to talk to my mom. A guard shouts something that I didn't pay attention to that stops the distraction. It's hot in my ears as I continue to push and pull away from guards. This isn't working but I know what will. Ice shoots out my hands and pushes me forward and I dash back down the hallway. My hands are surrounded by cold smoke when I'm standing a few feet away from her.

I raise my arms and flex my hands into fists. Before I hit her with a burst of ice her stupid ass jumps out the way. I'm surprised the guards haven't caught up. *Where are they?* I could go run and see my mom now, but I'll get to the receptionist first. None of this would've happened if she let me by. I could also leave my body here but that's too dangerous now and I want my mom to know I'm here.

I missed once, I won't miss this time. Clouds form around my hands as I lunge icicles at her. She runs down the hallway but begins stumbling over her feet. I use my ice to slide faster and catch up with her. As I zip down the halls workers jump out of the way. Before she can turn down another hall, with a wave of my hand, I'm able to freeze her to a wall just enough so she can still see my face. I stop right in front of her and take off my coat and scarf, my body is hot though my arms are still cold.

"I will never understand why people make things harder than they need to be. I'm so nice! I swear I am, but no one listens to me until this happens." My fingers twirl a fridged knife in the air, right as I stretch my arm back to plunge into her chest I hear a familiar voice call my name.

She looks at me stuck in place, wide eyed with her arms stiff at her sides. The knife crackles back into my hand when I meet her gaze. I'm gonna get caught but she is the only reason why I came all this way.

"Mom? Hey." On my face is a half-smile and I don't even know what to say. She looks tired. In the bags under her eyes, maybe scared as they widened and in them, she could also be sorry, all at the same time. I hope this isn't a hallucination but what would be new about that if it was.

"Xandria, you're not supposed to be here." I shake my head vigorously before she can get through the sentence. I'm so tired of hearing what I'm supposed to do and not do. Doing what I'm "supposed" to do landed me in dire circumstances. I need a reason. A very good one to take a statement like that at face value ever again.

"Not supposed to—Mom, *we're* not supposed to be here. The day I left, what were you going to tell me back at the apartment? It's about BT and whatever they're doing to this place."

"You need to leave BT alone. The minute you do that, this all gets easier. Leave it be!"

"NO! I can't. I know you've noticed the cracks in this place." She looks around the hall, her eyes tracing every crevice. "The day I left home. I can't remember what you told me, but I know it was important! Mom, you know this isn't right. I don't know what happened to you but—"

"Nothing happened! YOU happened! Xandria, look around! I did what I did to stop this from happening. To stop you from venturing into problems bigger than both of us. Things that you do not understand, but you had to leave—"

"No shit I wanted to leave! You didn't make it easy for me to stay! Hell, you made me feel like leaving was the only way to get away from you! You made me leave; I didn't want to leave!"

She drew in a long breath before hanging her head. "The things you think are holding you back are there to protect you, Xandria."

"From what? It didn't protect me from you nor your mood swings. In fact, it put me somewhere worse"—*going back and forth with her is pointless. I need answers*— "Tell me how to fix this! And don't tell me any bullshit about complying with a broken world. You know something about getting out and I need you to tell me. I can't do this anymore." *Don't cry. Don't cry.*

"Xandria. If you're gonna keep pushing this you better hope I don't find you when your damage is done."

"No. You better hope I don't find you *again*." That's if she can even make up her scattered mind to do so.

I hear the boots of BT workers clunking from down the hall, and I shift on my feet to let the ice particles pack together to seal the hallway closed. None of my abilities can save me now. The bullets keep eating away at the wall. I can't keep regenerating this ice as the bullets break it apart. I can't keep feeding this wall and ending up dehydrated. I can't leave my body, I'll die. The new ability that keeps me on my feet when I should be exhausted isn't gonna last long enough to get me out of this either.

This could be the last time my eyes are open, or it could even be a way out. I don't know! Panic rises and I squeeze my eyes shut and allow my mind to take me back to the room that would allow me a smile or two. I can almost hear the music in the background but my brain pulses and when I open my eyes, I see... *the music room?* The music stops when I look over at the piano. *Have I officially gone mad?*

I rush out the room to find BT down the hall, so I run into the room to the left of the music room. As I run through the doorway I end up back in the beige hallway of the building in front of the wall of ice. It shattered after I ran away from it and turned down a different hallway. They stopped to look around before continuing after me. I wasn't hallucinating. That was from my mind, and they saw that school hallway too.

"AN ILLUSION!"

As my realization strikes, more people in blue uniforms cut me off but there's more approaching from behind. *They're just standing there though. They stopped running. Why are they—It doesn't matter.* I shake my head and my headache makes itself known, and my muscles ache twice as much as they did before. I can barely catch my breath. My lungs are wrapped in pressure. My head and chest pound as I scan the hall for an exit.

Before anyone makes another move. I'm shoved into complete mayhem.

The ice builds into a blizzard and the room distorts as if it were attempting to morph. My ghost rips in and out of my body knocking me to and fro. And to add to the chaos I see myself falling apart into tiny pieces drifting away. *Am I disappearing?* No. Disintegrating. I'm turning into dust and smoke. Maybe this isn't as great as I thought it was. This is exactly what I was afraid of—its what mom was insinuating. Tears prickle at my eyes hoping this isn't me proving her right.

All I can do is scream and cry 'cause it's too much. It shouldn't be possible to be burdened with this much. Ice rips at the building, my body is fading in and out, and I'm shaking. I can't seem to keep my soul in my body. This is all pure madness. I can't. This is too much. My throat hurts from yelling and there's warm droplets on my cheeks. I'm falling apart as each event ties one to another. Every motion is blurred, and vibrations are being mirrored, by what I don't know—I can barely see past my tears. I need to leave this building at least. The only way out of all this is to get far away from here.

Through all the madness I manage to get control of my arms, flail them around, and surround myself with ice. I can't stop now, they're shooting. I swear a few hit me as I knock into my ice wall but it doesn't deter me from the shock of my hands breaking down into dust. *What is this?* The only sensible thought that crosses my mind is the cabin. So that's where I end up. Somehow, I appeared here. How many abilities is that now, five? Six? I don't know, I can't count right now. There was a pinch of pain before I disappeared, but I did.

After I jumped back to the cabin, the madness ceased. Before I even have the chance to detangle my steps everything falls black as it fades away. I take note of the last words my mom and I exchanged. I need to find her again. Before she finds me.

January 20th, 2096
Past: 8 months ago

When I opened my eyes, the leaves that once covered the forest floor are replaced with white snow. I can't even be shocked right now, I'm still heavy. Rolling over to my back I look at the sky as it does what it normally does—splitting apart to tease at glimpses of the white room.

My mom's words still manage to haunt me despite pretending I knew what I was doing and being ok with it. I didn't expect to jump to the cabin or manifest several neo-human abilities. I still have a headache from the memory of it. I couldn't control it or make sense of it, but that can't be the only thing waiting outside this world for me. These are still my abilities, and I can still do this on my own. I'll end up hurt walking into another problem either way. I can't let her words stop me now when I've come this far. I'mma find out for myself then I'll stay true to what I said.

Maybe, I should go back to the apartment, there could be something I missed while I was there. The headaches and glitches were most erratic when I still lived with her. That'll bring me closer to an answer.

I don't have enough money for another bus ticket, maybe I should leave my body and then go? But what if something happens while I'm out of body? I did just appear here. My hands and arms drag as I move them to hoist myself up to my feet. When I finally roll my back to stand straight, I take a breath to shake off the nerves and burdens. When I appeared here, I was desperate to be somewhere else. Specifically, the cabin. I was thinking about it while I was disappearing. So maybe that's the rule for this one? That I can only appear in places I've been to before? Since I've already been to the apartment before I'm able to visualize it like the cabin. I squeeze my eyes shut and there's a slight burning sensation in my hands. I take a peek and squint enough so I can see them disappearing. It's happening too slow and as it pulls it begins to sear in my skin .

Mentally, I know where the disintegration started but it's not happening quick enough to—*Hush.*

Ok then. I'm in the middle of the living room staring out at the kitchen. It's empty here, so either everyone's sleep or no one's home. That's until one of the kids ran to me from the dark hallway wide eyed—he's hurt. In the corner of the room the light is shining from the lamp. When he steps into the light, I can see a scratch on his face so I take a knee to level with him.

"What happened? Are you ok?" Clearly, he's not and the panic in his eyes make it all the more obvious and familiar. He shakes his head—probably too shaken to speak—and he points to the hallway. A small knife of ice twirls in my hand, I tighten my grip around it and skulk down the hall. I look into the open bedroom door that was once my room expecting to see more children but there was no one there. *I thought she had more kids.*

Continuing to my mom's old room, the lady with the red hair flings the door open and stands in the doorway with a knife in hand. Before she can do anything, I throw my knife at her. It grazes her neck and she lunges at me taking a stab at my shoulder. I grab her wrist, stopping her before she can penetrate the blade. A light huff of laughter leaves my nostrils as she struggles to push, swiftly I swing a new knife into her side and she lets out a yelp. In an instant, what she's wearing goes from average PJs to a BT uniform.

They're literally everywhere. I let her wrist go and she clutches her side. I take a few steps back, shocked yet again by their ability to seemingly come out of thin air. Down the hallway, the wide-eyed kid is laid out in the middle of the floor. I watch as his body fades into a cloud and then into nothing right as the dome flashes into view for a moment.

"What happened to the other ones?" I ask, releasing a shaky breath. The red-haired lady doesn't respond as she leans on the wall gasping for air. I shove my hand on her shoulder forcing her to stand up straight and look at me.

"What happened to your other kids? There were three, one was older than that one," I continue, pointing to the one that disappeared into nothing, "and the other one was—was small. What happened?" I hate crying but tears roll down my face as I get a blank stare in response. They were so young. The oldest couldn't have been older than thirteen.

The ice in my hands doubled over and an icicle surges through the hand I grabbed her shoulder with crackling down to her stomach. The tip of the icicle pierced through her midsection, leaving a splatter of red on my T-shirt. She tries to gasp for air but fails, and I watch her body sit on the mess I made as it hangs lazily on the spike. I stare at her and wipe my face with my clean hand still feeling my stomach turn at the thought of the wide-eyed kid. I don't know exactly what she did, but I saw and knew enough.

This keeps happening. Where the people causing this mess seems to be hiding under BT's name. Is this what they all are? Is this part of whatever game this is? I turn around and see a laptop sitting on the bed. I turn it to face me and red dots appear all over the map on the screen. When I click the one closest to my current location, red-haired lady's face appears. The next dot I click is by Damien's apartment, and his face pops up. I scrunch my nose and shake my head. Memories plague aches in my skull as they're brought up when I see him, I can't deal with it.

Then I click the BT building—where my mom is—and right after I see her the spot disappears. Of course, it does. So, this is a whole thing? This is a regular thing they do to innocent people? Children?

Not too long ago I said to myself, anyone that's willing to do what was done to me does not deserve to live their life when they're stealing another. The only way I got out of Damien's prison was because I killed him. I got away from my mom because for whatever reason she stopped fighting for me to stay. *Anyone willing to cause this pain deserves to die.*

I'm gonna find them and I'm gonna kill 'em, and when I'm done with them I'm gonna get beyond this world and beyond that dome. Then I'll look for my mother. Before she can start looking for me.

February 3rd, 2096
Past: 7 months ago

More time passes by, but it doesn't process like time has moved at all, but what's new? The only thing I have kept track of are the amount of BT creeps I've found and killed. Sixteen to be exact. The cases I've come across make this new hobby of mine quite therapeutic. Nah that's not the right word. It's *deliciously addicting.*

Before I left my mom's old apartment, I wrote out a list of places to go. Though it took me forever, I wrote all the names down in one of the kid's notebooks without letting sleepiness weigh me down. I even made efforts to commit some to memory. However, I'm beginning to notice a pattern. Under these profiles they don't talk about the evil shit they're doing, they talk about different abilities. Mostly ones I have already. The ones labeled cryokinesis are ones where romantic relationships turn into hellscapes.

The ones labeled illusionists are where parents are no longer protectors but the reasons why kids need protecting. The ones labeled astral projection are where privacy and autonomy of bodies are violated. Teleporting are the ones where folks are trapped in various locations. The abilities are specific to the experiences I come across. Maybe that's where mine came from, *but I have so many.* Some of the teleporting cases could also be illusionist cases so how come they're only teleporting? *Why do I have multiple?* Then again, I haven't found any cases tracing back to me so I could be wrong about my theory.

I have been standing by this garage door wearing one of my many black sweatsuit combinations since the sun was in the sky. The house is huge, gorgeous even with all its big windows and large marble steps that lead to elaborate doors with swirls carved in them, but I don't have time to look around, I'm waiting. I like waiting it shows dedication to my craft. He'll come and all I'll have to do is lunge an icicle right through the window, but I need it to be clean, so nothing too big or fancy. Sometimes I'm fancy. It depends on the situation, and I don't know if I'm in the mood for it tonight.

A small silver car is driving down the road, the metallic colors glimmer every time it passes under a streetlamp, and there he is. The headlights shine on my face and I can see him panic, reaching for whatever he's reaching for but it's not like it'll matter. His regular suit combination phases into the BT uniform like it usually does. He knows my face, a lot of them do, but I'm not the one running away anymore. I'm not being hunted.

I am the hunter.

As he searches for the phone, I twirl my still bony fingers and an ice knife forms. When I'm done twirling it in the air—because I am, indeed, a show-off—I flex my fingers forward and it flies right to his chest. The ice stretched into a X across his body, forcing him to sit up. Now they have a new picture to show to their little friends. I take all the money and valuables he has on him, and I ice out the scene leaving no tracks. A familiar song plays from his car, and I hum along with the melody. The streets are empty and the only light that shines is on the monster in the driver's seat. "You, sir, are number seventeen."

***

They call me X now. Just X. I went with it and made it a thing. I like it, it sounds cool and mysterious. Xandria is associated with someone who still had hope in the world, who still trusted people. Xandria was able to love people who didn't love her back. I can't do that. Not anymore. I've seen too much and been through too much. People disguised as regular folk with their own struggles are as nasty as the next person. I'd rather not bother with anyone at all.

Even though I seemed to have figured myself out, I still struggle to sleep some nights. At first, I could barely get out of bed. Now I can't even fall asleep. If it's not nightmares, it's the weight of pain lingering on my body weighing me down. Despite that, I have grown strong and I'm still hanging in there. I should get more supplies but I'd rather sleep, I'm not really hungry as of lately anyway.

Tonight, though, when I'm in the cabin lying in bed something's different. I'm falling apart like the scenery does as it crumbles and glitches over and over again. It has been like this for a while. This place I've been confined to has been making me sick for as long I know, but it was never this bad. I roll over to sit up and haphazardly lean on the edge of my bed. My shoulders feel misaligned, causing me the inability to be comfortable in my natural state. I rock over to stand and drag my feet to the bathroom to wash my face. Before I turn the faucet, I freeze when I see my reflection in the mirror.

I haven't seen myself in so long. I didn't want it to be real, but I am sick. My cheeks are all sunken into my face, my skin looks like it's been washed with green dye, and around my eyes are so dark. I visually look unhealthy. I don't know what's been happening, but it is what it is. Even after all this, I still haven't aged much but now it's hard to tell with this illness taking over.

I don't want to go without taking those BT workers with me but if I do, I do. Whatever this sickness is it's sending aching pains through every muscle in my body, and it weighs a lot more than the rest of my burdens combined. Whatever it is I can't keep up with it anymore. It's draining the life out of me and taking it to a place where I might not find it again. As an illusionist not too often do I create peaceful scenes for my own enjoyment, but now I do as I lay back down on my bed replaying the songs I memorized a long time ago as the images of black notes pass my eyes. Then the flash happens again under my eyelids, but it doesn't return me anywhere familiar this time. A rush of heat runs up my spine and I shiver and sit up in a bed, but not in the cabin. *What is this?*

I'm in a huge white room with hundreds of other people lying in beds. They're all attached to cords, but one bed is empty. *I'm attached to cords. Why am I attached to cords?* There's so many all over me—too many to count. *The dome . . . This is what was behind the glitches and cracks, this is what I've been seeing. The place I couldn't seem to run to. The place BT was hiding.*

But I teleported by accident. It can't be that easy. I snatch the cords off, and my stomach turns as I do so. I just woke up. I don't know how I know. I never fell asleep, *but I just woke up.* I leave the flat mattress bed and all I can think about is launching into a much bigger problem. My locs graze the triceps of my arms and I freeze in place. When did my hair grow so long? I touch the top of my head and my locs are retied. *By who?* I whirl around to scan the room of all the bodies, and everyone's still asleep. *I need to get outta here.* This place is making my nerves act up and my soul is getting restless because of it.

I leave the creepy white room and walk down steel-lined halls hoping to come across some information. I don't know where I am but it's empty—other than the people sleeping in that room.

As I walk, the floor is soft but it's soft cause I'm wearing socks? There's a room made of dusty gray stone with flickering lights and a countless amount of file cabinets. Maybe I can find something of use in there. If I would find anything useful I would find it here. I'm supposed to be looking for something to help me find out why I'm here, but I get distracted when a screen cuts on displaying a man who's face I recognize. It's my dad, Xavier, from the story my mom was telling me.

Whatever was in my hand drops to the floor, and I squint at the blurry video clip. He's in a lab and he's like me. He has the same gifts I have, but he's already learned how to handle them. He talks about finding a way to help people through different types of traumatic events by aiding them in accessing their gifts. So, my theory is right! He continues talking about how one specific person gets one specific ability—he doesn't say anything about having multiple. So why do I? Why does he? I'm not complaining but I'm curious.

Then I see two people and I narrow my eyes to make sure I'm seeing the screen correctly. It has to be me, I'm a little younger than I am now and there's my mom. I'm sleep on a bed—table—whatever. It's like the one I just got off of.
As the video continues, I take in what I see. But—nah, that never happened. I don't remember that. Then again, I don't remember a lot of things, but this is not like that. The air is more potent here and it smells metallic like my mom's room. Even the colors. Everything seems more *tangible*. Even my legs seem to be a little shaky, like I was sitting too long—lying down too long.

Both my parents are arguing back and forth in one clip about something I don't understand when a round of bullets fly through the lab room. The camera falls and all I hear is my dad yelling at my mom to take me and run. My other self is lunged out of the scene by my mom while she darts away carrying my unconscious body. All I can see now is my dad who does his best to protect me and my mom before the screen goes black.

"That can't be it."

I whip around, my locs moving with me—I'm still not used to this new length. I shuffle through tons of drawers for another drive. I pretty much tear the place apart looking for something that may not even be here. I don't want it to end there, but I know it does. I don't know what that was about and all it did was bring me more confusion. I don't remember a lab, then again, I was younger. But if that were the case, how did we end up in an apartment building on the edge of the city? And why was my dad with my mom in the lab? Where did he come from?

After looking through about twenty something drawers, I find a drawer labeled profiles. I pull the latch to open it but it's locked. With all my strength I tear the drawer open. Locked means the good shit is probably in there. As soon as I find my name alarms sound and now I gotta run again. So, I grab the file and run. My heart is beating against my chest as my feet sprint against the tiles. *Does that say exit?* My vision's a little blurry, but I still ram through the doors. The exit takes me to a car lot where I find a van parked by the building. It's a BT van . . . The whole parking lot is BT vans. *I was with BT this whole time? How?*

I teleport into a van and soon realize I don't know how to start it. This one has no wheel and the controls are all different. Does it drive itself? If it does, I don't have time for that. There are too many buttons but I'mma push the green one. Why else would it be green? I push it and the wheel comes out of the metal compartment, but now what? In the distance, I can hear voices approaching so I pick the largest button on the wheel and the car starts, but it's not moving. I think I can drive it. My feet stomp on the floor searching for pedals but there are no pedals. Why are there no pedals dammit? They're getting closer. That was definitely a flashlight that flashed by the window. A message reads on the screen where a radio should be, and it says something about selecting a speed. *Who has time for this?*

I press 100 mph and the hunk of metal starts to grumble. I firmly wrap my hands around the wheel to gain some control. That way I don't fly out of the car on my way out of here.

The car speeds away fast enough for me to get away and I swerve down a road before they have any chance at finding me. That screeching made my ears ring but all that matters is that I get away.

For the first time I catch a glimpse of myself in the mirror and all my thoughts stop. *What happened to the scar on my face? It's gone.* And where did these gray clothes come from? I don't even look sick anymore. The only thing that hasn't changed is I still look the same. I didn't age at all, I look the same as I did when I started high school and when I graduated.

The giant sign above the road says Main City 27 in big white letters against a green sign but I've never seen anything like that before. What's a Main city? And street names. Did the streets back home have names? None of them did, there were no street names. I haven't seen those since . . . *I don't know. I've never seen street names.* What happened to me? What'd they do to me? My hands and arms begin to shake, and I shake my head wishing I didn't know what I know. But now that I know, I need to put this all together.

I remember the things that happened to me before but it's somewhere beyond this realm of consciousness. It happened. But it didn't happen here. In a place that doesn't glitch, in a place that's not missing details in its appearance. The air is filled with detailed smells of smoke and earth as I breathe. Everything is detailed and there's a clock in here with a date. *Shit. February 3rd, 2096.*

When's the last time I saw a date? A time? I know how to read time, but I've never seen it this specific. Marking the actual moment I'm living out? *No, no, no. I can't. Not now.*

I don't have time to figure this out. I need to keep driving before BT gets here. I assume I can press the stop button if I need to stop, but maybe I should slow down a bit first before I crash into something. I press sixty and the car slows down and I sit back unable to drive myself.

This is . . .

I just woke up. I just got here. If I just got here then what am I even driving into right now? If I just woke up . . .
How long did I sleep?
Mom, how much did you fail to tell me?

Chapter 22
X

Present day: September 2nd, 2096
Main city 27

Rest is important but being able to get away from a chaotic scene takes priority over resting. It's late and they're probably sleep, now would be a great time to wake them up and go for a night run. I wasn't gonna fall asleep anyway, might as well get something done. They've been doing better in the last two months but it's not enough. My feet hit the ground as I roll up from the couch. After shaking my arms out, I release my locs from the bun and leave them in a loose ponytail.

I appear in Venus's apartment and realize I need a phone. Teleporting to tell them where we're going isn't ideal. The floors are too creaky so I sit in one of the chairs in the living room and leave body knowing she would see me. To my left is Victoria's room, and though she has explained this room to me before, I've never looked inside. Not that she would know if I did. I hesitate to float through the door. I'll wait until she chooses to invite me into that part of her story. I know Victoria's missing, and I know it still hurts her, but she never speaks about why. It's not important for me to know so it doesn't bother me.

After floating through her door, I wander around her room for something to throw at her to wake her up. There's a spray bottle on her dresser filled with water and oils. I had one like this. What does it smell like? I spray it into the air about seven times, but I don't smell anything. Of course, I can't. I'm out of body, I *can't* smell anything. I'mma just put that down.

"X, what do you want?" Venus asks as she waves a hand in her face, wafting the mist into the air above her. Well, I guess that wasn't completely pointless.

"I'm sneaking you out."

"What? No, its 1:00 a.m. go away."

"Venus, it's important!"

"Not important enough for you to interrupt my sleep. Do you know how hard it is to fall asleep?"

"No, I don't." Yes, I do. Of course, I do, but I'm so used to saying no.

"Ok, forget I said that."

"What do you want?"

"Just come with me but bring your body too, you're gonna need it."

"X, what? Do you know how that sounds?"

That doesn't matter so I don't reply. Instead I open the door and point at the exit. We need to go before her mom wakes up, it's bad enough she calls and texts her on a schedule.

"If I get caught—"

"You won't. I'm a professional. Now hurry up before you *do* get caught."

She gives a reluctant sigh and walks to the dresser rubbing her head snatching her bonnet off to reveal a ponytail of loose curls. Briskly, she throws on a pair of sweats over her shorts. I pick a scarf up from the hook on the door and she thoughtlessly takes it. It's important to keep their faces covered if they can.

Once, I retrieve my body we make our way outside. Since we're walking at night, I keep vigilant for any and everyone. BT is terrible but so are most people. That's how we ended up being able to do what we do in the first place. We go to the hotel, and I was gonna go back for the others but—

"X, why don't I call them. That's better than walking around the streets. "Actually, it is. So I go back to my body and wait for her to call and argue with her friends.

✳✳✳

"You guys look terrible."

It took the others a half hour to get here. They pretty much dragged their feet into the room, rubbing their eyes or in the middle of an obnoxious yawn. Meanwhile a laugh bubbled out of my diaphragm. They look like tired toddlers.

"X. It's one in the morning. Whatever this is, it better be important because no one here is on fire or dying." I hope this works because Isaiah sounds more careless than usual, Aruni looks like she's on another planet with her slow blinks, and Liam walks past me to sit on the couch.

"Oh no, you better get up, Sleepy, we're taking a walk."

"X, you're joking..."

"Nope. I need more supplies and what better time to get some than one o'clock in the morning."

Aruni groans and flops face first onto the other end of the couch. They need to get it together, if they're going to be running with me on this; I don't want to get caught. "Why are we here again?" Venus asks, leaning on the wall staring at the ceiling.

"... Well, I don't know. Would you guys like to get caught when we go to New City, or I'll do you one better, what if you have to outrun BT because they found out about what you can do? You think you can outrun BT?"

Silence falls over the room and it's not just because Aruni and Liam are falling asleep.

"AY! Get up! We need to get moving!" I yell, throwing snow at them both. Aruni runs at me, but I step out the way. She stumbles a bit but finds her balance. Maybe we should postpone this for another week, this isn't gonna work if this is how they're gonna act.

"Really?" Liam asks dusting the snow off his T-shirt.

"Yes, really, the cold wakes you up. Are you woken up?"

"No."

"Too bad, 'cause we're leaving. If you ever need to run for a long period of time you can't afford to be sleepy, so figure it out and let's go. I want food to eat in the morning and I'd like to maintain my hygiene while I'm here." I leave the room and hear shuffling feet and heavy footsteps following me down the stairwell. That's gonna get annoying very soon.

"Ok, so there is a huge supermarket a few blocks straight from here. I'm sure you know what I'm talking about. Now here are the rules. First off, cameras. Don't worry about them because I can shut them off for a bit but it's up to you to pick up your feet and move. So, stop walking like that, y'all are killin' me with the *chhsh chhsh* sounds. Also, did everyone bring something to cover their face in case someone does see you."

"X, yes, what else?" Aruni asks, still leaning on the wall. I really don't have time for her whining about the task at hand. I can deal with them now during daytime practice, but *this* is a different type of dilemma now.

"Just don't get caught. You guys better wake up now, so you don't get caught slugging around the store like drunk idiots. And, Patches, please with the hoodies! How are you gonna see behind that?"

"I can see just fine. It's bright as shit outside."

"AT NIGHT? You know what, I don't care. Let's go, AND PICK UP YOUR FE—"This is gonna be a long night.

After we get there, I tell them each where to go. On our way there, I gave as many pointers as I could to make sure this training is successful. I don't know if they were listening but we're about to find out. The store isn't small but it's big enough. I sit in between the buildings with Venus, and we leave body to meet so I can tell her how I disable the security before I go shopping.

"Ok, V, so here's what I do." I learned how to turn off security and work with other pieces of tech through . . . experience. Well trial and error. Lots of errors. Got lucky those times but my skill doesn't go beyond the simple stuff. But that kid Isaiah might know more about this than I do. I've seen that giant computer he's been fixing, and the books and papers about different technology, it's pretty cool actually. Unfortunately, he hasn't had the opportunity to share it with many people yet. They don't have those kinds of programs out here, but they do in New City, and I'm gonna get them there.

After I'm done shuffling my way through screens I go back to body. Venus does the same, then we meet back with the others to inform them we're good to go.

"So, how are we gonna get in if the front doors don't open?"

"Get creative, Patches, punching your way out of this one would get us caught, so think about it before you do something irrational." He stood in silence, and I wait for him to do exactly what I expect him to do. He thinks he's being smart with me but not this time.

"Ok. Lee, can you— "

"No, Liam isn't teleporting you and I'm not either. Look around and find out."

"Why did you wait to tell me that?"

"Exactly, now we're even. Aruni, can you go with him to make sure he doesn't run into a wall with that *cloak* over his eyes."

"Take that shit off."

Instead of listening to Aruni he throws his head back, keeps the hood over his eyes, and drags his feet around the building. Again, a toddler, but at least I got a good laugh out of it. Earlier today, he threw a giant tree branch at me and then proceeded to say duck after it hit me, so yeah I'mma get my laughs in too. To keep it even, of course.

Venus leaves body again to get whatever she's getting. Meanwhile Isaiah and Aruni are still close enough where I can still hear them bickering about the best way to get inside. I hold out a hand for Liam to copy teleporting. As my hand starts breaking down, he takes a hold of it and disappears into the store before me. I hope he knows what he's doing.

When I get inside, I go to the canned foods and grab what I need. It's dark but the moon and streetlights shine through the windows with enough light that I can see the food names. It is pretty bright, I guess, but nothing would ever convince me to prove Isaiah right after an argument. Then we're not even.

I'll grab a can of beans, corn, and some body wash. *No, not that brand, I hate that brand. Maybe this one—it smells like lavender. OH, shea butter. I'll take that instead.* Of course, we need matching lotion and body mist and—what is that squeaking? I follow the noise to find Venus standing in the aisle with a shopping cart. What is she doing? While I was in the other aisle this girl grabbed a whole ass shopping cart and bags. Maybe I should've left from the start.

"Venus!" That came out as a yell-whisper.

"What, X?" she answers as she floats to the aisle I'm in. "You said we're going shopping so that's what I'm doing. My mom needs a lot of stuff, and my dad needs a new soap dispenser, and also, there's this new line of hair care products that work wonders for my curls! I'm gonna clean out the shelves cause when I tell you this stuff is expensive—"

"Venus!" I hiss.

"You do realize that security has to be back on in two minutes or we're gonna be noticed, right?"

"What? You didn't say that!"

"So, when I was talking for that whole walk"—I shake my head releasing the lecture that's brewing—"Where's Isaiah and Aruni? I haven't seen them yet."

By the time Aruni and Isaiah finally decide on how to get in, it was too late. The worst part is the only reason I know is because of the crash I hear at the back of the store. I run over to see Isaiah struggling his way through a small bathroom window. Half of his upper body is through the window and a rack of toilet tissues is spewed all over the floor. I can't tell if we should do this again for more practice or if I should run away now because of how bad they are at this.

"Isaiah, just stop! We're leaving. We have almost a minute to get out of here." Isaiah falls on the ground outside after pushing himself back out the window. The thud sounds like it hurt. Like that branch he threw at me. I appeared back outside next to Venus, and she actually cleared the shelves! *Ok sure, because that's not obvious at all!*

"Venus, gimmie the damn bags."

Before she can slur out a rebuttal, I snatch them from her and teleport the stuff back into the store. Now where's Liam? Why isn't he outside? What is he doing? I should put this back, but I don't have time to put it back! I have about thirty seconds to find Liam and get out of here before the system turns back on and we're surrounded by BT roaches.

When I finally spot him, he's by the tech station. Why is he all the way by the tech section? That's the last place he should be, that stuff is wired with security tags!

"Lee, we gotta go! And why are you here? This section is laced with security! Whatever you took put it back!" Never thought I would say something like that 'til now.

"Nah, I'm good." And he's gone. So, I disappear to meet them all outside, hoping this isn't the first and last run we do.

"We gotta run."

"Where?" Venus asks me. I look around past the buildings thinking of how to explain what to do. It's easier that they follow rather than attempt to listen to me. I jut my chin forward and start through the darkest parts of the neighborhood and they follow no longer dragging their feet.

Every now and then I look back hoping they're keeping up with me as I make sharp turns past buildings to get back to mine. I creep through an open fence and when I look back again Venus is missing, but not only Venus, everyone. They all stopped by the fence and I watch as Isaiah pulls the fence back further allowing Venus to run through and eventually the rest of them catch up to me.

Then it happens again but this time I run through an old warehouse. I notice headlights but when we push and kick through some of the wood the old framework topples above us, and the group gets separated. I was ahead of them and when I looked back, I saw Venus and Lee on one side of the wood that fell. Aruni's on the other side past the new wall. I was gonna teleport her away from the doorway to get her away from the passing headlights, but they drove right by. Looking in between the pieces of wood, she turned around with blank gray eyes and a thumbs up. By then Isaiah had simply moved the metal sheet the wood fell on rather than tossing the wood everywhere like I once expected him to. I silently nod to myself. *Who knew Patches was actually listening to me?*

Who knew there would be people who operate so cohesively in a crisis? They don't ever leave each other behind but they don't say much when they need help either, they just do it. And I can't be part of it.

***

Before I know it, we are back at 238 and we sit in silence for too long. They're gonna fall asleep starting with this one.

"Alright, Patches, don't get too comfortable. You need to wake up in your house tomorrow not mine."

His eyes are closed as he continues to sink back into the cushion of the couch. While everyone else hoists themselves out their chairs, he lifts up a heavy hand for someone to pull him up, so I take heed to the gesture and do so. He yelled a sarcastic 'Ow' when I pulled him up.

"You're welcome." And I gave a sarcastic reply.

I teleport Isaiah, Aruni, and Venus back home, but I have a question for Liam.

"What did you take? You could've gotten us caught just by being over there."

"Don't worry about it. Can I borrow the poof ability?"

"Don't call it the poof ability, because in that case, no."

"But that's what we do. It's like a poof." He mimics the sound with his hands, and I shake my head not caring enough to hide smiles anymore. My vision is blurry and tired as is the rest of me. I'm sure he is too after that.

"Alright, goodnight, Liam." Then I do in fact poof him back to his house. That better not stick.

Chapter 23
X

We weren't supposed to meet until later today since we did a run last night, but here I am pacing around my room debating if I should meet with them early or not. It's for practice because we're gonna be leaving to New City next week. It's not because I enjoy their company or want to be around them more. That's not what I'm here for. I'm here for business. Maybe I'll go see what they're up to or I'll just see what Liam's up to make sure they're still gonna be here.

I appear in front of his house and there's a button next to the door, but is that too formal? Well, this is Auntie's house so maybe it's good to be formal. But I don't see his friends use it, matter fact, they just come and go. I can't do that though, we're not friends; just casual, temporary work partners. I think I should ring the doorbell. I hear a voice come through the door. "Now who is standing at my"—I jump back when his aunt answers the door before I can ring the bell—"Well, hello, Xandria!". She might have one of those door cameras. "Lee, someone's at the door for you!" How did she know I was here for him? What if I came to speak to Aruni, I am here to speak to Liam but still.

"X? I would ask if you needed to warm up food but—"

"Yeah, that's not why I'm here. I'm here because um . . . I need to show you something. About your abilities."

Let me straighten my back, I'm too relaxed. I was crossing my arms but stopped so I recross them so I don't look awkward. I already look awkward. Why did I come here? He crosses his arms, leans on the doorway, and looks at me knitting his eyebrows together. There's a moment of awkward silence. *Yeah, this is weird.* I place a hand on his shoulder and we disappear to the borders.

"You can't lead with a warning first?" he asks, picking himself up from the floor. I didn't realize he was leaning when we disappeared. My hand flew to my face to stop myself from laughing and apologizing. *We're not friends.* This is work related.

"No, because you need to expect the unexpected when we get out there. You think BT is gonna let you be all lax when they're tryna catch you?" *Good save.*

"Yeah, but I was in my house."

"Good, now you're better prepared to be on guard at all times. Now I wanna show you something with the ice since you're still shit at using it."

"Do I need to learn that though? I'm good on everything else, right?"

"Ok then don't. It's not useful at all to be able to make weapons in your hand at whim, or to freeze someone in place before they get to you, or maybe using the ice to freeze a lock or maybe—"

"Alright, I got it, now what?" I hold out a cold hand which is enough to answer his question. He takes it and I drop my hand away after the icy smoke rises from his hand too.

"So, in a situation where you can't use water from your body to make ice you gotta find it somewhere else. I also think it may be better to start working outside rather than inside."

"How though? There's no water here."

"There's water everywhere. Watch me." There's water in the air and in the trees. I haven't gotten a hold on the air yet, but I've pretty much mastered the plants, underground, and in dirt. I wrap my locs up into a low ponytail at the back of my head before taking a knee in the ground. The dirt is a little more moist from the rain last night which makes it easier to find the water hidden in the dirt. My fingers dig into the ground and the water becomes part of me as it pulls from the ground. It rises into tiny specks of icy particles scattered over the forest ground, but the heat wouldn't allow this to last long. Already the tiny spikes run clear as they rumble through the dirt. I hop up to my feet to meet his gaze. Liam looks around at the tiny icicles glistening from the ground as they melt.

"I know it looks pretty but at some point, you might wanna try it yourself." I don't mind watching him take his time to analyze what I do, it's actually cute but I gotta keep it moving.

That's easy for me to say since there wasn't much standstill happening in my lifetime.

I sweep my hand across the view as the ice breaks down into tiny particles that resembles snow and seeps back into my hand. Right after he sighs and takes a knee as I did. I can already tell he's gonna mess this up, he's given up already.

"I don't feel anything, X."

"Well first of all your hand is barely in the dirt. You have to search for it. Pay attention to the pull of the water in your hand and then the arms." I take a knee next to him and dig my fingertips into the ground. His palm is pressing into the dirt but that's not what I said to do.

"No, Lee." I shake my head watching him overthink rather than just doing it. I slide my other hand a little closer and place it over his. I can't only show him, he has to experience it to understand it. He's not gonna be able to do that if he continues to over analyze everything.

"Close your eyes."

"Why? Please don't freeze my hand to the ground again."

"Tempting but I won't. Follow the water. I'm gonna show you where it is." When he does follow my instruction, The water is pulling at my hand like it did before. Since we're using the abilities at the same time, he should be able to follow the pull of the freeze.

I close my eyes too so I can get a better idea of where he's pulling the water from as it freezes. The ice he's pulling at traces behind mine but it's slow and patchy along the surface.

"Liam."

"Hm?"

"*Relax.* You do half the work, you guide it, it goes and does the rest."

"I am relaxed."

"No, you're not. I can literally feel the tension as the freeze passes, and your hand... You're too tense." I don't know how to help him at this point. I tried everything but he worries too much. I understand though. With that a brilliant idea comes to mind.

"You listen to a lot of music?"

"Yeah, why?"

"Ever heard someone play piano?"

"Barely. I thought they stopped making those." I take the phone from his pocket.

"X, give my phone back," he demands rising.

"Calm down," I say, stopping him, "I'm not gonna steal it." He cuts his eyes at me and in obvious defeat he closes them. Good. I use the search bar and then scroll through all the artists to look for the songs I used to listen to. *I haven't heard this in ages.* After I hit play, I put the phone down between us and refocus on keeping up with the freeze.

"Listen and follow it with the water freezing over." Maybe that'll give him something else to focus on other than whatever is keeping him tense. It helped me focus when I was running even when I didn't have the iPod anymore. It takes about thirty seconds of listening before the patchiness in the freeze meets a point of solidifying. While his freeze crystalizes, it is still slow, but it's moving and it's consistent. A few more seconds pass and the ice stops freezing by my intentions to let him take over but to keep up I didn't move my hand. The ground rumbles a bit and I see small icicles forming. HA! It worked! Who knew?

"You can open your eyes now." When he opens his eyes as they find sparkling ice dripping and melting back into the ground. He didn't say anything but by the way he studied the icicles and feeling his hand loosen was enough for me to share the experience.

"See, you're not half bad when you trust yourself." It takes him looking back at me to notice how close we are. Close enough that all it would take is a lean forward to close that gap between us. I didn't notice at first how good he smells, it's subtle but sweet. My mind starts to wander into senses it shouldn't. His eyes fall to my mouth, for a moment I don't realize my face is heating.. *Yeah, let me get up . . . it's time to get up.* It shouldn't have taken me that long to make that decision, but it did.

After I stood up and dusted my hands off, so did he. More than likely because he had questions.

"But why do you trust me though?"

"What makes you think that I do?" I don't need to keep dusting my hands off but I do. I attempt cleaning my nails though I know it's gonna take more than me picking at my nails to get the dirt out but I do it anyway; so I don't have to look at him. He needs to not look at me like that again, but I'm not gonna tell him that because I don't want to. *But I should want to!* I hate him.

"Well, you could've just given up, but you didn't. You didn't give up before I did."

"That's not trust that's belief. It's different."

"Trust is a form of belief. So?"

"So, I still don't trust you. I trust that I'll kick your ass though." It wasn't supposed to come out as a joke but it did. A smile crept across my face as I looked at him and crossed my arms. To make matters worse he smiles back. I turn around to pointlessly look at the trees to ignore the warmth in my chest. I need to get it together.

"Alright, X, is that your favorite song?"

"What?"

"The song you played."

"Oh, um not quite. It's my favorite instrument though, like guitars and um, the golden ones. Saxophones are what they're called, I think. They're nice but I love piano. I had—Well no. My school had a piano and I used to hide in the piano room and play it when I didn't wanna go home or meet with—Yeah. But it really is a beautiful instrument, you can play all types of stuff on there. I don't think y'all listen to music like this anymore but music genres like Jazz, and R&B, and really ancient stuff like classical, but I love

Jazz piano, but the sax is a close second to—I'm sorry I'm rambling." There I go getting too comfortable. He stood there leaning against one of the trees surrounding the empty space watching me ramble off about silly shit. Shit I haven't talked about in a very long time. I haven't talked about it all actually. Why is he like this? He makes it so damn difficult to hate him like I said I would.

"No, don't be. It's cool. You should show me what you listen to."

"I don't really listen to it anymore, but I don't need to. I memorized it from an old iPod I found. I lost it when Damien . . . never mind." I should go back to the hotel room but instead I sit down against a tree at the mention of him. He took so much from me and for what? I didn't need to have ice and astral projection abilities. I'm glad I have them now but at what cost? Was that all that was for? I have so many, and it wasn't worth it. I would give up all my abilities to undo that whole simulation and live the life of my dreams and have a childhood I could actually recall. What I would give to be a blissfully ignorant kid and part of a family that left me whole instead of broken.

"I don't think they make pianos anymore but when we get to New City, I can almost bet they have one somewhere." Another reason why it's difficult to hate him. I was on the verge of falling apart as hurt rose behind my forbidden tears, but then he sits next to me.

"We're only going so we can get information from the BT worker," I reply, sniffling and wiping my face before tears stream down.

"Yeah, but after that though. We're gonna get information, find your mom, and then we're gonna move to New City. Then maybe you can teach us something aside from how to run away or defend ourselves against people who want to kill us."

"Playing piano?"

"Yeah, why not? You don't think I could learn?"

"Lee, you could barely get a handle on your abilities."

"C'mon, X, what happened to believing in me?"

"I never said that." There goes my smile again, but I forgot to wipe my nose.

"You did but indirectly. But seriously though, after all this we're gonna get the hell up outta Main City. There's a better life out there and all five of us are gonna make it. We're gonna have one of those really nice black cars that hover without the wheels. Isaiah would love that, he loves cars. Also, I heard New City citizens travel all over the country to other New Cities and believe it or not they're so different, X, you gotta see it but not in pictures. I mean we gotta go. We could start at the one close to us. Number 27 and then we could—"

"You keep saying we." I can't stay. I know I can't stay. I don't want to get his hopes up knowing that truth. I have to go after this because I'm always running from someone or something. I can't stay. I can't have a home especially not here, where BT would be led right to them.

"So, you're really just gonna leave after we get into the BT worker's house?"

"Yeah, that was the plan, right? Lee, it's not you at all. I wish—I can't stay. It's not meant for me to stay. You—*none of you* deserve to carry the burdens I carry. Me staying may bring about that result, but it's ok! When we do get into this guy's house, we're gonna see what we can find to get the four of you in. That way I know for sure you'll be safe."

"And what happens to you? X, the door is always open for you to be around. You don't have to fight by yourself."

I hate him so much, at least I want to right now so this wouldn't be so difficult. "I know and thank you but let's go back to the room, I don't want the others to come and wonder where I'm at."

It wasn't supposed to be this difficult to leave. I remade myself to be detached from this and I was. To my surprise they brought something out of me I thought died in that apartment. Creating spaces for me to exist where a smile isn't dangerous, where relaxing isn't a risk, a place where peace is invited, and bonds are catered to like the pink flowers in the window.

I've fought a lot in my life but while this fight brings me pain its different because now the ball is in my hands and I'm supposed to let it go, but I don't know if I can. It wasn't supposed to be this difficult to leave, it's supposed to be easier to be alone. It's part of me to run alone but this warmth is digging up the very thing I thought I would never find. Two kinds are growing, but whatever this is that's closing the gap between me and Lee cannot happen. It's not him, I can't bring myself to do that again after what happened last time. Yet, I still look at him a little too long unsure but entertaining the thought of closing that gap.

Chapter 24

X

Present day: September 8th, 2096
New city 27

The day we were supposed to go to New City I stayed in my room all day making sure I worked out every detail to perfection. I visited that location twice more to make sure I got everything right. I've been counting time with music running in my mind. I hope the time I spent at that BT worker's house while he was away, was worth it. I know what I need to do. I don't need to plan anymore. The only reason why I'm pacing my room and choosing to overlook everything is, so I don't have to be reminded about leaving them when this is over.

After this I run again to find my mom—that's what has to happen. These last several months were a surprise gifted to me and while I'm grateful it is not mine to keep.

Venus got to 238 early because I made the mistake of telling her when I wash my hair and now here she is two hours before we're supposed to meet. I washed it this morning and then realized I should've took her advice about snatching up that product on the last few runs we did this week. Matter fact, did Aruni walk in too? "It's retie day! Ok, go sit!" Venus shoos me away and I sit down in the folding chair because talking her out of this is pointless.

"Hey, X, we're both gonna work on your head because I'mma put some um . . . box braids on Venus when she's done." I would argue but I can't. Instead, I'm too busy fighting back tears at this being a last time thing for us. They're having conversation and while they do ask me questions, it's hard to be in it right now so I remain quiet. *It shouldn't be this difficult.*

"X, you ok? You're more quiet than usual and you haven't cussed us out once."

"Yeah, I'm just thinking about tonight." Unfortunately, that was enough to stop the conversation all together. I don't mean to make them uneasy but that is the appropriate reaction to the shit we're about to pull. Isaiah and Liam arrive right as Aruni is completing Venus's last braid. They continue their chat and I sit; thinking while small conversations and hushed laughs crept in and out of my mind. They're so uneasy. They're not acting like themselves after I mentioned tonight. *What if they mess up?* In haste, I quiet that thought. They'll be ok, I'm gonna make sure they're ok.

The silence stiffens as the moonlight shines through my window. Let me drink a bottle of water before I go out there. I'm gonna need ice and a lot of it. I can't stand this type of silence. Silence with them is ok but not this kind. I keep watching Aruni smooth her puff one-too-many many times. Venus has been staring at her phone since she sat down to get her hair braided. Isaiah's pulling at the strings on his hoodie and it's eerie that we haven't had a single pointless argument since he got here. Liam's always overthinking but still, they moderate that but now it's—

"Are you guys ready to go?"

"I am. I don't know about the rest of them." Isaiah waves at the rest of the room from the old rocking chair Liam insisted on bringing back here. I told him it was too bulky but it's honestly a nice chair. I've sat in it a few times.

"Ok . . . I know I asked a lot of you all, and if you want to leave now you can. I don't want to put you out there if you're unfocused."

"X. We'll be fine. I think its best if we hop right into it rather than talk about it right now." At that I nod my head, I'mma take Venus's advice. The group follows me to that car I stole, hidden in the back of an old garage of an abandoned house. No longer shuffling their feet but keeping up with mute steps not too far behind.

Teleporting there would take too much out of me before we even get in. The man I'm after lives in a two-story mansion with a good amount of people guarding it which is why I needed them. I need someone to keep them busy while I get the information.

The entire ride is how it was at the room. Pure silence. Aruni is unusually quiet. On a normal day she'll have something encouraging to say but not right now. Now she looks out the window taking deep breaths and twiddling her thumbs. They could've left weeks ago when I told them where I came from yet here they are sharing a burden meant for me with me.

Then again, they're getting something out of it too. I wanna find them a way into New City. They didn't have to ask me. Even if Isaiah hadn't brought it up, I would've looked because they agreed to be here before I offered them anything from this mission. It revealed their intentions and proved that, maybe, they're not so bad after all. We cross the borders and I can see the moment we enter into New City.

It's easy to get distracted here. Everything they don't have in Main City they have out here. They have the fancier cars with less buttons inside, their roads are built to stop traffic so sometimes they wind upward into higher levels. They have self-driving buses that actually work, but not only do they work I have heard rumors about them having dining cars side. The buildings are all lit up with all kinds of technology I haven't even seen prior to coming here. To a large extent, everything here is built better. It's optimized to move people forward and it caters to neo-humans. *What could life be like out here?* Maybe they'll know after tonight.

The part of New City we went to is darker and hidden on a road shadowed by round 'too-perfect trees' which makes it difficult for us to be noticed. We're leaving the car far enough down the road so no one can see where it's at. We don't leave until I finish re-explaining exactly where to go and what to do. When I get what we need I'll know where they are, and I'll be able to bring them back before things escalate too far.

Venus, Isaiah, and Aruni leave first, but before Liam leaves I hold out a hand to let him copy the ice and teleporting ability. I told him mimicking everything would be convenient, but we ended up agreeing on two because of what happened the first time he copied my abilities.

"Lee, if I'm not back—"

"You'll be back. We all will." Yeah, but I may not be if I choose to look after them first. I'm not gonna tell him that because I already know what he's gonna say. We both leave the car in a puff of smoke, and when I reappear, I breathe out all my emotions.

I'm inside, and I can already hear the commotion outside. Past all the golden statues of people I don't know and the luxurious furniture, the BT worker I'm looking for is being led away to steps that go down both ends of the dome shaped room. I should've teleported but I need to save energy for when we're leaving.

I run up the steps and the ice shields me from whatever they're shooting at me. I'm close enough to reach for him from behind the wall of ice to get answers about the cube but I get hit into the wall by the masked people in blue uniforms. The ice broke from my hand and slid down the steps. Before either of them can stab me with the needle they're holding, my eyes go gray and I disappear. He's down the steps so I appear in front of him at the doorway on the other side. Whoever was next to me shot me with something that sent burning electric shocks through my neck. Leaning into the wall I refuse to react to the pain. I grit my teeth and yank out the metal. He sprints down the long marble hallway and I watch him do his best to get away. Before they shoot again, I throw two ice knives. The knives pierce two BT workers in their stomachs and I take off.

The other one's footsteps echo down the hallway. Thrusting my hand towards the ground, I freeze the floor and watch her fall on her ass as the ice spreads under her feet. Got you this time. The first time I tried that it didn't go well.

I skid into the hallway the blue suit ran into but there's a metal door closing. *This little shit. Is that screaming?* I run to the window closest to me hoping no one I know got hurt. It's Aruni but she's not the one screaming, it's the BT workers and they're terrified by what Aruni is projecting. I've met a few illusionists, but I've never seen one stand so still in the middle of chaos. She's off to the side watching them panic. One is scratching their face so much they're leaving skin raw and another worker runs into a wall. Note to self, don't ever piss Aruni off. I don't wanna know what would drive someone to ram themselves into stone walls like that.

Shaking off the sight, I rush back to pull the door down. With all the strength I have I bend the metal, gritting my teeth in the process. Damn this is heavy! I hear more footsteps. It's almost open, I can hear it creaking; I'm good. "HA!" Alright! I keep getting better and better. And I just saw a flashlight. I run down the steps, and I'm faced with a bunker made of steel—hard cold steel—that's thicker than the door. The door was difficult but this? I can't open this. Maybe I could ghost but then how would I use illusions too? This is taking too long and one of them could be hurt and I wouldn't even know. *I promised.* I promised, I wouldn't let that happen. I gotta check on them then I'll figure this out.

    I appear by Venus first and hide behind the green hedges but it's quiet. The guards are standing around. So, what happened to Venus? Is she ok? Did they take her? No, they didn't ,they couldn't have. I gotta find her, she has to be here somewhere. I hear a gun blast from the right of the green field. I leave the top part of my body to look around. I see her face, she's focused and she doesn't see me. She hesitates while she shoots and doesn't intentionally hit anyone. I would joke with them about not being capable of such things, but now I need them to be but they're not like me. With those thoughts heat rushes my head and chest.

    I need to hurry up. I swish back into my body and my back knocks against the wall and snaps forward again. After I catch myself, I teleport again to finish checking on everyone.

    Now where's Isaiah! Why can't I see any of them? As I ask that question, I look over at the three guards walking by and one of the pillars shake. I'm behind hedges but if that thing falls it's not just gonna hit them. As the pillar crumbles, one tries to warn the others but they're too late as the pillar crashes on top of them. I poof out the way and end up next to it. That was so loud, I know people can hear that! Before I can call Isaiah, he runs off, but it's a weighted jog rather than a run. I didn't think it would get this bad this quick. Why are they slowing down so soon?

We need to go, I miscalculated something. I scan the area for something, a device, a liquid, whatever it could be is in the walls. It's putting pressure in my head and fatiguing my body. It kinda reminds me of BT, but they're not supposed to have this stuff out here. I'm going to find Liam and take them back. I'm not risking it. Maybe I'll find another way.

When I get to Liam he almost throws a knife of ice my way but he just misses and curses under his breath. He whirls around and continues to keep a look out for danger.

"Liam, we need to get out of here. I'm gonna get Venus and Isaiah, you can bring your sister back."

"Did you get what you needed?" he questions as he throws ice past me hitting one of the guards. He doesn't dwell on it too long and neither do I after I fling a knife past him to hit someone else. Too many are showing up, there's more here than there's supposed to be, and I don't like how lightheaded I am.

"Don't worry about that go get your sister!"

He listens and disappears and so do I. After I appeared by Venus and then by Isaiah I reached for their arm or shoulder before they could see me. Neither of them got a chance to question me before they were back in the car. Wait, Aruni is here, but Liam is missing, and Aruni snaps her worried stare to me.

"He went back, X. He's probably looking for you."

"Idiot! Stay put you hear me? I'll be right back!" He knew that if I wasn't back all he had to do was get them out of here. I could get away on my own. Somehow. I look in the front yard and he isn't there, not in the back, or the sides, so he's inside. Why would he go inside?

What is he doing? I ran into the hallway I was in before and a crunch echoes down the hall to my right. When I run down the hall, I find a BT worker in blue shivering, but he's not wrapped in ice. Taking a knee, I put a hand on his arm and he's freezing cold. I tighten my grip on the arm and it *crunches*. Is that ice inside his body? How come I didn't think of that before, did Lee do this?

Footsteps huddle by the staircase and I see him run down the steps and I fall in line behind him right before he freezes it back closed.

"What are you doing? I said to go back! That's it!"

"I didn't see you in the car so I thought you were still here." I don't have time to argue so I continue down the rest of the steps and we're met with the steel door.

"You need to open this?"

"Yes, but by the time we do that we're gonna be dead thanks to your spontaneity."

"It'll be fine, X, if you let me help you."

"Whatever then." He must've been with Isaiah earlier because he didn't stop to copy the ability he needs to help me open this door.

He pulls at one side while I pull at the other and the door creaks like the other one did. My joints and muscles stretch to their limits as heat and aches rush up my arms.

When we finally get the door off its hinges I ignore the burning sensation. Instead, we wait 'til they were done shooting. When it stops, my arms drop with the door before I poof in front of the man in the suit. I should've checked for the other BT workers but the four that were here are silent as I turn to the sound of that same crunching. When did he teach himself that? I didn't teach him that. I look down at the shivering bodies and he's already back up the steps holding the ice door. *Focus.*

I don't bother to ask for anything concerning the cube because he's not gonna tell me. An illusion of siren screams echo throughout room. I hear it in thought, but he flinches to cover his ears.

"The computer cube on the table next to us, open it." He doesn't respond and he'll regret it in a minute as my arms grow cold. I don't have time for this and he doesn't deserve to eat up my time. I look up the steps at Lee, wondering how he did what he did. *"There's water everywhere."* I told him that but little did I know that lesson would make a full circle back to me.

"Have you ever gotten brain freeze?" My hand grips the top of the BT worker's head. He kneels over in agony. Using three abilities at once *could* be straining, but it's never too staining when BT is involved.

"There's no password I could give you."

"Why?" I tilt my head as my face drops cold. I have no heart for them. They aren't people to me, I wasn't a person to them. I study the blue lines of the cube long enough to notice the slight dent for a hand to sit in. He doesn't have to answer.

" So when you hold it, it opens, correct?" The ice crackled past his skull and he's shivering too much to give me a coherent answer.

"How is it that BT workers can't handle what they deal? No worries, I answered my own question. Now raise your right or left hand so I know which one to take or I'll take both." I shrug and let go of his head. The illusion falls away and he crumples to the ground falling on his back. Long knives of ice crackle over my hands before I swing them and chop both hands right off in a clean sweep. Not too clean though. After ignoring the screaming I pick up both hands—now pale, purple, and blue—and walk away from the blood so it doesn't get all over my sneakers.

"What a mess. Thank you for lending me a hand though. Get it? Because I have your hands? "I turn and laugh at my silly joke. I went to open the cube with one hand but that doesn't work so I toss it back to him.

"My bad, hold that real quick." But this one did work and already I'm seeing the information I need. Just in time too because Liam is struggling to keep the door open as he shifts from holding the door with his back and turning around to push it back closed. I search for my mom's name on the computer with the little keyboard that reflects on the table. I need to find this now. I should've found it already. All these cities are so far away but if she's looking for me why is she bouncing around the map like that? Shouldn't she be closer? There is one place in Main City 27 that she may be in at some point, but I don't know when or if she's even going to be there. It's a randomized list of flashing locations on a map of the land. What is she playing this time?

I leave that folder, disappointed, and there's another folder titled NCD? "New City Defenses?" That's how they'll get in! They can apply there! But how and when? I read as I scroll through the information. The amount of time it takes to process the applications, the amount of rejected applications— it's going to be too difficult to get through. *Damn.* All four of them barely have a chance if they're gonna do this, they need to at least have a place to stay while this is getting processed and are they really ready to make it there?

"X! Did you get it?" I look behind me to see Liam looking between me and the steps, by that look alone I knew to teleport him back to the car. We poof and dart for the car. He gets in the back and I get in the driver's seat and skid off the road. I need to breathe so I snatch the scarf off my face.

"So, was this whole thing worth it or what, X?" Isaiah asks. I don't know how to answer that. I mean—I got something but it's not enough and they could've gotten hurt for it. I'm never going to do something like that again; it's bad enough that we almost got caught. BT is gonna increase their numbers in their adjacent Main City because of this. People are gonna talk. I didn't think this through well enough. I did but at the time I didn't care about them how I do now.

I didn't care if BT increased their numbers in their city or not but after this, maybe, I should stay? They'll be ok, right? I need to stay because they could use my help and they need to be ready for NCD applications if they do want to make it out here. Yeah, that makes sense. They haven't found me in months and they won't find me now. I can stay to make sure they're ok.

"I got enough. Don't worry too much about it, I'll explain more later. Thank you, truly. You gave them a good fight."

"Of course, we did. BT is gonna have a problem on their hands."

I look in the mirror to spare Aruni a smile for her sentiment but behind that is the reality that they do have a problem on their hands. *They are the problem. I looped them into my burden and didn't consider its aftermath. BT will be looking not only for me anymore but them too.*

I wasn't supposed to care this much. It wasn't supposed to be this difficult to leave. I wasn't supposed to share my burdens, my life, or myself. This is why. Now I've dragged them into my pit, and I can't let it consume them too. I have been a killer for a long time and a lot of people have died due to my proximity to them, but I should've known that this virus would spread to them. To people I would never wish this virus on.

Present day: October 10th, 2096
Main city 27

"Venus, you can't leave body all out in the open like that. What if someone finds you before you can get back?"

"Clearly, I know that, but do you see where we are? Of course, you'll see it out here!" Venus contests, stepping out of the bushes. We've been at this since morning and they've been asking me to take them back, but not yet. I've seen the BT trucks and vans increase in numbers here. They need to be ready, no mistakes. Mistakes are too costly.

"Well, I need to not see it because that's not safe. You need to be more discreet; people can see the objects you're carrying floating in the air."

"Whatever, X."

"NO! Not whatever!" They have no clue what they're being threatened by. There's so much more to BT than the back of that van or truck. They don't deserve that. I can't know what they're facing and watch them make mistakes that could kill them or worse. They end up stuck with them. People die slow in BT. I can't let that happen.

I shake my head and look at Isaiah, he's on his phone leaning on a sphere of ice I left him with. That pissed me off which spilled over into icicles being thrown in his direction. He ducks out the way once and swishes to the side to dodge the next one and snatches the last one out the air. He could've done that with the other two had he been paying attention! Which he isn't! Which is how they can get hurt or taken! I can't.

"What is your issue lately? Can you relax?" he argues, tossing the icicle to the side. For one extra month I stayed here, and I've been arguing with them more and more every day. It's not even them that's causing me to react the way I do it's the nerves. I keep seeing more of BT here and memories of my time with BT keep creeping up on me. It's unsettling while I'm here—while I'm here with them. The warmth that wraps around me when we're here is the reason why all these hostile emotions are seeping through what once seemed to be a safe place for me. This is why I'm not meant to have a safe place look what follows me when I find one.

"No, I cannot relax! You've seen those vans out there! They're after people like you. You think they're gonna give you a minute to catch your breath?"

"X . . . Maybe let's take a break . . ."

"We don't have time for a break, Aruni!" I say, barely turning away from Isaiah.

"Yeah, well I do, so you can either take me back or I'll walk myself." Venus disperses from the bushes and they all lean up against the trees to catch their breath. I get why they would be frustrated and tired, but they don't know what it's like to be stuck with BT. If they get to them and put them under the simulation the way they did me it could tear them apart, and they may not survive.

What if they don't have space and they're stuck in one of those cells I saw? I don't have much else to give them, maybe that's why I'm pushing them so much.

Am I being selfish by staying? Am I staying for their own good or mine? Maybe if I get BT to follow me out of here they might loosen up and leave them alone. I'm going to get their attention—I have to—even if that means losing people I care about, again. At least this time it's for a good reason.

"Ok, fine." I take Venus back to 238 first and then Liam follows behind with Aruni and Isaiah. Before the door can close Liam stops it and tells the others to give him a minute.

He knows.

"So, you're leaving?" he asks, closing the door behind him.

"Lee, it's nothing against any of you. I don't have anything else to teach you. This is the last thing that I can do for you at this point. If I leave, BT will leave and that'll make things safer for you guys and any other neo-humans that may be out here."

"Ok, but what does that mean for you? What if it could get better?"

"Right, but it's not getting any better, it's getting worse and you guys could get hurt. I don't know what I would do with myself knowing that I was responsible for that. I made enough mistakes already and I've lost enough people already. I'm not risking any of you. I can't."

"But what about you?" I don't know about me, but I know enough to know I can be responsible for myself. That's what it is and what it has to be—chaos follows me wherever I go. I knew that and still got closer than I should to people I was supposed to use and leave. This was a place that was supposed to be another detour in my journey. For the first time, a detour in my path consumed me in a way where I get to choose to leave or stay. I can't bring myself to entertain what I really want to do because my past informs me otherwise. That never works out for me. That's how it ought to be.

"I'm not telling you that you have to stay. You don't have to do anything. It's just that, you keep saying you have to leave, but do you really? You can leave if you want but that's not the only option. We can figure this out."

"We can figure this out and then what? Go to New City? Lee, even if we were to make it into the NCD when they find out about all the people I killed what are you gonna tell them? Hm? When they find out I've been rummaging through BT personnel and breaking people out, what are you gonna tell them?"

"I didn't think that far ahead yet, but how do we think ahead if we can't even get past this. X, you told me you didn't wanna go back. You said you couldn't. So, don't. We're right here. *I'm* right here. We're not going anywhere. We said that already."

"It's not that simple."

"How? How is it not simple to look at what you have and fight for it?"

"I don't have anything! Liam, I have *me*! That's what I have! You—you have them, you have each other. I have myself! I watch my own back, I don't need anyone to do that for me! I'm good! Alright?"

"No, you're not good. If you have your own back, why'd you need our help to get into that house then?

"See, this is why I don't ask for shit. *What do you want?* You expect me to stay because that's what you want?"

"I don't expect you to do anything. Do you know what it's like to watch that on the other side? Being told to run and looking back to see those people gone? You said you can't go back. You said you can't lose us, but you're quite literally doing that to yourself and you thought I was gonna watch that? *Again?*" I wish I could say something but knowing what I know about the day he left home and losing everyone but his sister to BT in a day, what am I supposed to say? *It wasn't supposed to be this difficult to leave . . .*

"I'm not telling you what to do, I'm telling you exactly what you told me, and I'm watching you refuse to give yourself the grace you give to everybody else. I'm not running this time, X. I'm right here because I can be, but you won't let me be."

It's silent again and I part my lips, but no words form. No one was ever there. I was always there and now we're here and I can't even receive it because I never got it. What a twisted mind game to play on someone.

"Just think about it, alright? It's up to you, but I want you to know that I'm here if you need me this time." The door closes behind him and I sit on the couch burying my face in my hands. I know they're there. They've proven that over and over again and it's been months. I kept pretending that we weren't friends. Pretend that I didn't care but I do. It's more than caring. That's why I stayed longer than I should.

This is home.

I haven't called a place or people, home in a long time. With that understanding, tears push past my eyes.

Why am I crying right now? I knew this would happen. It wasn't supposed to, and I let it happen anyway, but they make it so difficult.

How do I walk away from this now? Most of my memories were jaded by the broken ones but I've collected so many yellows. I've smiled so many times and laughed even more. Even now as I pull my locs away from my face more tears squeeze through my eyes at the thought of the memories I've created with Aruni and Venus. My hair has grown so much since they've been retying my locs for me. Their care for me permanently etched into my scalp. Those memories in the segments of my locs and now I have to leave.

Dragging my hands across my hair memories dance across my mind of Venus's cosmetic advice and Aruni's stories. The ones she would make illusions of as they fazed by in my line of view. Where's that book she gave me? I get up and reach into a drawer for the book. It's banded together with rings instead of glue which is odd. *Wait. . .*

Is that her name on the cover? *She wrote this and I didn't read it?* She didn't tell me. I wouldn't even know because she acted like everything was cool when she came over to help me out.

I'm a terrible friend I swear. I lean on the counter and begin to read what's on the first few pages and my tears stain one or two of them. I should've read it while I was still here. I'll take it with me that way if I see them again I can tell her I read it. After closing the book, I stuff it into my backpack. I sit on the couch and look around at the chairs and more phantom memories pass by as I remember the laughs, jokes, and petty arguments we had here.

I swing the bag on my back and poof to the edge of the roof to watch the sunset. I look next to me remembering Lee's feet swinging over the ledge.

"When we get out of here, we're gonna go to New City and make a better life out there." He's said that to his old friends, he said it to his new ones, and he said it to me.

But I have to leave. There wasn't supposed to be a "we," it wasn't meant to be. I went back to the room and used a piece of cardboard to leave them a note for when they come here to meet me tomorrow. *Try* to meet me here tomorrow. I'll see them again one day. Hopefully, the next time I see them it's in New City and we'll be there together and we're gonna see everything like Lee said we would.

Then, in a puff... *poof* of smoke I leave my last chance at a new life behind, and I appear right in front of a BT van.

I was made to fight, and I was made to run, and it's time to do that again.

Chapter 25
Liam

I can't keep watching BT close in on all of you. I've seen a side of it that most people shouldn't see. I have nothing left to teach you and I, in fact, learned just as much from all of you and I will never forget it and I'll carry that memory with me.

Venus, I still have your hair grease and I took it with me. I'm sure you don't mind though, you know I have sticky fingers. Patches, if you got that damn hoodie over your eyes take that shit off before you run into a BT van.

I took your book with me, Aruni, sorry I didn't read it yet but I'll read it while I'm gone then I'll have a story to tell you if we meet again. Also, I understand the mythological creatures thing now, thanks for the guide behind the cover.

Lee, do not go looking for me, you're not gonna find me, you said to look at what I have and I did, and I appreciate every second of it. But you need to look around too, they're gonna need you to get to New City and live in one of those fancy houses you were talking about.

I ran and lead a few BT vans away as they chased me so it should be a little clearer down there but I'm sure you'll give them a run for their money. This was one of the greatest years I've had

in my life, so take this as a thank you for everything. One day I'm gonna cross the border with y'all and you can show me the wonderful lives you built.
- X

We stood over the box reading the goodbye letter X left and out of all that the only thing running through my mind was BT being led away by X. If that's the case, did they catch up? When did she leave? She said not to look but why wouldn't I? How am I not supposed to look knowing what I know?

"What does she mean by leading BT away? She ran right into them?" Isaiah asks behind me.

"That's what it says, right? . . . Lee, you ok?" Aruni asks resting a hand on my shoulder. X looked me in my eye holding back tears, saying she couldn't go back and then leaves this? She could've stayed. I told her she could stay. She couldn't have gone far; BT couldn't have caught up that quick. She doesn't even have to stay here but I know she can't go back to BT. I can't watch someone else get taken by BT when I know I can do something about it now.

" Isaiah . . ." He walks up next to me as I continue to read the letter over and over again.

"I need to borrow your abilities."

"Not 'til you tell me why you need them."

"You know why."

"Liam, you can't fight BT. We can't fight BT. Especially when it's been hours since she's left. We don't even know where to start."

"Then let's find out. We did it at the house we can do it now."

"I don't think we should. Guys we barely made it away from there. I know you felt your abilities fading too." Next to me, Aruni shakes her head and Venus stands up out of the chair. If they aren't gonna go I'mma go. She has to be somewhere and standing here isn't helping anything.

"I'll go with you, but I have a feeling we aren't gonna find much." Isaiah leaves and I waste not another second to follow him. I hear Venus and Aruni follow us afterward. We need to do something better than running. It has to be better than running.

Chapter 26

X

I don't know how long I've been walking past these trees. The rain soaking my clothes makes me heavier and the breeze passing by sends shivers through my body. I have no idea where I'm going or how much time has passed, but I need to find a place to stay. Where am I? I'm in the middle of nowhere and all I see is green and brown. I can't make anything out through my blurry vision. I need to sit down. I hope I gained enough distance from the BT vans I led out of Main City.

I hope Liam, Aruni, Isaiah, and Venus are okay. They have to be ok; I didn't leave without reason. My hearing is buzzing as shapes turn into fuzzy clouds. My eye lids are heavy from my run, my vision now narrowing into darkness, and I think I see someone in front of me. I hope it isn't BT. My feet scrape across the dirt and my arms prickle as if white noise is running through them. still, I attempt to push myself up but fail inevitably. Then I see nothing.

***

Where am I? When I sit up against a wall I notice I'm surrounded by stone. This is a cave. My arms push me up leaning more than usual on the wall for support. When I get to my feet they drag across the rocks drawn to the view of the Luminescent moon. How did I get to a cave? Crumbling pebbles are to my right, and when I look I still see them moving. Something—someone is out of body, but my abilities are not functioning as they should.

There's a weight in my chest where heat is usually drawn to when I'm doing anything that requires an out of body experience. Let me sit first.

My head leans back and a song leaves my lips as I coax my soul back out of my body. It pulls me forward a bit but not enough to hurt me. *What just touched my hand? Held it in fact.*

"Xandria," a voice says gently.

"You're not real so let me go!" I know this face. He's not supposed to be here, and he called me by the name I don't use.

"Don't call me that." I replied snatching my hand away.

"Don't call you by the name I gave you?"

"I don't go by that anymore."

"Ok Xandria." The look in his face as he shook his head at me reminded me of the nickname I gave Isaiah; Patches. He got over that though. My own stubbornness isn't gonna work that easily on me. I turned away to leave after seeing the dead man I saw when I woke up in a lab. But I stop in my tracks when he speaks to me again.

"Ok, fine, but I need you to listen to me."

"No, I'm not falling for anything like that ever again. You died I saw you die!"

"X, it's not a simulation. Do you see a glitch anywhere?" I don't actually, but I would have to go back to my body to make sure. I need the air to hit my face to show me I'm alive. When I get back I keep an eye on the ghost in front of me so it doesn't fade from my purple-tinted vision.

"I need to show you something." I could run again but what if he's like my mom and knows something about why she acted strange or why I was in the simulation. What if he's actually able to tell me? As we walk, there's a well-lit campfire we stop by and a body. It's his body lying next to this fire. Scarred from the fires that happened in the video where he died. He was supposed to be dead after something like that, but I guess if he's like me . . .

"Why are you showing me this? How are you alive right now?"

"You still don't believe me." Why would I? All the events that happened in my past keep crossing my path. Every time I go about my business and run away from another problem or into another one something else comes up. I can't keep detouring like this but I had to let this one stop me. I thought my mom was the only family I had left.

"If you're my dad then what happened? Why are you out here in the middle of nowhere? Or better yet why'd you let them do this to me?" I squint at the lights around me as they flicker in my view. Turquoise, guilt.

"Xandria, it was never my intention for it to go this far. I was going to talk her out of it, but she wasn't listening."

"What do you mean? Like she would flip flop personalities, right? Do you know why?"

"No, I know that the simulation became more of her idea than both of ours."

"How so?"

"You might wanna sit."

I don't actually, but I'm gonna be here for a while so I might as well.

When I was born, I was very sick. At the time, my father was working on the simulator to keep me alive. Eventually they put me in it, and it bought me more time.

Apparently, the original purpose of the simulator was to help people process their trauma to help them learn about their abilities. Now it creates their trauma so they can have them. The system glitched and went bad and he doesn't know how, but it did and when it did, I was in it. That's when my nightmare began. From that point on the episodes of trauma only intensified over time and did so in haste.

My dad explained that this was meant to make a rageful machine. That's what growing up in a loveless world would do to someone. That's not all I am. It can't be after all that happened back home in Main City 27. The four of them proved to me that I wasn't. They proved to me that I was worth more than the colors of the parallel.

When I was twelve the lab was attacked, and he doesn't know who was responsible for that either, but he does know that BT had something to do with it. That was the video I saw of my mom and I running away while he stayed behind to make sure we made it out ok. When I left, he didn't know what abilities I was manifesting or if I had any at all. He didn't know until he caught me snooping around the night I woke up in the lab. He was the one that turned on the TV and showed me the video, he wanted to know if it was really me.

My father revealed that when the attack happened, he barely made it out alive. He presumed his survival rate was low so ever since then he has been hiding out in the cave doctoring himself while he's out of body. He tries not to stay out of body too long, because of its condition he could die. So, he stays long enough to make sure he doesn't completely disconnect.

I didn't find my mom but *I found my dad.*

Since I'm with him maybe this time BT won't be able to take me—that's if they catch up. I know he's still healing but imagine two neo-humans with multiple abilities together. I can hide here without worrying about the consequences of my mom finding me.

6 months later
April 27th, 2097
Main city and New city 27 Borders

Out of all the things I have learned from my dad this is the one thing I can't seem to get right. When we leave our bodies, the place we end up in is The Parallel. I didn't know I could take my whole body into The Parallel with me. Which explains the reason we can't see orbs without these abilities. It's on a whole different plane of existence. The first time I tried to take my body to The Parallel I realized that The Parallel's energy just doesn't agree with me.

    I close my eyes and hold my arms out to reach for the violet lights of energy that now tint the walls of The Parallel as it takes shape of the cave. Orbs of all colors lit the space here, but that's not my focus right now, which is why I closed my eyes. Violet wires of light wrap around my arms and it's warm against my skin. When I open my eyes to peak at it, the clamor of multicolored orbs swarm my arms. I squint at the bright multitude of lights and shake my arms out as the orbs spring from my arms and the purple wires vanish.

    "X, you need to focus."
    "I am focused, The Parallel is . . . temperamental."
    "Probably because you're temperamental."
    "I'm not temperamental!"
    "Really?"

Ok, maybe I proved his point but I'm temperamental because of The Parallel. All the spherical colors that spot the area are the result of emotions I don't always sit in. It's too open and vulnerable.

The red lights pulse nearby, and I swat a hand through it. This is exactly what I'm talking about. I know I'm frustrated I don't need the lights to give that away.

"Can we do something else?" I ask after kicking at another red light bobbing near my foot.

"Sure, right after I get back."

"You need more supplies already? I thought we were good. You brought stuff back yesterday. We still have some food left over too." I insist as I watch him finish packing a backpack. Where is he off to in such a rush every day?

"I'll be back later tonight—I can't be away for that long anyway. I gotta go back to body. Just keep practicing."

"But where are you going?"

"Main City 27."

"Right but New City 27 is closer, and you could probably find better supplies there. It's a little more difficult to steal stuff but for medical supplies—"

"Main City is good enough. I'll see you later." He rubs the side of my shoulder, and his ghost leaves the cave and into the trees.

I don't get it, it makes more sense to go to New City for what he needs. Why go to the Main City this often for supplies that aren't even up to par on quality? It works but New

City is closer, and they have better supplies. Then he gets here and barely brings back anything. Sometimes nothing at all.

Maybe he couldn't find what he needs? But then. . .I'll leave it alone. Clearly, he's doing fine.

Chapter 27

X

6 months later
October 10th, 2097
Main city and New city 27 Borders

My dad doesn't flip like my mom does. He answers most of my questions about my abilities. I've shown him what I've learned on my own, and watching his impressed nod drew a smile from my face. I've learned a lot from him too. Now I can teleport objects to my hand now. He's also shown me how to freeze the water in the air—particularly when there's a heavy fog. Which is what I was doing when tiny spheres materialized in the air. I hear my dad woosh past me. For someone who's been hiding in a cave, he moves with a lot of urgency all the time. I stopped asking why because that's one of the few questions he doesn't answer.

"What's wrong?" I ask him as the spheres of ice crumble into snow and swish into the palms of my hands.

"BT is rounding up folk in the Main City—a lot of them too." Another reason why he should go to New City for supplies. What's over there that he needs to travel back and forth so often?

"Wait, why are they there? Is the crime rate up or something?"

"Yes, but they don't know who's responsible, and whoever it is, they've been making a lot of noise over for the past year. I don't want to worry you, but leading BT away isn't enough to keep them away from your friends anymore."

"So, who is it? I'll get rid of them, and it'll stop."

"I just told you I don't know, no one does. BT is rounding up a large amount of people to find out who they are. It's happening a bit too quickly for my liking." I didn't want to go back before because I didn't want to risk attracting BT back to Main City, but it seems like they already went. Why? Neo-humans in all types of Main Cities do stupid shit, but why pile up at that specific city? Did they find out who was with me in that BT worker's house? What if they're looking for them because of what happened? But that was a year ago, though, why now?

"You're gonna go back?" My dad asks and it snaps me out of listing more questions.

"Yes, it looks like it. They um . . ." He doesn't know what I did. He doesn't know who else is a part of it. He said he used to work for BT, but after what happened with Damien and my mom, used to is still too much.

"They what? X, if these folks are into anything that'll—"

"They're not, they're good people and don't belong in a cell." This past year here hasn't been bad, but it was nothing like the time I spent with Isaiah, Aruni, Venus, and Liam. My dad will be fine, if the group gets caught, they won't be.

***

I walk through the borders which took three hours and then poofed to Isaiah's backyard, grateful for the abilities both he and I have in common. I couldn't walk that far and not be fatigued without them. I hide behind the shed and wait for the group. It's filthy of course, so I put my hair up in a bun so it's not touching the dirt.

I left body to peek past the backyard door where I spot a kid approaching. I don't know this girl, but he once said his little cousins come by quite often. Either I've never seen this one before or they've grown since I last saw them. If he can't keep up with all of them, I can't either. She takes out her phone from her pocket and video calls someone, asking where they are.

"I'm busy. Why are you calling me, anyway, is something wrong?" Isaiah.

"No, but whatever you're doing your parents aren't happy about it. They're just worried about you. You know?"

"I'm fine. I'll be home in a minute."

"Where are you now?"

"Not far. I'll be home soon."

"Isaiah —"

I think he hung up on her. What is he up to? He said he's not far so where is he? I looked by the diner, the deli, and the small park closer to their houses. I patrolled several streets for an hour while I listened to a playlist of songs in my mind to track the time. Maybe I should retrace my steps, maybe I missed him. But, I swear I saw Aruni turn the corner. I know that hair puff. Maybe she went back home?

Rushing back to my body her book crosses my memory. I read it. Twice. I find myself taking urgent steps to talk to her about the book like how she used to talk about the stories she read. At her door I knock instead of ringing the doorbell.

C'mon now, answer the door. What's taking so long? I swear I just saw her. The door swings open. It's Auntie. The same auntie who was always happy to see us opens the door with tired eyes. *What happened to them?* "Hi, um, is Aruni home?"

"And you are?" It would help if I took the hoodie and scarf off.

"It's Xandria." She stands up straighter and waves me in shutting the door straight after.

"Aruni is out, I don't know where she is, but she might not be back 'til tomorrow."

Tomorrow? "Well, where's Liam then?" The question lingers in the air as she takes a breath and sits up in the single chair in the living room. She eases into the cushion that hugs her body and crosses her legs. My hands reach for my locs, but I need to focus. Letting the worries crawl through my nerves isn't gonna help anything.

"Liam went to another part of the city; he left a few months ago. All I know is that he's in the upper part of this city a lot. That's the last piece of information I got about him from Aruni."

He hasn't spoke to Aruni? His sister? No that's not right. What happened? "Wait, so you don't know where he is now? Well, shouldn't Aruni kno—"

"Xandria, they haven't spoken since he left. I don't know what happened but neither of us have heard from him and Aruni refuses to reach out." That doesn't sound right. I need to leave, I gotta find him. Why would he leave them now? The whole point was for them to stay together and not get caught up.

Before I can leave, I hear Aruni's voice scattered amongst what sounds like children. Why is she with so many kids? Following the sound of the voices I peek past the hall to get a good look at her. She got taller but the puff didn't change. Aruni's asking if the three kids could stay. They can't stay here though. Wouldn't they be orphans now? I can't get all those details right now but at least I know she's ok.

I know where Liam could be. I somewhat heard about Isaiah earlier through that phone conversation, but I don't know anything about Venus. I'm gonna come back because I need to know why he left without his sister. Why he left without any of them. He was convinced they were going to make it out together.

***

With that memory still fresh in my mind, heat bounces around in my chest causing my soul to be uneasy.

I knock on the door of the apartment and someone with a thicker body shape answer the door. Who is this? She looks like Venus but older. It's not her mom because she doesn't look old enough to be, is this her sister? The one they couldn't find?

"Victoria?" I ask squinting at her like that would turn her into Venus.

"Do I know you?"

"Well, no, but I'm a friend of Venus."

"Oh, you're looking in the wrong place. She moved out a few months ago." *By herself? How? With what money? Does she have a job?* Focus! "Where is she now?"

"Ok, I don't know who you are or why you know my name, and with everything that's going on I think it'll be best if you leave."

Alright, she doesn't know me. Instead of losing my mind, I take a breath. "Let me speak to your mom, she knows me."

She studies my face squinting at me, like Venus does, before she decides to call for her mom. When Venus's mom comes to the door her face has more lines and her curls—that are shaped like Venus's—are speckled with grays. She can't ever seem to have both her daughters with her; she gets one and loses the other.

"Hi, its Xandria from Venus's old school, I just want to know where Venus went."

"*Xandria.* I wish you would've stuck around. Things seemed to be going a lot better while you were here."

I mean, was it? BT was closing in. Me leaving could be the reason why they survived . . . but they were together back then. *Something's wrong.*

"Do you know where she is?"

"West Point. A good bus ride from here. I can write down the address for you, she'll be glad to see you."

"Thank you."

She hands me a piece of paper with Venus's address on it and I shove it into my pants pocket before I leave. Why is everyone so far apart? Isaiah is into some shit for sure. Venus left in who-knows-what condition. Aruni isn't doing anything bad but how is she going about it? And Lee.

I take another breath to calm my nerves that flare up under my skin. I'm concerned about all of them. None of this seems right and it's so out of character for Liam to just . . . *leave.*

Chapter 28

X

I ended up sneaking on the bus after walking onto it inside of the Parallel. I rested my head against the window to catch a nap before looking for Venus but barely fell asleep. Instead, I open my eyes to the sun beaming in my face. A memory of the roof of the abandoned building I stayed in floats from my memory as I looked out the window. It's the five of us sitting together on the roof when they told me they weren't giving up on me. If I wasn't afraid of tears I would've let them fall.

I'm not one to be optimistic about lasting friendships outside of school but after everything we went through together for them to separate like it never happened raises concern.

The bus halts and everyone jerks forward. The people mutter about whatever stopped the bus and I look out the window.

A BT truck.

I run off the bus to get a look at the people in cuffs, but I don't know their faces. One of the people BT took mumbled a name I know. . . . *Patches.*

Down the block I can see a shadow as if someone were wearing a hoodie, so I follow it. I followed the hood to town hall and walked through the purple luminescent doorway I cut through with my hand. It's best to walk through the veil of the parallel to stay hidden.

I can't keep my body in The Parallel but for so long. It's not meant to be here like a soul is. The 'Misplacement Sickness' upsets my stomach and squeezes my skull, but I can ignore it long enough to see where he's going.

When I get inside the town hall building he's talking to someone behind the counter and they hand him a stack of money.

Shit! That's a lot of cash! Wait, that's a lot of cash. Is he the reason BT is swarming out here? Are they here because he's collecting bodies for them? No. He wouldn't do that. I massage my temples as I walk away from the scene. I told them what BT did to me, why would he send anyone there! I could've set them up for money, but I wasn't that shitty of a person! I'm missing something. From what I know people give hints at neo-humans all the time, but not too often does it go well on all ends. He's setting this up, planning these disappearances, but for what? What would he need that money for when he's pretty well off. Maybe it's New City money? But how do you stay in New City without working in New City? What the hell?

Where's Liam? I need to find him and get them together or tell them what's happening or something. This can't stay this way.

So, I make my way to the upper city by traveling through The Parallel and this place is gorgeous. All the buildings are made of glass and reflect off each other. It's nothing like New City. Though, I've never been out here before, but it's nicer than where they're from. How'd Liam end up out here? I leave the parallel when there are less people around because my body starts to get sore from staying there for too long. I need to remember that my body isn't supposed to be here, if I stay too long, I'm going to fall apart, literally.

A whole day of searching and he's nowhere to be found. Maybe I taught them a little too well. I walk out of the alley I hid in and there's a puff of smoke down the block but before the body can fully form it disappears again.

That can't be him, he was never good at that. He could barely walk the first few times he tried teleporting. Then again look at how much everything has changed.

There it is again—the roof. In the shadow's grip is a mush of red that drips. Nope there's no way. There's no way they have the stomach to do shit like that. I do shit like that. The body crumples to the floor and the silhouette begins to disappear but not before I grip the shadow's shoulder. When we reappear I see him and tilt my head at him as if I don't see his face clearly.

"Liam?"

He turns around and looks at me, raises his eyebrows and does a brief squint before he recognizes me. He tosses whatever was in his hand on the table and a clean hand poofed me to an apartment. One that smells of fresh wood. I whirl around taking in the place and everything down to the light fixtures embedded into the white ceiling is brand new.

"X, why are you here?"

"Why am I here? Liam what the hell was that in your hand?" Instead of answering my question he wipes his face and walks away. "Liam. Why aren't you talking to your sister?" I asked poofing in front of him.

Poof! He's gone again and appears in the bathroom behind me reaching for the knob on the sink to wash his hands.

"What's going on?"

"Nothing really. Why does it matter? I thought you were good on your own."

"*I still am* but you aren't, nobody is. Do you know what's happening back home?"

"Yep. I can't do shit about it. And I'm doing pretty good, actually. So, I think I'm good on my own too." He walks past me, pulling the hoodie off over his head, and I watch him walk back down the hallway noticing the difference in his arms and back under the black T-shirt. He doesn't have the same abilities as Isaiah so how is he doing this? Why is my face hot? Doesn't matter. I shouldn't even be looking at him like that.

"What about everyone else and your sister?"

"We don't talk."

"'*We don't talk?*' What do you mean y'all don't talk?" He was about to leave the apartment and I fling my arm upwards freezing the door shut. "Liam, when's the last time you spoke to them?"

"Almost six months ago. Can I go now? I have to get back to the borders since you just about used up all my time with the last ability I had."

"What happened?" He throws his head back and puts his hands in his face. I cross my arms in response. I'm not letting him off that easy—he's so dramatic—just answer the question.

"Venus left without warning after her sister got back. Isaiah did the same a month later and I haven't heard from him since. And Aruni insists on making headlines, so I left, because I didn't want to be part of it. Everyone was doing their own thing anyway. Now unfreeze my door please."

Aruni's making headlines doing what? We're going back to 238, I need answers. Swiftly I grab his shoulder and teleport. As soon as we appear in 238 I step back before he can copy any of my abilities. He flops on the couch rubbing his face again. I take a chance to go find Aruni before she left Auntie's house. There she is! In an instant, we're right back right in 238 with her brother.

They don't say a word when she gets here, instead they stare at each other. I've never been to Venus's apartment so I can't appear there to find her.

"Can you call Venus?" I ask Aruni who's already shaking her head no.

"No, X, what is going on?"

"I'll tell you when you call Venus." Aruni sighs and takes her phone out her pocket. Now I'mma go find Isaiah.

I waited outside the town hall building for about twenty minutes. When he finally appeared there was no need for questions.

When we get back, the silence is heavy and I'm gonna find out why.

"X? You can't be serious."

"Very serious, Patches, now what the hell is going on?"

"I was about to leave my house! Why are we here? Why are they here?" Aruni waves a dismissive hand at them and Venus points her red pointed fingernail at her.

"Don't wave your hand at me like that."

"No actually, we didn't do shit to you."

"Piss off, Isaiah."

"Gladly."

"Why? You gotta go collect your BT money?" As soon as I said that he turned away from the door.

"How about you mind your own shit."

"What BT money?" Venus glares at him and I can see the argument erupting before it even starts.

"*My* BT money." After Isaiah's reply Liam asked him another question but it fuzzed in my ears.

As their bickering grows faint, I notice Isaiah has scars too fresh for someone with abilities like his own. There's so many of them, where is he coming from that he's scarred up like that?

"Isaiah, what happened to your arms and the back of your neck?" He stops yelling at whoever he's yelling at and does a double take at me before answering my question.

"Nothing happened."

"No, where'd that come from?" Isaiah darts his eyes away from me and back to Liam. I straighten my back already knowing the answer as I shove it away from my thoughts.

"You should be the last person worried about that. You don't remember me calling you?"

"What does me answering the phone have to do with—"And there it is. Liam looked away from Isaiah putting the thoughts together at the people who could do such a thing. How did he get away? Those scars should've been healed by now. Was this recent? If so how recent? And I wasn't here, apparently, nobody was. At that a looming guilt drops in my chest.

"Exactly. What happened to 'You're gonna get yourself sent to BT, Isaiah? You remember that? Where were you this time? Cause you didn't pick up that's for damn sure."

The room fell silent as the tight energy wraps the room uncomfortably allowing the new revelation to settles in our stomachs.

"I called you. I called Venus, Aruni, shit I would've even tried to find X if I knew where she was but no answer. Nobody needs to worry about what I'm doing. Matter of fact what I'm doing keeps BT focused on anyone outside of this room."

"When did this happen though? Like did you—Were you in a lab?" Aruni asks smoothing her edges back.

"Recent enough. Obviously. Everybody's so worried about what I did wrong when all I did was send the people that put me there back to where I came from, and I made money off it. See, I took your advice, X."

"Yea but now BT is flocking here."

"Oh, no, that's not all me. Ask Aruni about those fancy headlines floating in everyone's notifications. OR Lee, tell them about why you're in the upper city so often 'cause I've seen you around there before. What about Venus's very *obnoxious* post about being anti-BT? No? Or is it still on me this time? *Everyone* brought BT here. I'm doing y'all a favor. Which I shouldn't be, but lucky for you it keeps my pockets heavy. Now I'm gonna go make sure my pockets stay heavy so I can get into one of those fancy buildings Lee drops bodies in."

"Why didn't you pick up your phone?" I ask Liam. This grabs Isaiah's attention enough to stay. He closes the door leans on it folding his arms, listening in.

"*Me*? No, you don't get to ask me about this, X."

"Why the hell not? I explained everything to you before I left. This isn't about me, it's about this! Look around you! This whole city looks like a ghost town!"

"You wanna know why I started doing what I was doing? I was at the borders looking for you, but I happened to find plenty of neo-humans who were willing to give a lot of what they don't have to do what I do."

"Nobody told you to do that! I told you not to look for me!"

"Alright, X." *Alright, X. Who the fu—*

"Wait, wait, wait! We're already here, we're gonna settle this now. Isaiah made a good point. We're all partial to blame and if we don't fix this now it's gonna get worse."

"Why? You're tired of attracting BTs attention, Venus?"

"You are too, Aruni, and *it is* getting worse . . . *clearly*. And I'm hungry." She swung a handout at Isaiah before her last thought. We all look at each other before following her. We know we're going back to that old diner.

✧ ✧ ✧

"Does anyone want ice cream?"

"No," we all reply to Isaiah after sitting at the table in the same spots we always sat in.

"So, you're gonna answer my question, Lee, or no?" He looks over at me and then addresses Isaiah instead. Why is he acting like this right now?

"When you called me, I was in the middle of looking for someone. I couldn't answer, I would've got caught. So, I put the phone on silent."

"How convenient."

"How was I supposed to know? You said you were staying by your uncle's house so I thought you decided to stay."

"And it didn't occur to you that I would say that at some point if that's what was happening?"

"Well, Venus did disappear a month before that so we both assumed that you did the same," Aruni replies, handing off the tablet to Isaiah.

"I left to get out of that apartment. It was sudden but I couldn't stay there." I can understand why Venus would feel that way. Her mom hovers a lot. Even though its for a good reason it could be quite overbearing as well.

"So, you couldn't call?" Aruni continues. "No, I was looking for someone. It was different from what Liam was doing." From what Venus told me I could take a solid guess at who she was looking for. She was looking for the one that brought on her abilities.

"Did you find him?" I ask, remembering how I got my revenge back then.

"No. He's very far off the grid, but one day I'll catch up. I'm patient." And I believe every word of that. It's silent again but it's not the same, everyone's a little more laxed leaning back into their chairs, looking at their phones or the menu screen.

"Guys, BT is everywhere and don't start with the pointing fingers! I'm gonna lose my shit." Isaiah hands the menu to Liam, and he keeps his eyes glued on the screen.

"Yeah, I think I'm over that," Liam replies, handing the menu to me. He's barely looked at me since we sat down.

"Same. I think we've collectively screwed everyone over. I talked my shit with no plan," Venus says.

Well, that's one thing we all agree on as we share quiet nods. I shouldn't have left, I didn't even want to leave in the first place. I hand Venus the screen.

"So, now what? "*I have no clue, Aruni.*

Not yet.

Chapter 29

X

I always pay attention to where I'm going. However, being here and falling back into an old routine had my attention before I realized we're by Isaiah's backyard. That's not bad, though it's dark. Now's the time to figure this out.

"Has anyone else had bad run-ins with BT?" The thought of it makes my spine run cold.

"Almost. When I dropped the kids off to the group home the other day. I'm fine though.
Is it bad by you, Lee?"

"Not as bad, but bad enough."

"And this means what? It's gonna get worse. This is already a hot spot."

"It means we fix it, Isaiah. I've never liked talking about problems without having the means to fix them. But now we do. We brought them out here. We can bring them back out." Venus sits in the lawn chair and crosses her legs staring at us. Her hair has either gotten fuller or it's the fact that she pulled it back into a ponytail with two curls framing her face. It's only been a year, but they all look slightly more mature than when I left them. They're all dressed in black more than likely because we've all been hiding.

"So do what we did in another Main City?" Aruni asks as she sits on the bench at the table. A memory of her bringing ice cream outside passes through my mind.

"No. I mean we can fight back! It's like Lee said about the house, we made it out before, right? Maybe we could do it again. And to be frank I've gotten pretty nice with my abilities so I think it could work."

"That was a year ago and, clearly, I was wrong."

"Well, you're wrong again and, Venus, you're absolutely right. The only way this is gonna stop now is if we push back. We just need to slap together a plan and we can get the city back." He can ignore me or act petty if he wants. It's like I said, I'mma do what needs to be done with or without them, and right now I have Venus. Not only is it a good idea, but it's also tempting to scratch that addiction I picked up in the simulation. It's been a while. It may have something to do with what my dad told me. Maybe all BT wanted and needed from me was rage. If I didn't know of the experiences I've had here, all I would know is spilling blood.

"I don't have a problem with it but I gotta cash-in with the people I sent in yesterday."

"C'mon now, Patches."

"Don't do that. I get to cash-in because now they'll know how I felt. They can get a first-class experience in BT's graveyards, plus the money is real nice. So, that first, then we kick their ass."

"I still live at Auntie's, so I'll be there. Aside from the wrecked homes I have seen, the kids are getting snatched up now. They keep dropping the age." It makes sense she would have a soft spot for children. I do too after what happened to me and seeing what that red-haired BT worker did to her children. I would ask Liam but he's still acting pissy and I don't have patience at this point. So, I cross my arms, lean back in my chair, and watch the other three watch me—they're probably wondering if I'm gonna ask him.

"My shit! Lee, are you doing this or no?" Isaiah throws his hands up in the air fed up with our version of the silent treatment.

"Yeah, we should start by the borders on the east side. A lot of neo-humans gather there from multiple cities."

"Good." Venus replies and both her and Aruni look at me and then at each other. I'm not talking to him, so I don't know why they're looking at me like that. Aruni sighs and follows Venus as she walks out the backyard.

"Alright, listen. I don't know what your problem is with each other right now but everybody but you two has stopped acting an ass. Whatever it is, pack that shit up before tomorrow because I'm not playing messenger." Isaiah walks into his house making sure to guide the door shut so it doesn't slam. If his parents are up, they're gonna have a fit if they see those scars. They're good people. Parents, I wish I had.

"So, are you done acting like a child now?" I ask as I head toward the exit just in case I wanna leave mid-conversation.

"I'm not acting like a child."

"That's what a child would say." He takes a breath and looks at me. He steps in front of me, and I cross my arms but he crosses his back.

"You're still irritating." I say, doing my best to not allow a smile to leak through. At this point it would be bad timing, "What is your problem?" I ask refocusing the conversation.

"X, this whole time I thought you were back with BT or worse."

"Well, I wasn't. I'm fine. You're mad at me because I'm ok?"

"I'm not mad at you."

"Really? So, walking away from me while I'm asking you questions isn't you being mad at me? Or what about this?" I throw my hands over my face and toss my head back, making fun of his dramatics earlier.

"Alright, I didn't do all of that."

"Yes, you did." And there goes that contagious smile. I'm still mad at him though.

"You never mentioned running right into BT."

"Because if I said that you would've followed me which you tried to do anyway. So, I left without notice and didn't mention that detail. I did hint at it pretty clearly though."

"Yeah, but I didn't think you meant tomorrow or that that's how you were gonna go about it. I'm not mad, I'm glad you're ok, but you operate like people don't care about you."

"Well, there were certain folks in my life who were supposed to and didn't, and you know that. But I am sorry if that doesn't always register. I—I didn't mean to hurt anybody. I just wanted y'all to be ok. I promised to look out for all four of you."

"Ok cool, so I'll make the same promise to you."

"No you're not; it's different with me. I'm gonna run if I have to."

"And I'll be right there with you. I told you I'm not running away this time." *No, he can't! That's the whole point!* Those words were supposed to be said out loud, but they're caught in my throat. Behind all the times I said I wasn't supposed to have that, I knew what I wanted. I can't bring myself to say it and now I can't bring myself to say the latter either. It's a nice idea 'til I lose someone, 'til I lose him along the way. That's why I operate the way I do because one way or another everything and everyone I'm involved with ends up caught up in chaos. Then I end up hurt *by* them or worse, *losing them.*

"Lee—"

"Promise is a promise. See you tomorrow."

I hate him. I hate him so much that I don't wanna be forced to let him go. No matter what I say, he still wants to follow me and my chaos everywhere.

Chapter 30

X

When we got to the border it was the same as what we left behind. An open section of green grass shielded by trees and scattered abandoned houses covered in vines and roots. Junk metal peppered throughout the ground but the only difference were the whispers hidden behind leafy shrubs and decrypt insides from the houses. As the five of us walk through the area, I catch wind of whispers of people explaining their circumstances or abilities to one another.

Rumors are floating through the air about New City and how suffocating BT has been to our city. I watch some of the people pass by us and notice how some stay hidden. The same warmth that enveloped me with the people I found is the same warmth that calls to me as I watch the people here. As I watch the community, I see they are like me, they are like us, hiding so they can make a life out of what they have in between two places that do not make enough space for them. *A community of forgotten people.*

"How'd you find them?" Lee and I had slowed down from the rest of the group as we watched the people hiding and talking.

"I was looking for you and found them instead."

"Oh, so are these the people who made making those requests?"

"Some of them. Otherwise, being here is alright."

"It's more than alright, this is amazing."

Ever since I've been out of the simulation there are pinpricks of yellows amongst shaded areas. I came out believing this was all hopeless and that everyone and everything was inherently made to bring about the downfall of others who don't deserve it. Then I see this. *I meet them.* I did what I did driven by all the hurt people brought me, but being here with this community, *with good friends*, I have a new reason to fight. This reason carries me in a way that cradles me before throwing me off a cliff. It's a lot less lonely, but it's so new.

"Remember when you woke us up in the middle of the night to steal stuff from that supermarket?" A breath of laughter escapes my smile as memories dance through my mind of them completely screwing that over.

"Of course, I do. You were gonna get us caught being in the tech section."

"But I didn't. You know what I took?" I cut my eyes at him and he pulls a blue rectangular case out his pocket. Inside of it is a silver-blue bracelet with two small earpieces that almost resemble tiny crystals on the inside.

"First of all, I don't know what that is, secondly that looks expensive! You sure you weren't setting us up to get taken? I know that thing was laced with security."

"Yes, it was, but I got it though. It's to listen to music, the two crystals attach to the back of your ears."

How? This has to be New City tech—all the more reason why it was probably very pricy and not even worth the risk.

"Oh, I see but it's never that serious, Lee, I'm sure you could use whatever you have already."

"Yeah, that's true. Can I see your wrist?" He stopped walking to take the bracelet out the case and dangles it in front of me.

"Lee, I can't take that! It's too expensive!"

"Why not? It's a good replacement for the iPod you told me about." *Don't cry. Don't cry.* "Why?"

"Not that I mind hearing you hum the songs, but it might be easier to keep track of time by listening to it in a situation where you can't do that." He heard that? Did they all hear that? I was so quiet though at least, I thought I was quiet.

Nevertheless, I give in and hold out my arm. The Bluish-silver bracelet snaps around my wrist and I take the two crystals and place them behind my ears. Cold and tiny hints of metal wrap around them and a familiar song starts play. It's the song I played when I explained how water is everywhere.

No words form and none are necessary; even if I had any to share I couldn't. I'm too busy staring at the grass beside me while listening to a song I haven't heard clearly in a long time. Sure I played it out loud, but having it this close to my eardrum is different. "Um. Thank you." I sniffled and held my head up high to will tears back into my eyes as my words piece together in a whisper. *Who knew a new safe place would bring an old one back to me.*

"Anytime, X." Most of the time hearing cars screech in the distance is exactly what I don't want to hear but I'm glad to hear it now. I was able to sneak away a couple tears when we both turned around to see BT is here. They pull up on the road behind a few trees and immediately I look for Venus, Isaiah, and Aruni who are not too far ahead quietly warning others to run. Lee and I run in the opposite direction ready to protect something BT didn't know we were capable of building. Now that I know, they're gonna have to get through me before anything happens to them or to anyone attempting to maintain the safe places they've created for themselves.

Chapter 31
X

November 3rd 2097
Main City 27 Borders

The abandoned houses that lie in between the cities make good hideout spaces to keep a lookout for BT. Though the people who stay around here are consistent in their rotations around the nearby borders, BT still seems to have a knack for finding them wherever they are. That's why we're here because when they run, we fight so they won't have to.

Here they come. Seven . . . nine BT vans line the block not too far from here. The second the vans are in sight Liam and Aruni get in place to occupy them with illusions. He's not as good as his sister but two is better than one. The moment I hear people panicking, I hop out of an abandoned cottage through a broken window running past plants and trees to get to the people. I guide them to the safest way out of the borders as I point in the direction that would get them out of BT's sight. Every now and then BT workers attempt to cut us off by hiding in different spaces, but little do they know we can see them. Another reason to know how to run and hide. Based on what I know now, it's easier to find anyone in hiding since I know where to look. The only thing that has changed in the past few weeks is it's not only us fighting anymore, others are joining in, in small ways, but it makes a big difference.

I've seen people with abilities I don't have, like duplicating themselves or others who can give life and take life away. Lee knew someone like that. I've seen those people obstruct the view of the workers using the grass and plants growing them into thick green walls. Multiple faces of the same person revealing themselves. I've seen more ice being thrown in BT's direction. Ghosts I've never met snatching up BT guns into the Parallel. This reminds me of the time at the lab when I freed those neo-humans. Though, these people didn't react the same way.

When I was at the lab a lot of the neo-humans broke away from the group when they felt they got what they wanted. Here it's different. They stay together—most times. I've caught people ready to sell others out for money, but little do they know they could be next. Besides that, money must be running short because of what's happening here. Less money is being given for rewards, but more BT vans keep showing up. They can be backstabbers if they want, at the end of the day BT works for BT.

I caught the eye of a girl hiding in an abandoned house through a broken window. I care about everyone here as a unit, but I know what it's like to be where she is right now. Watching everyone go by and being afraid of calling for help. I walk inside to the terrified girl clutching her leg with red stained hands against her tan skin. She couldn't run if she wanted to.

"I'mma help you get out of here, ok?" I go to wrap my arm under her shoulders but the way she shook her head "no" almost made me jump back.

"I'm not gonna hurt you, I promise. I wanna help. There's a medical center nearby that can fix your leg for you." She shakes her head "no" again but this time with too much weight in it for someone her age. She seems to be about the same age I was when I left BT. As I watch her, she leans her head back and closes her eyes. She looks like she's giving up on running and I don't blame her, she probably didn't plan on getting help.

"What are your abilities?" She looks at me with tired eyes and holds out a blue orb of light from the Parallel. So, I hold out a yellow one.

"I know it doesn't seem worth it now but it is, and it could get worse but it could also get better. You deserve that chance like I did. Here"—I hand her the yellow orb—" you can have this, it helped me, and it'll help you for now." She taps an index finger on the orb, and it flows into her arm, I place a hand on my chest so she knows she can put that where her heart is. She rolls her shoulders back and in the next second her head pops up a small smile creeps onto her face.

"See and there's plenty more where that came from."

All at once either bullets or those neo-human numbing darts shoot through the wall behind me. Right away, I wrap my arms around her and poof to the front of the medical center. She'll be ok here, if not today then one day. I poof back into the chaos and the area is nearly empty. "X! I think that was the last of them but that was pretty quick, right?" Aruni asks.

"Good. I'd rather them leave than stay and cause more trouble," I reply. In the distance I see Lee, Venus, and Isaiah. "238!" I yell before teleporting Aruni and I back to the room.

"Guys I don't like that those trucks left like that." *Me neither Venus*, but I'm not gonna say it out loud.

"You think they followed us?"

"Not likely, Isaiah," I reply, knowing I'm not being honest with sharing my thoughts. We all know something's off. My gut is twisting to tell me something's off. I learned not too long ago to trust it when this happens, but I wanna sit in this for a bit on the off chance that everything is ok. I don't believe it is but please let it be.

The silence lets me know The Parallel is spotted with gray lights as we sit and wait for whatever went wrong under our noses.

I hear trucks skirt to a halt outside ... one ... two ......
... five trucks. *No.* We meet each other's eyes and waste no time rising to our feet. We rush down the steps and just as we hit the middle of the stairwell the pests pour through the doors.

They found us. BT is rushing in through the side entrances and I shield the five of us with two walls of ice on both sides leaving the entrance to the stairwell open. I said I would protect the people at the border. *I said I would protect them too. No matter the cost.*

"You all need to leave now!"

"Yeah right, Alexandria."

I don't have time to bicker with Isaiah right now. "Listen to me! I know you want to help but they're here because I came here. I brought them here. Let me handle it.

"X, but—"

"Aruni, I'm sorry. I'm sorry ... to all of you." Tears shove through my eyes but, tears won't save them, so I hold them.

Sorry for leaving again. Even though I know that they're willing to run with me. I'm accustomed to running alone. I swear I'mma learn but now's not the time. They can't go where I came from, I can't let it happen. Running with them will risk me losing them in a place I know the burden of too well. It's ok at the border but not when BT is this close. They all stand along the stairwell staring at me and I can hear the ice cracking from the shots it's taking on. My arms are tensing the longer I hold this wall up.

"What are you guys waiting for? GO! Take the fire escape and take one of their trucks!" I look at Lee and he leaves first. *Why did he leave first?*

When they've made it far enough up the steps, I shove the walls of ice at BT and do my best to project an illusion. There's so many of them. Having to project an illusion of this magnitude is stretching my brain so far that a headache begins to cover my skull. *What if they're outside too?*

Bullying my way through them—hoping they don't shoot me instead of one of the fake duplicates I made—I make it out the door. There's a truck being driven down the block. *They're gonna be ok.*

The illusion doesn't hold up because I'm forced to defend myself with more ice again when they come outside. You mean to tell me they're all inside? A BT van goes after the van Lee and the others took. They knew I was gonna send them away. I teleport into the truck and punch the guy in the driver's seat and stab the guy in the passengers' seat in the chest with an ice knife. I leave the truck and there's two other BT trucks filled with the idiots rushing toward me. Gripping the front of the truck as the steel crushes in my fist the truck slides across the pavement and crashes into another. There were more though, where'd they go? If people didn't know my face, then they know it now. Dozens look out their windows watching all the commotion. Their parents are gonna kill me when they find out.

Several BT uniforms rush out of their trucks and there's no way I'm not gonna get taken, there's too many. Well, I did it before and if it means the four of them get away then I'll go back but I'm not gonna make it easy.

I lunge at one of them with my ice shield in full as they shoot at me causing stingy wounds to open across my body. There's a frail BT worker in front of me. I snatch the gun out his hand and shoot the rest of them down. I disappear behind one of the other buildings to pick the metal that hit me out of my skin. The road in front of me is clear but I hear tires screech. I walk out to the road to see where the noise is coming from, but the weight of fatigue forced me to take a knee on the ground. Still, I managed to look up the road.

I need to get up, I see more fuzzy blue bodies in the distance. But one stands out—a white coat.

Get up. I need to get up. Wait, I know this person. They walk up to me, familiar black heels heavy stepping on the street as my hands are digging through the cement responding to the aches panging through my muscles. This person is blurry all the time for many reasons but not because I recognize her face. My stomach aches threatening to throw up nothing.

She found me, she found me first.

"Mom?" I whispered the question hoping what I see isn't true, but it is. I know it is. I would be scrolling through all the questions I have like usual but I'm too busy fighting not to collapse on the ground. As I fight heavy eyelids, she leans in and the words slur through my ears.

"Found you."

Burning, tears shove through my eyes as a yell crackles from my gut. *I thought I got away. I was so close. I thought I was gonna make it. I thought I was gonna cross the borders with them and leave this all behind. I was ready. I was ready... I was gonna make it. I was gonna have a life... I found my people... I found my home. I was gonna make it and she found me.*

She's watching me scream and cry and fail to force myself up to my feet while whatever was in those bullets weigh me down. I could've gotten up had I not felt like I lost everything. I would've been able to fight if I wasn't too heavy to lift myself back up one more time. I really believed what Lee had once told me. *I finally believed it a little too late.*

What she made me will be her undoing. Almost on cue I hear more tires screeching and a truck slams into the workers standing behind her. I strain my neck to look up and the four of them hop out of the truck. That's where the other trucks went, they were leading them away. That's why he left first. I stand up almost failing to ignore the soreness in my bones, but I'm filled with new energy as Aruni, Isaiah, Venus, and Liam run to me. Isaiah and Aruni meet my gaze and step out of the way as they follow my eyes to the white coat fluttering away from the scene. She's never gonna find me again and *I'mma make sure this time.*

I stop as my hand raises with no rush. My locs are all in my face but I can see her just fine. A pole of blighted and haphazard ice crackles through the skin onto my palms and through fingers. Harsh spikes snap from them as it forms toward her and wraps around her body.

The ice flurries and crunches back into my hand and up my arms. As it disappears she gets closer to me squirming in the cold grip. When she's close enough she drops to the ground. The memory of her dragging me across the room by my arm mirrors when I pick her up the same way to toss her into a wall. She manages to stand up and lean against it despite the red stains dotting her coat. I wave my hand packing snow together encasing her in ice, freezing her to the wall.

A gentle hand grasps my shoulder and when I reach for it. I pause when I finally realize who it is.

"I said to leave, Liam."

"You would've been taken if we didn't."

"X, let's leave." I was gonna turn to Venus and repeat what I said but more eyes began to peek through windows and curtains and they were all on me. They could be like us or not, they could even be enemies waiting for me to slip up so they have an excuse to justify more people getting kidnapped by BT. As much as I hate to admit it, we need to leave. I need to leave without ending her life and quenching this blood lust that's been resting at the back of my mind for so long.

"Don't ever come looking for me again and I won't be looking for you." Lucky for her the people by my side reminded me that I'm more than what BT claims I am.

Hush. I appear into the driver's seat of the truck, my face still tight after being face-to-face with my mother. I don't ever wanna see her again. I don't need her anymore. I need to keep them safe and treasure what I have.

We drove in silence heading toward New City until a BT truck turned onto the same empty road we were on. She's not gonna give up. She's not gonna give up 'til she has me, and they can't be with me when that happens.

"Venus, you take over." I pull over and appear in front of the truck but there's two more right behind it as they separate into three parts on the road. Suddenly, there's a poof next to me.

"Why, Liam?"

"What? Do you want to go back to BT? Might as well hop in the truck yourself." Well, that's not a bad idea but I can't make it that simple. Not on the off chance I can get away. I shouldn't entertain that hope again but it keeps whispering to me.

As we stand in the road watching the trucks get closer, he narrows his eyes, I can tell he's thinking. A few seconds later, Venus, Isaiah, and Aruni join us.

"Actually, don't take that literally." At that a genuine slight smile passes my face. *He knows me well.* The trucks get closer and Aruni steps in front of us, I can see her eyes glazed in gray as the BT trucks swerve off the road.

"Well get to it! Don't watch me!" One truck swerve's back but before it speeds up Isaiah runs over and crashes into it to force it to stop. I'm taking full credit for everything I saw—I was teaching them at one point.

The BT workers get out the truck and I dart into the trees, Liam and Venus follow my lead and track close behind. Hopefully, they chase us. Venus shouts and I don't understand the words but an icy sphere forms around her body when she leaves it. Even though one of the workers seem to be catching up to us, when Liam and I look back the BT uniform is snatched up into the purple haze of the Parallel and so do a few others. A few other people circle in front of us and I put us in a sphere of ice using the bit I have left. I hold out a hand to him but he pauses like usual.

"Just a few abilities." He can't keep hesitating like this. I don't fully understand what it's like to bear a burden like mimicking abilities but one of these days he's gonna need to copy more than three at a time.

Ice, teleporting, and being ever so slightly bullet proof is enough for now. They're all pretty convenient. I took half the dome down and he took the other. Slices of ice from both of our hands fly out at the remaining workers as they jerk back and fall to the ground. We're so close to New City. If we can get past these guys we can run to it. They're not gonna go in there—they're not *supposed* to.

"Lee, we need to go back! We just gotta get into New City territory and we're good." Look at me saying *we*. I wasn't supposed to belong anywhere but, now I belong wherever they go.

He gives me a nod. "Watch out." Startled I duck immediately as Liam lunges an icicle at a BT worker but it's thin. *We gotta run.* Teleporting is gonna be a strain but not impossible. We flicker a few times and eventually he disappears and so do I. I appear by Venus, and I stick my head out into the Parallel to call for her as my physical head slumped to the side.

"VENUS!"

She answers and I see her holding the head of a BT worker between her palms, filling their head with a ton of orbs. *Alright she's a little nice with her abilities.* She rushes over to me zipping through the air and I explain the plan. I take the ice from the sphere back into my hand and Venus stands after getting back to body.

She takes one of their weapons with her and we run over to meet Isaiah and Aruni who are holding their own pretty well. Isaiah snatches a worker charging at Aruni by the collar. By the time I got there Liam must've explained everything. Isaiah runs over to one of the new BT vans and snatches the driver out as I run to them.

"You better not crash!" Venus says from the passenger's seat.

"I'm not gonna crash!" He says as the car swerves and screeches.

Yeah, ok. He gains control but now I wish I was the one driving. We drive as close to the border as we can before BT can catch up and by the time we see New City we hurry out the truck and run. We can't go into New City with this truck, it'll without a doubt, bring too much attention.

It's so funny to me that New City has no guards at their borders, they let people run straight in. *False hope. A false promise.* Sure, we can go in, but will we survive in a world much more different and advanced compared to ours? We don't know and they don't care but at this point we are out of options. My bet's not on New City, my bet is on them—they're gonna be great out there. We could do great out there if I make it . . . *I'm so close.*

But first we gotta make it in. We're gonna make it. I'll make sure of it. I promised that I would look out for them.

I hear someone bristle through the trees not too far away from here. Scanning the area, There's a blurred figure knelt behind some bushes and in between some trees. By the time I see their gun raise I hadn't reacted fast enough. Isaiah collapses to the ground. My abilities are growing tired as is the rest of me.

Though the newfound adrenaline allowed me to find water in the ground and immediately, I shoot ice through their body. I wasn't paying close enough attention to unblur the figure before but I see them so clearly now. The spikes of ice shoved up behind their back and the screams did not last long. Their body sits on the ice dripping with red. When I rush back to Isaiah my shoulders drop when I see he's okay, it's only his leg. Well, they still shot at him but he's ok. Then, air returns to my lungs. *That was too close.*

Venus and Liam gather Isaiah and I hardly notice the lingering smoke in my arms 'til I saw the smoke in the corner of my eyes. I stay back to keep an eye out allowing them the opportunity to gain some distance but Aruni stays too. *She knows what Lee knows.*

"X?"

"Look out for them for me, Aruni." I can't go with them. *I'm right here and so close but I can't stay.* My eyes flickier from the New city lights and back to them carrying Isaiah. BT...My mom is not giving me up. Two things can be true at once. I belong here but I can't be if my past won't let me go. That one shot was one too close. I need to run again; I want to tell her I'm sorry but sorry won't fix this nor the hurt I'll be leaving them with. *They'll be ok.*

"X, at least come with us to the hospital, I promise I won't tell them about a thing until later but—but if you leave now . . ."

She doesn't need to finish the sentence for me to know. I need to make sure they're safe. So, I nod and we run to catch up with the others. I tell them to wait because I'm about to do something they're not gonna like. BT is gonna catch them on foot, but they won't catch them if I teleport all four of them to the nearest hospital. I know where that one is too—people that are dealing with abuse end up in the hospital more often than they should, so I was around these areas a lot. It's a good thing I was. They probably got kicked out of the city by whoever the NCD is afterward. I hope that doesn't happen to them. *They'll be ok. Please, be ok.*

I grab Aruni's hand and she holds onto Venus's shoulder then I reach my hand out to Liam, but he knows what I'm up to. I can tell by the way he looks at me and shakes his head before he asks me the same question I asked him earlier.

"Why?"

"*Promise is a promise.*" The same one he made back to me.

"Can you guys decide already? Look at my leg!" Isaiah yells at us and this is the one time I can't retaliate. Liam grabs a hold of my hand and I give everything I got to get us out here. As the smoke builds, I flicker. I'm searing apart by giving energy I don't have. I let out a painful cry. I lean my head to my shoulder so the silver at the back of my ears can play the music Liam gifted me. The notes swell in my brain as I take a breath and manage to piece myself back together in front of a New City Hospital.

Shit! I stumble a few steps backward into Aruni. She catches me and helps me stay on my feet. "Thanks." I whisper. Venus and Lee look at me and I nod at them to tell them that I'm ok. I'm ok as I can be right now.

After they head inside, I look to Aruni to ask her for one more favor, but she's done more than enough already. They all have.

"Give this to Lee for me. I'll come back and get it one day." I take the earpieces off and reattach them to the bracelet I hand to Aruni.

"Ok." She stared at the bracelet, appearing as though she was searching for words. See, Aruni pauses sometimes when she speaks but that was a different type of pause. She knows her brother well, but I know that and I know her too.

"*After* today you can give that to him. Ok?" She doesn't answer, instead she gives me a tight hug. I stiffen, my eyes widening and back tensed as the warmth relaxes me and allowing me enough vulnerability to return the hug. *It's safe, it's safe with the friends that helped me find my yellow.* I let go of her, unable to let go of them. I was so close, but my memories are close too, but I won't forget this time. *Never again.*

Tires screeching, is it BT? I guess they decided to take the risk. When I run to one of the small alleyways, I'm surrounded by people in dark blue uniforms. Here we go again. I'll make it one day, just not today. Guess she found me first after all.

They won't see me cry so I go back to what keeps me afloat. Black notes overlay memories of them as a needle stabs into my neck and fades my vision and the music slows from my thoughts.

***

What made me jump like that? I'm still jostling a bit as I sit and my head moves too much feeling heavier than usual. I raise a hand to wipe sweat off my forehead but I can't take my wrist apart. BT, I'm with BT. In the back of their truck, I look away from the cuffs lit with blue lights to see a blurry figure standing at the truck doors.

"Lee?" Aruni, she gave him the bracelet anyway.

"Good, you're up, I have an idea, but we have to work quick because I'm losing the abilities." *He shouldn't be here. Why is he in here?*

He sits down next to me struggling to make ice in his hands. *Only one of us can make it out of here.* He uses the little ice he has to put it on the cuffs and snap it off. Everything that was happening stops as I hold both his hands, he needs to leave. He looks up at me, I look at him and shake my head no. Weary from the fatigue of the drugs riddled through the walls of this truck.

"Listen to me, you can't stay here, I can't let you follow me there."

"I'm not. We're both leaving."

"You know that only one of us can leave. Lee, I don't know what BT has been up to but they're changing. Whatever is in this truck is stopping us from using our abilities, it's bad enough we're burnt out. If we both try to leave, we both won't get out." *He's not gonna leave so I don't let go of his hands.*

"I'll figure out another way then." I look down at our hands and it's apparent that we were both thinking to do the same thing.

My hands don't begin to disappear because I was gonna leave on my own. His hands don't begin to disappear because he was gonna leave on his own. He was gonna put me back at the hospital and he would be left here. Luckily, I still know my abilities better than he does.

I look at him and he says what I thought were my last words to him.

"Promise is a promise." He gives me a reassuring smile and of course I mirror it back hoping it distracts him from the fact my eyes are glossy for so many reasons.

"And that's exactly why I'll be keeping it. I'll see you in your new life, Icicle Boy." We both particle away as the breakage travels up our arms. When I open my eyes. I'm the one that's still in the truck. Which means he's where I left him—in the hospital with his friends and sister.

My hands press against my wet face as the knot forms in my throat. This is a new reason why I didn't want to get attached. I didn't want to lose anyone again but now they don't want to lose me, and I don't know how to handle this when all I've ever been given was the opposite.

Chapter 32

X

BT
13 months later

Five hundred songs play through my mind in the same order the entire time I'm here. So I don't lose track of time. If it stays the same, I'm not in the simulator. If the order or number changes then they put me back in. When I got here the smell tossed me into a recollection of bad memories. The first ones I had from my mother—Marie's apartment. That metallic smell, the vial in Damien's pocket, whatever that was riddled throughout that apartment. Now they want to give it to me, and I have no clue if it's what brought me under the first time or if it's something else.

Now is the only time where I can catch a break. If it's not a needle being jabbed into my neck, it's the "doctor" that comes in for testing. I have tried to wiggle my toes multiple times hoping that I was being dramatic about the aches in my legs, but they don't move. When I do walk, I drag my feet—maybe I shouldn't have kicked the worker in the ribs.

I knew that wasn't gonna get me out but I saw him and did it anyway as soon as he approached me. We were walking down the hall so I could go wash up and before he handed me off my foot snapped his ribs. He doubled over and I pressed my elbow into his neck against the wall while Marie watched. That didn't get me out, but it was cathartic. Maybe not worth the numbness and aches in my legs and ribs now but still.

I may not be able to reach my abilities but that didn't stop me from running before and it's not gonna stop me from acting up now. They took more from me than I had. She took more from me than I had, and she let this lab continue to do it. She's a part of it.However, what they can't take are memories—they did before but never again. *Not the ones from home.*

I wonder how they're doing. Do they still go to that diner? Well probably not if they live in New City. I didn't even get a chance to make sure. *They're ok. They have to be.* They can make space for them somewhere if they can't make it into the NCD. I sit in silence scrolling through memories I have with them and every now and then a smile or laugh passes by as I ignore the pain in my abdomen. Smiles and laughs I used to hide. The ones I was angry about sharing. *I miss them.* We were so close, but they made it and they're ok.

The door slams open and I don't react because it's 4:00 p.m. and that's my appointment with Doctor Stickman. Look at him, his head is too big for his body. If I had five seconds with these cuffs off I could t—

"You can leave, Doctor," Marie says interrupting my thoughts. Why would she send him away?

"You got bored?" Never too tired to attempt to piss her off.

"No, Xandria, I have a new idea today."

Xandria. I lost track of the number of times I corrected her. So, I stopped. What's this new idea though? What is she up to now? I would say it can't be worse, but they're proven that it can always be. As she continues on the more my stomach turns.

"I know where your friends are at this exact moment."

"Yeah, ok, Marie." But what if she's being serious? I'm here, I can't do anything, and I thought they were in New City 27. They had to be, why would they go back? Maybe for their family? Ok, maybe, but they wouldn't stay. They couldn't stay. BT isn't supposed to be there, but they did follow me into the city when I left.

"You want proof?" I briskly look up and my locs fly away from my face. She raises her eyebrows at me before she turns around to the screen on the rolling table behind her. What's taking her so long? What is she gonna show me? Are they in New City? Did they take them? No, they couldn't have. *They're ok.*

She slides away from the screen and I see them driving in a car on a road. One of the fancy floating ones Lee spoke about, but that's Main City. Why are they over there? How close is BT that they're able to get that footage? How do they know where they are? Are they being tracked?

"So, you have about ten minutes to make a decision before my people stop the car when they cross the border. They'll be sitting in the same position as you, Xandria. We'll make sure of it." Maybe . . . maybe I was wrong. I was wrong again. I should've stayed and I ran again. I can't help them here!

"Why do you want them so badly? I'm here, I can do everything they do, why don't you leave them be?"

"Because Xandria, you and I both know your friends are special—one in a million like you."

How? Do they have multiple abilities? Liam is a mimic but she's not just talking about him, so did I miss something? My eyes dart around searching for something I missed but it's not adding up. For now.

It doesn't matter either way, I'm gonna let them give me the metallic silver serum and hope for the best. But that's even worse. What if I'm not conscious? I can't watch them take them. What if she's lying to me? What if she's not and she's depending on my mistrust of her to take them, anyway? To take them and still put me under. Is it bad that I'm hoping they'll find me first this time?

If I allow them to be brought here, I don't know who else would come looking for me and they can't help me if they're here too. Even if they can't look for me if I'm somewhere else they're the only people who would fight to get me back. This is the dumbest decision I've ever made. Depending on anyone but myself makes my nerves hot but I don't have a choice. I gotta believe they'll be around when I need them even if I'm not in my right mind. I at least gotta believe that Liam meant what he last said.*" Promise is a promise."* I whisper the statement to myself remembering all the times he welcomed me with open arms even though I ran in the opposite direction. Now I hope that hasn't changed because now I need the help and they do too.

"Ok."

"No fighting it this time."

"No fighting this time."

They stick the wire in the back of my neck and connect it to the computer cube. As I watch the live feed of the group driving on the road bordering one of the new cities the gray serum is plunged in the side of my neck for the hundredth time. I inhale as I reject the urge to fight the silver duplicate from the mindscape forming. It almost killed me once.

On that day I had left a chamber of glass stumbling. I fell on the floor struggling to get up. I hated that; those were one of the worse days.

My vision distorts but I still caught the car running red lights and a laugh leaves my last conscious exhale. *Patches is driving for sure.*

The black behind my eyelids doesn't flash into a white dome. There are no glitched holes in the darkness like the ones from the simulation. This time it's silver and silent. As my intentions change a new goal plasters in my mind. Hold on.

"Wait no, you didn't tell me that! You didn't tell me that! WAIT! Shit, shit! No, no, no—"

My vision leaks silver . . .

Everything is white or grey. The door is six feet away from where I lie. Each wall is the same distance apart.

"Xandria?"

"**Hi, Mom.**" *There are faces on the screen to my right. That is what she's pointing to.*

"Who are these people, Xandria?"

"**Isaiah, Aruni, Venus, and Liam.**" *She remembers them. I remember them.*

"Do you want to see them?"

"**Yes.**" *But why? Why does she want to see them. It doesn't matter, I'll have a new why.*

"What are you gonna do when you find them?"

A strange, strange addiction. I know what to do now. I see her memories. I see my memories. Never forget, Xandria...

"Bring them home."

To be continued...
in
Conquer: Reborn

Acknowedgements

This is probably one of the most difficult things I've done. It's right up there with college. I was going to quit on this book more times than I remember. I rewrote this book 4 times and hated it an equal amount of times...at times. But thankfully through answered prayers, tears, lots of hard work and a community I stumbled upon on tik tok this was made possible.

I want to thank my wonderful editor @_thestorymaestro for her detailed commentary and critique. I want to thank her for challenging my ideas and changing my stubborn mind about a lot of things in this book. I want to thank her for her compassion, empathy, and mostly her patience with me as I was very anxious about publishing my first debut novel. I'm grateful for her fun and funny commentary every now and then. She truly wasn't just an editor but one of the few people I call a booktok big sister. Thank you for correcting me and talking me down from quitting when I needed it most.

Thank you to my cover artist project manager Alisha with ebook launch covers for the absolutely amazing book cover! Thank you to my Queens College professors who heard the idea and encouraged me to take the leap of faith and go for it. Thank you to my Fictional Workshop professor, for all those writing prompts at the beginning of class. Thank you for the workshops and thank you to the classmates who participated in it. Thank you to my fellow Peer Counselors of 2021 for encouraging me to change my major and pursue what I was passionate about.

I'm thankful for my alpha-reader Melissa, a good friend from high school who read the very first version of this book back when it was a very different type of hot mess. I want to thank her for being honest in her critique and then encouraging me to keep going. I wasn't even going to share this, but she offered to read it and then straight up said 'you gotta publish this'. If you know Melissa, she does not BS she tells it like it is, no matter who you are. That's part of the reason why I even made it this far because she said that it meant something.

Thank you to my mama who held me while I cried about all the rejection letters and lost competitions while I first started my writing journey. Thank you to my pops for being the idea man and encouraging me to create too. I got my drive, focus, and 'Don't tell me what I can and can't do' attitude from my mama. I got my imagination, creativity, and a brain built for ideas from my dad. I grew up watching Spiderman, X-men, Avengers, Star-wars, and Star-trek, with him since before I could remember. My dad used to be called the TV guide because of all the shows he could watch and remember. We both love a good story. Thank you to him for being the first blerd I met, before I knew what a blerd was. Thank you to my mama for drilling the 'don't talk about it be about it' attitude into my mind. That encouraged me to make my dreams tangible. My mom's realistic mind and my dad's creative one was the perfect mix to build this.

Thank you to my lil brother for letting me vent and bullying me to get it together and lock in when I wasn't fighting for this. That's my lil homie and do not tell him I said that. To my best friend of 11teen somethin' years (it's been so long that I lost count) Delanna. I know you don't understand not a single thing about all this publishing stuff but thank you for listening. Thank you for trying to understand and sending me information to help anyway. You're literally my sister for life for more reasons outside of this book so thank you.

To every single Beta-reader, Ruby, Kay, Johnathan, M.C, and Sky. Thank you all for your feedback and critique. Even while this process was difficult you were able to tell me what I needed to hear in a way in which I could receive it. I couldn't have done this without you, and I mean that so honestly. Thank you, a thousand times, for believing in this stranger from the internet, that loves a good story.

To my mutuals on the clock app. I hope you never hesitate to reach out to me for help, because I can't give a genuine enough thank you no matter how many times, I say it. Thanks for believing in me when I had no IRL community to cheer me on. Thank you for trusting me to share your space with me.

Thank you for encouraging me when I didn't want to work on this anymore. Thank you for reminding me to take a break when I needed it. A big thank you for all the advice you took time to share. Thank you for making me laugh all the time, sometimes it's right after a really bad day and there you are. It is truly an honor to take this adventure with all of you.

To my entire following on social media. Y'all are the coolest. The absolute coolest folk for allowing me to dream again as cheesy as that sounds. Little me never thought people would stop to watch me create and the fact that you did means so much to me. Not only that but, you guys stick around when I am myself. Who would've thought two-thousand people would want to hear from me. You are not a number to me. I know your lives are as busy as mine so thank you for spending some of your time and money to come chill in Slim's World for a bit.

I hope this book Conquer was able to give you all what it gave to me during quarantine. This book was my therapy. Conquer is my song I never got to write before I stopped pursuing vocal music. Conquer and I grew together. I started healing with my characters, and I learned with them and from them. This book gave me another chance at dreaming big right before I was ready to stop believing in dreams. It snatched me up before my creativity ran off a cliff. My characters promised not to give up on each other and their community. And you guys chose not to give up on me when I was ready to give up on me. That's crazy to me. It's so much to process that I can't find enough words to express the overwhelming gratitude I have for this gift I just so happened to find. So, I'll put it this way:

Thank you for being my found family.
Thank you for helping me believe in fairytales again.

Imperfect Black Characters
Blog post about Conquer

My Social Media

Tik tok and Instagram:
@SlimWrites22

My Website

My website:
Slim's Universe (slims-universe.com)

Abilities Guide

- Cryokinesis- domestic abuse

- Astral projection- Sexual assault

- Teleportation- isolation

- Illusionist- Child abuse

- Strength-excessive bullying

- Life manipulation- grief/grieving

- Self-multiplication- missing persons

A Rough Sketch Map of Where the Gang has Been.

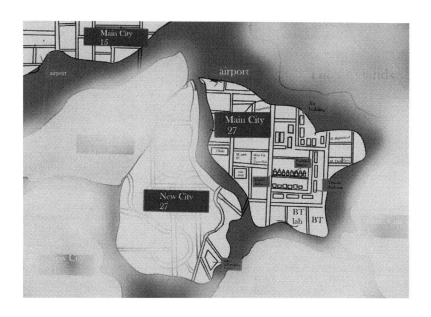

Made in the USA
Columbia, SC
04 August 2024

4dd9cc6c-cb33-445a-acee-c9caaba3154fR01